"Weitz's assured debut follows the trials one painfully shy college student faces when she ventures beyond the safety of the library. . . . Weitz masterfully captures the collegiate atmosphere as seen through the eyes of a troubled, sympathetic young woman."   —*Booklist*

"This debut novel unwraps an intriguing downward spiral, deftly portraying social and psychological implications of college life. Natalie's needs to come to terms with her history, slowly revealed throughout, is well worth the read."   —*Library Journal*

"Natalie will remind many readers of their own awkward youth. A deft . . . coming-of-age tale."   —*Kirkus Reviews*

"*College Girl* is a sensitive yet laser-precise look at the joy (and indignity) of college life. Weitz's prose is lovely, direct, and wincingly honest."   —Diablo Cody,
Oscar-winning screenwriter of *Juno* and author of *Candy Girl*

"With *College Girl*, Patricia Weitz has created an everywoman for our bewildering times, a woman who transforms before our eyes into a philosopher of heartbreak and redemption."   —Nick Flynn,
author of *Another Bullshit Night in Suck City*

"A raw and resonant debut novel. Readers will recognize themselves in Weitz's very real narrator—I know I did. Like Natalie Bloom, I hovered on the fringes of frat parties, wondering why everyone was having the time of their lives except me. In the end, Patricia Weitz's novel is not only compelling and compassionate, but a page-turner. Natalie's transformation, drawing on strengths she doesn't even know she has, had me cheering."   —Megan McCafferty,
New York Times bestselling author of
Second Helpings and *Fourth Comings*

"Sharply observed and unflinchingly honest, *College Girl* is a sexual-coming-of-age novel that will resonate with anyone who remembers the bittersweet emotions of their first love affair. Weitz's depiction of the underbelly of the student dating scene is so uncannily perceptive that it will make you squirm."
                                                                    —Fiona Neill,
                                                        author of *Slummy Mummy*

college girl

*

patricia weitz

Riverhead Books
New York

RIVERHEAD BOOKS
Published by the Penguin Group
Penguin Group (USA) Inc.
375 Hudson Street, New York, New York 10014, USA
Penguin Group (Canada), 90 Eglinton Avenue East, Suite 700, Toronto, Ontario M4P 2Y3, Canada
(a division of Pearson Canada Inc.)
Penguin Books Ltd, 80 Strand, London WC2R 0RL, England
Penguin Ireland, 25 St Stephen's Green, Dublin 2, Ireland (a division of Penguin Books Ltd)
Penguin Group (Australia), 250 Camberwell Road, Camberwell, Victoria 3124, Australia
(a division of Pearson Australia Group Pty Ltd)
Penguin Books India Pvt Ltd, 11 Community Centre, Panchsheel Park, New Delhi–110 017, India
Penguin Group (NZ), 67 Apollo Drive, Rosedale, North Shore 0632, New Zealand
(a division of Pearson New Zealand Ltd)
Penguin Books (South Africa) (Pty) Ltd, 24 Sturdee Avenue, Rosebank, Johannesburg 2196,
South Africa

Penguin Books Ltd, Registered Offices: 80 Strand, London WC2R 0RL, England

This is a work of fiction. Names, characters, places, and incidents either are the product of the author's imagination or are used fictitiously and any resemblance to actual persons, living or dead, business establishments, events, or locales is entirely coincidental. The publisher does not have any control over and does not assume any responsibility for author or third-party websites or their content.

Copyright © 2008 Patricia Weitz
Cover design by Monica Benalcazar
Cover photograph by Polka Dot Images/Jupiterimages
Book design by Michelle McMillian

First Riverhead hardcover edition: December 2008
First Riverhead trade paperback edition: November 2009
Riverhead trade paperback ISBN: 978-1-59448-404-9

The Library of Congress has catalogued the Riverhead hardcover edition as follows:

Weitz, Patricia, date.
College girl / Patricia Weitz.
p. cm.
ISBN: 978-1-59448-853-5
1. Young women—Fiction. 2. College students—Fiction. I. Title.
PS3622.E4616C65   2008   2008015236
813'.6__dc22.

PRINTED IN THE UNITED STATES OF AMERICA

10 9 8 7 6 5 4 3

For Jane

In memory of David

college girl

※

one

UCONN: HOME OF THE HUSKIES AND NUMBER SIX
PARTY SCHOOL IN THE COUNTRY

A snapshot: Hazel eyes. Long brown hair. Not short, but not tall, either. Curvy. Considered attractive—maybe not by one and all but by some. More than a few. Most.

More details?

Fingernails chewed down and bare of polish. Eyelashes that curl up naturally. Strong legs with defined muscles, especially in the calves, which some might call bulbous. A nose that is maybe slightly too broad but otherwise normal-looking. Crooked bottom teeth; fairly straight top teeth. Poor posture— a mild case of scoliosis. Full lips, symmetrical. Rough feet and elbows, in need of moisturizer. Occasional acne outbreaks, usually at the hairline. Hairy arms. Hairy legs, too, but luckily those get shaved. Eyebrows that benefit from a good plucking now and then, but can pass as somewhat exotic-looking. Oh . . . and a basically flat stomach with a single fat roll when seated or slouched.

Who do you see?

Who do you want to see?

It was the early nineties and I was a college student—a big surprise, given the path my six older brothers had paved for me. Starting in kindergarten, whenever I entered a new grade and the teacher took attendance, he or she almost always paused on my name and said, testily, "You're not one of *the* Blooms, are you?" It was like wearing a neon sign that read "Slacker," and so I complied and was one, soon rooting myself in the world of Average Kids, where the general philosophy regarding schoolwork was thus: Just because we are *capable* of doing assignments, why on earth *would* we?

Days passed. Years passed.

I yawned a lot during classes.

I got *a lot* of C's.

And then, during my junior year, one of my teachers woke me up.

Mr. Smith was by no means a role model. He was a sociology teacher with dyed black hair and an overgrown mustache, and he didn't take me under his wing or nurture any long-dormant intellect. He was a straight shooter, though, and gave me some smart advice after a particularly bad performance on a pop quiz: The world could care less about me; it didn't care if I succeeded, failed, or died tomorrow. Then he dangled a carrot: Good grades were the great equalizers. I could be the *same* as the college-prep kids, those well-dressed class treasurers and presidents of committees who walked the halls oozing self-satisfaction. But without high grades, he sighed, glancing furtively but appreciatively at my breasts, I would not only *not* be like them, I would undoubtedly become, in society's estimation, a loser.

I hated Mr. Smith. Still do, in fact, and I think it's because he knew that I was *already* a loser, *before* I'd flunked his little pop quiz . . . But was it possible I might sink *even lower* after graduation? I stared back into his beady black eyes, frightened, and yanked on my cardigan, determining that I would *never* allow him to sneak another peek, and after that I slowly did better in school. Not stellar, but better. And by my senior year, once I'd had time to truly taste the confidence that came with a grade, it became like a drug. I barely talked, then, but my grades gave me a voice because an "A" spoke volumes. I started to raise my hand in classes. I began to read my textbooks willingly. I even began to like *math*. And Mr. Smith was right: High scores made me more like the guys and girls I had always been intimidated by from afar. I wasn't less intelligent! I just hadn't tried! But the damage had already been done. The good grades I achieved in my last two years of high school couldn't sway the college of my choice, the University of Connecticut, to admit a former slacker like me. So, as a poor Connecticut resident, I did what every other aspiring student does in my situation: I went to a worse state school, Eastern, driving back and forth, until I was able to transfer into the one I wanted to go to.

This took two and a half very long years.

Was it worth the wait? Was it worth the struggle?

Yes and *yes*.

UConn, to me, was this beautiful place filled with the kind of preppy, solidly middle-class students I had always envied and—let's admit it—despised. The sprawling lawns, the rolling pastures and hills around campus, the brick, ivy-vined buildings and the pond of overfed ducks. I had wanted to be a part of it for *so long*, to once and for all break free of the Average Kid straitjacket, and so I kept reapplying and maintained a GPA that wavered between 3.7 and 4.0, and eventually they let me in.

They *let* me in.

But even after I willingly plunged myself into debt in order to attend and moved into McMahon Hall, midway into my junior year, I still felt as if I were looking in from the outside. Getting my own mailbox and brushing my teeth alongside others in the bathroom gave me the trappings of belonging, but that was it. By junior year, students are firmly entrenched in their cliques, roommates have been carefully chosen and study partners picked. This isn't to say that a newcomer can't break in with a winning personality or a mystique of cool. I just wasn't one of them. And after my years of commuting, I was less than skilled in the art of making friends. I'd lived at home and generally left campus as soon as class was over. My only true friends were the family dog and a neighborhood cat I occasionally fed! When the cat disappeared after a snowstorm, I cried for a week.

No. It was easier to hang back than to actually attempt conversation with girls I assumed would rather I didn't. I had missed the boat. There was nothing I could do about it. But . . . in truth . . . I didn't feel worthy to be friends with those who had gained admission at the right time: as *freshmen*. Not that

I let on about this. Hardly. It made me even more determined to excel in school, to place my grades at the forefront of all my efforts. In the cafeteria I sought out corners and stared at books as I ate, hoping it sent the message that I *wanted* to be sitting alone. While they were all busy laughing and talking and eating sugary cereals, I was *studying*. I was *serious*. I was even (I hoped this was what they were thinking!) an *intellectual*. I decided my reclusiveness was a choice; girlfriends would distract me from maintaining my still-perfect grade-point average, the number I revered with the fear and love I had once offered God.

It was different with guys, though. They approached me. They talked about me when I passed by and even made animalistic noises. And I hated them for it.

That night—it was a month into the first semester of my senior year. I went to the dining hall, took my tray to the least-occupied table, and listened to the hum of voices for a moment before focusing on a text. I was reading, absorbed, blocking out the ever-rising volume, pausing occasionally to highlight a sentence here and there, when Linda joined me. Linda liked everyone—even socially awkward people like me—because she took it for granted that people were generally nice, which of course we all know is not true. Linda had a pretty, round face which she glossed with shimmering, pale eyeshadows and a special powder that left traces of glitter on her skin. Her hair was brown and curly, but she was also short and dumpling-shaped. Her laugh was constant, and alarmingly high-pitched, but her main quality was that she bragged. She'd say things like, "I was the best baton-twirler in the state when I was in fourth grade," or "I once saved a family of raccoons who were going to get hit by a car." She would segue from a conversation about classes to her natural acting skills and the play she had starred in in high school. She inserted herself into other people's cliques constantly, with no inhibition. It was painful to watch. I would see girls smile and guys feign interest—but as soon as Linda turned away the eye-rolls and whispers began. She prided herself on being a "floater"—nonjudgmental and sweet to one and all—but everyone else, I think, just read her as naïve and annoying.

"You're going to a frat party with me after dinner." She slid onto the bench across from me in a red scoop-necked sweater that showed off her ample bosom. Small gold hoops hung from her ears and a matching gold chain decorated her neck, and the scent of vanilla wafted across the table. It was Linda's belief, she had once explained, that men couldn't resist girls who smelled edible, in the same way that she couldn't resist a powdered doughnut.

"Sorry," I replied, glancing around to see if anyone was looking at us, "I'm going to the library."

"*No.*" She pouted. "You *always* go to the library, and it's a Friday night. I can't find anyone to go with me, and there's this guy from my poli-sci class who told me to come, and I *have to* go. I really think he likes me. Guys like him *always* like me. They have a thing for big boobs."

"I really don't . . . like frats," I said uncomfortably. "But you should go anyway since he told you about it."

She scowled. "I can't go *alone*," she gasped. "Come on—we

haven't gone out together in *ages*. Bring your backpack, and if it's totally lame we'll leave and you can go to your library."

The truth is, I had only been to a few parties, all with Linda. The previous semester I'd gone to one where I'd gotten drunk and made out with two different guys . . . although one didn't really count because he had grabbed me as I passed by and laid a whopper on me, tongue and all, without my consent. What's really noteworthy about this is that I had never kissed anyone before that night. What's perhaps *more* noteworthy is that I hadn't kissed anyone since that night. After that party I was certain that everyone had dubbed me—the new girl—a slut. Would it have been better or worse if they had known I was really a virgin? I walked around for days without looking anyone in the eye.

I finished my meal—lasagna sagging under far too much mozzarella—and replaced my book in my bag. Linda sat staring at me, waiting for a verdict, her hands clasped together as in prayer. I felt hot and jittery, and this is how I knew that I was going to say yes.

"Isn't it too early for a party?" I stalled, picking up my tray and carrying it to the conveyor belt as Linda followed. The clock on the wall read eight p.m.

"Pete—that's my guy's name—told me to come early, before it gets too packed. Besides, he said he and his brothers were going to start drinking in the afternoon."

We went outside and steady gusts of freezing wind pushed against us; within minutes my toes and fingers burned with pain from the cold. It was an unseasonably frigid October night, but I was at least warmer than Linda, who hadn't even bothered with a jacket because she didn't want anything to detract from her breasts.

"But shouldn't I . . . get ready or something?" I asked.

"You always look good," she said, teeth chattering. "But forget about you: How do *I* look?"

Now I began to sweat, even with the cold. I was going to a party. I was going to a party with Linda. I smoothed my long dark hair and tucked it behind my ears—then reconsidered and let it hang loose. I felt stupid carrying a backpack, I felt huge in my winter coat. We neared Frat Row and joined a swarm of students out on the lawns and drifting in and out of each house. Linda's face glowed with anticipation, whereas my face, I was certain, was clouded with nausea. About ten guys stood on the front porch of the party house, surveying those—like us—who wished entry. Dance music thumped. We hung back as Linda tried to determine if Pete was one of the guys outside, but when she was sure he was not she grabbed my hand and led me to the foot of the stairs.

"Hello, girls," a short guy with a beefy neck purred. "What can I do for you? Or better yet, what can you do for *me* . . . and my brothers?"

Laughter. Drunken laughter. I lowered my eyes, heart pounding.

"I know Pete," Linda laughed along. "Is he inside? Can we come in?"

"Oh, you can come in all right," he said. "But, again: What are you *going to do* for me and my brothers? Forget about Pete. Do you know *Johnson*?"

This time I shot Beefy Neck a nasty look and started to walk away, and as I did so the guys on the porch yelled out things like, "Wait! He's just kidding! Gary's an asshole! Don't go!" Linda grabbed my sleeve and I stopped. "You know guys," she whispered. "They're *pigs*. Let's just go in. Please? I'm *freezing*."

I looked back at the house. My hands were actually shaking. But it was college. I was supposed to go to parties, and now that I lived on campus I finally *could* go to them. I nodded and we climbed the stairs, avoiding eye contact with the frat's sentries, still laughing at Beefy Neck's audacity.

It was dark inside except for a strobe light that flashed across people's faces in spastic streaks of white light. There weren't too many people on the dance floor, though, because most were congregated around a keg, filling their cups and mouths with beer. Linda gestured for me to join them, but I shook my head. She shrugged and got in line, and I shrank back into a corner and removed my backpack and jacket, stuffing them down on the floor behind me. Without my puffy coat of armor, though, I didn't know what to do with my body. My breathing speeded up and I had just decided to follow Linda to get a beer to ease my nerves when a baseball-capped guy approached me. He stopped in front of me, beer cup in hand, blocking me into my corner.

"Hi," he said with a smooth smile. "Welcome. Can I get you a drink?"

He was cute in a pleasant but generic way, like a sitcom actor. I shook my head.

"Then, here, take mine," he said, holding out a red plastic cup. "I just got it, and I haven't touched it. I swear. Not that I have germs. I mean, all people have germs but mine are okay. I promise."

I didn't want his drink, but I took it anyway. Alcohol, I had learned, was something not to be feared but embraced—a social crutch that provided an invaluable, tangible service: It either made both you and whoever you were talking to instantly more attractive, or it made you *not care*. Of course, for it to work its magic it had to be taken in excess and with abandon, and so instead of thanking him or smiling I downed half of the beer in seconds. When I lowered my cup, he was grinning. "What's your name?" he asked.

I again took a long drink, swallowing the bitter contents quickly. "What's yours?" I asked.

"Oh, okay." He smiled. "We're going to play the 'you show me yours and I'll show you mine' game."

I stared at him blankly, and he crossed his arms and looked past me, eyeing other girls. "That was a stupid thing for me to say," he shrugged, giving it another go. "I'm Quincy. I'm premed. What about you?"

I flushed. If I stayed and consumed more liquor there was a good chance that I would be kissing Quincy before the end of the evening—whether I wanted to or not. I looked over his shoulder where Linda was chatting up a guy in a white "Coed Naked" T-shirt. Probably Pete. He had a hand on one of her shoulders and, like Quincy, you could tell he was checking out other girls even as he listened to her.

"I have to talk to my friend," I said, edging away from him.

"Will you come back here after you do?" he asked while smiling at a long-legged blonde in the keg line.

"No." I shook my head. "I have to . . . go."

"Well, can I call you? I still don't know your name."

"I have a boyfriend."

He walked away. He didn't even smile before he moved on. I watched him follow after the blonde, and when he tapped her shoulder she looked elated to have his attention. Like him, she was attractive, but in a familiar, forgettable way. In an hour I would have no recollection of what either of them looked like, but by the end of the night, I was sure the two of them would be making out. Frenzied. Only to never speak to each other again afterwards. I felt a twinge of disappointment, and yet I also hated this baseball-cap-wearing frat boy. I hated him for looking at my lips as he promised me his germs were okay; I hated him for checking out my chest. I took another long drink and felt the warmth of the liquor flow through my body, and then I grabbed my coat and bag and pushed my way over to Linda to tell her I was leaving, but she was so engrossed in telling Pete, or whoever this was, a story about how her dog once flew—literally flapped his floppy ears and flew—that she just nodded as I walked away.

Outside, my coat zipped, the familiar weight of my back-pack firmly in place, my legs taking me quickly and confidently in the direction of the library, my discomfort collapsed into a tiny kernel of embarrassment and I knew I wouldn't think about it for too long. I hadn't done anything bad. I hadn't lost control. I was already pushing Quincy out of my mind. No, I had a more important date, a date with my books, where there would be no pressure to drink, kiss, or make bad conversation with anyone.

The library's many windows glowed with fluorescent light. It was the tallest building on campus and at the very center of the campus lawn. It was under construction, with half of the brick building covered with what looked like Saran Wrap, but despite the daily articles in the campus paper condemning this, it still looked beautiful to me. The plastic quivered with even the slightest of breezes, and colors flickered across it, like a giant, transparent insect wing. I smiled and buried my hands in my coat pockets. I liked imperfect things. The other buildings on campus were too collegiate-perfect for me to ever feel truly comfortable in, whereas the library—newer and more common-looking—was the one place where I felt I legitimately belonged.

Two girls were chatting on a bench just outside, and I avoided making eye contact on my way in. I pushed through the revolving doors and was happily blasted by a gust of heat, then walked to the middle of the main lobby and waited with two others for an elevator. The surrounding walls and bulletin boards were plastered with UConn athletics posters, the Siberian Husky mascot salivating in every ad and reminding me that I had never been to a single basketball game—something akin to sacrilege on campus. I never cared whether we won or lost, but I always knew how the team was doing on game nights by the loud cheers or boos that exploded the silence as I trekked the deserted path to and from the library. Dorm rooms glowed with the ghoulish blue of television sets while I throbbed with loneliness. I always passed Gampel Pavilion, that white-domed stadium, as quickly as possible.

I rode the elevator to the library's fourth floor, which was virtually empty. Midterms were still several weeks off and the only people roaming the aisles were either employees or social outcasts like me. I took my usual spot, a carrel that gave me a view out the window and an equally good view of the book stacks, lit in the stark glow of the fluorescent beams lining the ceiling. Fridays and Saturdays were normally my favorite days to use the library because it felt so . . . *private*, like when you go to a movie theater in the middle of the afternoon and have the whole place to yourself. I'd put my feet up on a chair or even on the desktop and take frequent bathroom breaks just to look at myself critically in the mirror. I'd fantasize about living in the library and plan out the logistics: a knapsack of food, a flashlight, a sleeping bag. Then I'd add a few details: A great-looking guy would show up, a smart, non-frat, non-jock type, maybe an artist, who'd also stowed away in the library, and we'd end up talking and kissing and . . . well, that was about as far as I let my imagination carry me.

I pulled out a Russian history text and began reading. The silence was powerful for the first hour but then, during the second hour, the library—*my* library—was invaded by two others who were laughing and talking like children on a field trip. I leaned back in my chair and peered around my carrel. A guy and a girl were seated at a long rectangular table, and I shot them a disapproving glance just as he stood to use the water fountain. He was extremely tall, and I presumed he was a basketball player. Really tall people can look almost freakish, especially at first, and so I watched him return to his table, transfixed by his towering height. He was attractive, but not conventionally so; his eyes were spaced too far apart and his forehead was never-ending, a slope that extended far up into the strawberry blond hair on his head. He was very thin and wore a loose-fitting white oxford shirt with a pair of tan khakis that struck me as very J. Crew but was at least more interesting than the University of Connecticut apparel most guys wore religiously. The girl—a dirty blonde, slightly pudgy—who stood to leave when he reached the table, appeared almost midget beside him. I watched them. I liked the way he kept bending down to hear what she was saying; there was something self-effacing and gentle about it. His face was animated and friendly. He looked nice. A pang of envy shot through me as he went on talking to the blonde—who began laughing so hard her pale face turned a beetlike crimson. I didn't think she was particularly beautiful, but I guessed she might possess other qualities that could charm . . . or maybe it was just the super-tight white sweater she was wearing. I became so engrossed in trying to determine what, exactly, it was about this girl that he liked that I completely failed to notice that he had begun staring at *me*. When I did realize this, he smiled, invitingly; I, in turn, hurriedly ducked back under cover of the carrel. But when I dared to look again he was alone, and he was approaching me.

"Who are you?" he asked simply, directly, pulling up a chair.

"Sorry," I replied coldly, turning my attention back to my text, "I'm busy."

"I'm Patrick," he replied without insult. "Patrick Dunne. So, again, who are *you*?"

I sighed, heavily, conveying that I was finished with the conversation, and yet he still didn't leave. I could feel him examining me, and I dragged my long hair over my right shoulder in an effort to veil my face.

"You're pretty," he said. "Do you like being pretty?" His tone was scientific and his expression revealed *nothing*, and there was something in his delivery that unnerved me. It was almost as if he had insulted me—like his flattery was instead a way to patronize and denigrate. Perhaps he had used this tone because he felt snubbed, but whatever it was, I am sure, now, that this is why I immediately liked him.

I looked him full in the face, with open curiosity. "Do you like being tall?" I countered, using as straight a tone as he had.

He smiled then, and his smile gave me a surprising jolt, a little thrill. He liked me, he liked me for using the same tone he had used! It made him look at me in a way that was more interested and less playful. He leaned back in his chair and our eyes locked for two or three seconds too long, and in those two or three seconds I felt unmoored and . . . known. I averted my eyes, fast.

"No," he finally answered, "I hate it. I'm six-five. Wherever I go people comment on my height, saying things like, 'Hey, you're really tall,' as if I had never noticed. That's why I walk with a permanent slouch and will be a hunchback by the age of thirty."

I laughed. I thought what he'd said was funny. "Basketball?" I couldn't resist asking.

"No," he sighed. "I got the tall gene but not the coordinated one."

I smiled, weakly, and pulled my book to my chest. Was it the beer I'd consumed earlier that had allowed me to banter with this guy? I wasn't quite sure how to put an end to it, but I knew I had to before it became the kind of conversation that made me squirm. I couldn't flirt. Nothing was more unsettling to me than the idea, even, of flirting, and yet I had left an *opening*, I had exhibited *interest* by asking a question, however slight it might have been. What was I supposed to do now? Toss my hair? Blink my lashes? I could never be that person, and so I had learned to avoid this kind of talk altogether with an air that dissuaded approach, an iciness that failed to be moved by hurt feelings, rejected egos. Most guys gave up at just the simple frown or the brief but severe look—both of which I had mastered. And when I *was* attempting to be sociable I had perfected the art of not giving anything away about myself. This isn't to say that guys were falling at my feet, but they noticed me. Maybe it was the way they nudged one another as I walked by, but I knew I was looked at, leered at. So what if I, myself, couldn't even look in a mirror without squinting with displeasure? *They* didn't see the flaws that I thought were so evident. To them my soft curves must have seemed seductive, while I, myself, yearned for a lean, hard, athletic body. And my face must have seemed pleasant to them . . . but I detested my thick eyebrows and would have preferred a more conventionally pretty face, one that blended in better, an ivory-skin blonde with pink, perfect lips. And then, of course, there was the tit factor. I had them. Not giant ones like Linda's, but nice-sized, anyway.

I should mention here that I despised my breasts.

One of the pages in my book started to tear from the pressure I was exerting on it. I could either tell Patrick, outright, that I wasn't interested, or I could leave. Neither option was satisfying. I glanced at him and saw that his eyes were barely blue and lacked something definite or solid—the color of white-washed mornings that couldn't decide whether to turn gray or blue. My heart was thumping.

"You're shy," he stated then, and again I felt his eyes inspecting me. "You don't make eye contact and you keep crossing your legs. Are you nervous?"

He frightened me, even then, but in a way that was still childish. I forced myself to look at him. "I'm here to study, in case you hadn't noticed, and you're *really* staring at me," I replied. "And I suppose that *is* making me a bit nervous. That doesn't mean that I'm shy. Although I am. A little."

He smiled, gathered my hair together, and gently tossed it behind me. "There. Now people can see your face," he said, looking over my head and exaggerating a lack of eye contact. "So, is it better if I talk to you like this? I can, if you want, but it seems a shame to deny me the pleasure of seeing you. Plus, people might think I'm blind."

Again I found myself laughing and, without thinking, I playfully shoved his arm. It's not enough to say that this was unlike me. It *wasn't* me. He reacted by grasping the point of impact in mock pain, as if I'd just clobbered him.

"Stop it," I said, laughing. "That didn't hurt at all."

He leaned back in his chair and grinned. "Come study with me at my table," he said, gesturing behind him. "We'll take a break every fifteen minutes to share something . . . personal. Since we're the only ones stuck here, it'll make it more fun."

My laughter stopped. "Oh," I replied stiffly, "I don't . . . do that."

"Um . . . do what?" he asked.

"I don't study with anyone. It doesn't work."

He frowned. "Okay, please tell me you *have* to be here right now. Please tell me you're not here on a Friday night by *choice*."

I blushed as my muscles tensed. "Why are *you* here?" I challenged.

"I have to take a makeup exam tomorrow morning," he answered. "And you?"

I closed my book and dropped it into my backpack. "I don't take makeups," I said more harshly than I'd meant to. "I prepare for the original exams."

I stood and slung my bag over my shoulder, knocking over my chair in my eagerness to leave. Patrick set it back on its legs and grabbed my wrist as I tried to pass him. I stopped and stared at his hand, at his touch, dumbfounded. He was looking at me with new interest, and it was a look I had seen before: I was going to be a "challenge."

"Just tell me what your name is," he said, seriously. "Then you can go."

I hesitated, but only a moment. If he wanted to try, which I doubted, he would fail. "Natalie Bloom," I replied.

He released my hand and plunged an imaginary dagger into his chest. Again, I laughed. Then I did an about-face and walked away.

. . .

The campus paths were lit with lanterns. I wrapped my scarf around my neck and, despite the chill, slowed my pace, enjoying the solitude of the darkened grounds to think. About Patrick. My heart raced and I resisted an urge to simultaneously sprint and scream at the top of my lungs. It had felt really good to laugh like that. But I knew the sensation would pass and, most importantly, I would never see him again.

I accepted this fact with ease and, truth be told, relief.

When I reached my dorm I took the stairs to get some exercise. The distant sounds of a party traveled through ceiling and concrete—intermittent thuds from blaring music, and a soft, musical din of people talking. I paused and listened. It was strangely beautiful. Then I quietly opened my door and shook my coat off into a heap on the floor. Faith, my roommate, was in bed on the bottom bunk, fast asleep, an ashtray perched precariously near her head. The room reeked of cigarettes. I turned on a small desk lamp and glanced around. Faith and I both had flower-printed bedspreads. Mine was lavender, Faith's pink. A border of pastel hydrangeas, daisies, and stargazers ran around the rim of the room; the rug was plush, a creamy white. From the bureau I picked up my heart-shaped wooden jewelry box and traced its shape with my hand. My father had given it to me for my tenth birthday and I had loved it—not just the shape but the red crushed-velvet inside, and the *Moonlight Sonata* it played when opened. It embarrassed me that such a keepsake came from my dad and not a boy. Most of the time I told myself it was insignificant that I had never had a boyfriend. But it was beginning to feel as if the longer I went without one the more impossible it would be to ever get one. How does one explain virginity in a twenty-year-old? I wasn't ugly, I knew that, and though I'd grown up Catholic, it wasn't religious beliefs that were getting in my way. Mostly, I tried not to think about my lack of experience, but it was always there. Sex was one thing I knew nothing about. This ignorance scared me, and I filled it with fantasies, but even I knew that my fantasies were too idealistic to ever materialize.

I changed into a loose T-shirt and stood before the full-length mirror against the door, assessing myself. I lifted my shirt a few inches. My stomach looked soft. I drew in a deep breath and tensed my muscles until it flattened. I brushed out my hair and arranged it to fall on my shoulders. Red highlights glistened within the chestnut. The dimmed lighting softened all of my features, like one of those glamour shots you can get at the mall, and I wished I could go through life in that exact lighting. It made my cheeks look pinker and my lips look darker, like I'd smeared them with lip gloss.

I thought again of Patrick, and I wondered if he would approve. Then I closed my eyes and pictured his face, his broad shoulders, his pale eyes. Yes, Patrick would be my new crush. Crushes I could do. You didn't need to speak to a crush, you didn't need to *see* a crush. Even better, you could make a crush into whatever you wanted him to be. He could become better-looking or more sensitive or more passionate with time. He could become *yours*. An idea. An idea worth thinking about, but nothing more.

I studied my reflection. *You're pretty,* I aped, taking in my face, hair, eyes, and body. *Do you like being pretty?*

I focused, hard, but what I saw bothered me.

No, I mouthed to the mirror, *I don't.*

Then Patrick—tall, dashing Patrick, with his blue eyes that had already grown bluer—leaned in and kissed me, and when he was done, when he had pried himself away from my lips, I climbed into bed and went to sleep.

two

My mother once told me I slept through an entire fireworks display as a baby, and I don't doubt it, because I'm sure I could do the same now. Growing up the youngest of seven and the only girl in the bunch, I learned early on how to block out noise. I even blocked out the gunshot that killed my brother, Jacob, when I was ten. It had happened in the middle of the night and a quarter of a mile away from our house. My father heard it, though, along with two of my brothers and a few of our neighbors, and an aunt who lived in another state claimed to have sat up in bed at the exact moment the gun was fired. But me? I never heard a thing.

The alarm was buzzing, bleating, piercing the silence, but it sounded distant, too, part of a dream. Faith kicked my bunk from beneath and I rolled close to the wall, trying to escape her jabs.

"Get up," Faith moaned. "Please, get up, for the love of *God*, get up. You're killing me!"

I opened my eyes. The alarm clock was wedged between the wall and my bed, and I hit snooze, immediately falling back to sleep.

"Natalie," she warned, "don't even fucking hit snooze. Either get up or turn your damn alarm off altogether!"

"Sorry." I forced my eyes open and stared at the ceiling, cursing myself for signing up for eight-o'clock classes, then swung my body over the side of the bunk and stepped on Faith's bed to ease my drop to the floor.

"Why don't you ever use the ladder?" she hissed, burrowing her face into her pillow. "Did you ever consider that stepping on my bed is a little disturbing?"

I ignored her. I ignored her a lot, which was okay because Faith never really noticed if I heard her or not. Generally I liked Faith, but we weren't *friends* in any soul-baring way. A mechanical-engineering major, she was a twenty-five-year-old college senior who looked like an eighties chick straight out of a Poison video: the frosted, feathered, and oversprayed blond hair, the acid-washed jeans, the constant cigarettes dangling from her lips and saturating our clothes with their scent. She had mixed with a heavy-metal crowd in high school, dropped out, done hard drugs, gotten pregnant, and had an abortion. She bartended for a few miserable years before earning enough credits and good grades at a community college to transfer to UConn, but by then she looked hardened, and despite her mere five feet, she was intimidating. Everyone in the dorm steered clear of her. She didn't belong among the L.L. Bean or Husky cliques, and felt no shame in this. I admired that about her.

When we'd first met, the previous semester, both of us brand-new to the school, I knew that I had lucked out. I'd worried about rooming with a stranger, but when Faith arrived and pulled out of her duffel bag several plastic-framed photos of roses lying atop violins and kittens peeking out of a bowl, I breathed a deep sigh of relief at the bad taste. In that moment I stopped worrying what my new roommate would think of me and the money and nice things I myself lacked. Faith's family background, it turned out, was no different from mine. Both of our fathers worked in factories (mine was a retired mechanic, hers was still in shipping); both of our mothers were waitresses. Winters were cold *inside* the house, fights occurred over food, and groundings happened over spilt milk—literally. I'm sure there were plenty of others like us at UConn, but it didn't feel that way when I was sitting beside girls scanning clothing catalogues, circling all the items they intended to order, or seeing the mountains of CDs littering dorm rooms, or overhearing students complaining to their parents that *everyone* was going to Cancún for spring break. It was a relief to come back to my room with Faith and feel free of all that. Our poor backgrounds were the only thing we had in common, but it was enough. Sometimes it was everything.

Gray light filtered into the room, promising yet another dark, possibly wet, morning. I sat at my desk and quietly opened a Russian history text. Professor Anderson was giving an essay exam that morning, and I was still unsure of early dates during Peter the Great's reign. I scanned the chapter, absorbing them:

1695: Russian navy begins; 1697: conquest of Kamchatka;

1700–1721: the Great Northern War with Sweden; 1703: the founding of St. Petersburg.

History. I'd chosen it as my major while still at Eastern because the A's came easily to me in that subject. At first that was my sole reason for choosing it. I was good at remembering details. I could give the broad overviews—I could succinctly recount the main points that led to the American Revolution, say—but my real passion was for the trivial facts, like what the soldiers' uniforms looked like at each stage of the war. It's safe to say that history satisfied this need I'd always had to obsess, only it was wonderful because the obsessing wasn't about me or my family but about others who were vastly more important. So I wanted to know everything, particularly when it came to individuals: the color of their hair, what their childhoods were like, who their first loves were. Everything. And once my focus became Russian history, it was as if I spent days with Trotsky and Lenin and Gorbachev in snow-covered places like Moscow and St. Petersburg. I felt as if I *knew* them, but what made it perfect was that they would never know me. And I loved the idea of bringing people back to life—bringing an eighteenth-century figure into my twenty-first-century mind. There was something magical in that.

I don't know. I guess when your studies are your *only* source of pleasure, there might be a problem.

Faith coughed, or rather hacked, drawing my attention. Pushing herself up in bed, couched by a mass of pink-hued pillows, she glowered at me when the hacking subsided.

"Jeez," I said, astonished by how haggard she looked, "did you get wasted last night?"

Mascara ran down her face and her mousy blond hair was a tangled mess. Despite this, her brilliant blue eyes still shone brightly through the black sludge. She reached over and grabbed a pack of Newport Menthol 100s from her desk and lit up.

"I got into a fight with Keith," she replied, referring to her boyfriend of nine years, the same one who had convinced her to end her pregnancy at the age of seventeen.

I ignored her and went back to my book. I ignored her not only when she directed complaints at me but also whenever she talked about Keith.

"It was the usual," she said wistfully, as if I had inquired and was still facing her. "He got jealous because I was talking to a guy at a bar—or, actually, a guy was talking to *me*, but he wigged out and attacked the guy. I threatened to break up with him afterwards, but in the end I couldn't. I love him too much, I guess."

I heard stories like this from Faith, on average, about twice a week, and my interest in helping her had by now diminished to nil. I instead pictured Patrick's intelligent face next to Keith's dim-witted one and then sighed, audibly.

"What should I do?" she asked.

"Find a new boyfriend?" I suggested.

"*God*," she snapped, whipping a pillow at the back of my head, "why do I even try talking to you? You have *no* compassion. But then, you've never *had* a boyfriend, so it's not like you have any experience to go by, anyway. Must suck."

I grabbed the pillow from the floor and whipped it back at her, though more gently than she had thrown it at me. I got up and hid behind the closet curtain to change, pulling on my red terrycloth robe. Then I fished out my toiletries, grabbed a towel, and gripped the doorknob. I wanted to retaliate with "I guess I should feel bad that I don't have a great guy like *Keith* in my life—my *high school boyfriend*," but I didn't. I was already justifying her remark in my head. Faith was right: What did I know? I did have zero experience in the bedroom.

"Sorry," I muttered and went out the door.

In the shower, the hot water knocked me fully awake. I put my face directly into the jet stream and brooded over my sexless past.

Why was I so abnormal?

Before long the water began to cool and I twisted the knob to make it hotter. I washed my face, roughly. Of course I hadn't had a boyfriend in high school. I'd gone to school with most of my male peers since kindergarten; the idea of kissing most of them seemed incestuous. There had been crushes along the way, mostly on out-of-reach guys who were grades above me, but I wasn't popular, and only popular girls got those guys. My years as a commuter college student hadn't provided many opportunities to meet anyone, and the guys I did meet I fled from, or spurned. Something about the rituals surrounding male-female attraction revolted me. I didn't want to be looked at. I didn't want to be touched. And I didn't know why. I rinsed the soap out of my hair and rubbed my eyes. Maybe I just hadn't met the *right guy* yet. I was holding out for perfection. Patrick. Was he perfection? I smiled and decided to look him up in the student directory later. Just think! I could pick up the phone and dial his *number*. I could speak to him again. I *wouldn't*, of course, but I *could*. That was something. It was more than I usually had.

I pressed my body against the peach tiles of the shower, trying not to think of how many other girls had done the same with their own naked bodies. Then I reluctantly turned the water off. My robe was hanging over the shower door, and I dragged it into the stall. Most girls hung their robes on the hooks outside, but I preferred the privacy of my system. Before leaving the bathroom, robe safely knotted, I looked in the mirror. The harsh white light made my skin look sallow, and two new pimples were developing on my chin. I smiled, hoping that might make me look more attractive, but it just made me notice how crooked my bottom teeth were.

"Take your seats," Professor Anderson called out, holding a packet of blue essay books in his hand, "and put away all notes and study materials. There are two essay questions, worth thirty points each, and four short-answer questions, worth ten points each. You have an hour to complete the exam. Good luck."

My knuckles whitened as I gripped my two pens, both needed in case one ran out of ink. This was always the worst moment: learning what the essay questions were. You lived or died by the essay questions. Professor Anderson—stoic gray suit, furrowed brow, white hair, and cold blue eyes—stood at the end of the row, passing out the booklets and the sheets of photocopied questions, and I tried to catch his eye. Would he be reasonable on this occasion, or tyrannical? He was harsh, but

I adored him as a teacher. His approach to the world and to his students was one of airy disdain: Nothing fazed him, and I had seen him send more than one tearful student away without so much as a glance after they'd received a poor grade. I admired his impermeability and I wanted, desperately, for him to like me. What did I care if he liked *no one?* It was better that he didn't, since Anderson was one of my secret crushes. Not a romantic crush, but a scholarly one. Unlike romantic crushes, I could talk to the scholarly ones. There was no real intimacy or sharing of personal information. I did have one philosophy professor at Eastern who had made a pass at me, but luckily it had happened at the beginning of a semester and I quickly dropped his class and signed up for another. *Old men.* That was the key. Old and somewhat decrepit, asexual men. They were the safest.

I grabbed the questions from the girl sitting in front of me and scanned them, breathing a sigh of relief. The first dealt with Rasputin, a favorite of mine, and the other was a broad reflection on three of the five major developments under Peter the Great that led to a more modern, westernized, Russia. I glanced up as Anderson sat at his desk, heavily and with effort. He looked old, too old, and for a second I was worried about him. As of that semester he was my adviser. With his guidance, I planned on figuring out what to do after college . . . and if he should retire or fall ill, I worried, there was no one else I could imagine myself talking to.

"Grigory Rasputin," I began confidently, setting pen to paper, *"arrived in St. Petersburg in 1911. Within just a few years*

he would become one of the most powerful men in government, se-
curing his position through his close relationship with Alexandra,
Nicholas II's wife . . . ."

I was still writing, fast, when I realized I was the only one
still left in the room. This was not unusual. Anderson sat on the
desk at the front of my row and impatiently ticked his pencil
against the metal base.

"That's enough, Natalie," he said sternly.

"Just two more minutes," I pleaded.

"No," he stated firmly. "Time's up."

I dashed off the last sentence and handed the two blue books
I had filled over to him, then flexed and shook my cramped
right hand.

"How do you think you did, Ms. Bloom?" he asked, almost
rhetorically.

"I don't know," I said, shrugging, "but I hope okay."

He smiled and shook his head. "And what unimportant facts
did you report on this time?"

I blushed. "I just repeat what you tell us in class," I replied
hopefully.

His barely there smile succumbed to a frown. "But remember, Natalie," he warned, "don't get mired down in the details
so much that you lose sight of the question. The point of history is not to know what outfit Rasputin wore on the day he was
murdered. It's to know *why* he was murdered, and how his life
and actions affected the Imperial Dynasty and the course of
history. I do hope this is the issue you've addressed," he finished, rising, "or else you will be graded accordingly."

I nodded and bit my lip to prevent myself from blurting out what Rasputin *did* wear on the day of his murder: black velvet trousers, leather boots, a white silk shirt with a gold sash tied loosely at the waist that was a present from his benefactress, Alexandra. I looked at Anderson. He was hunched over his desk and seemed lost in thought as he stacked the blue books in his briefcase. I think he thought I had left, because when I next spoke, his head jerked up with something like fear.

"I was wondering," I said, feeling like an especially irritating pest, "if I could make an appointment to speak with you."

"About what?" he demanded, sounding flustered.

"Um, about *me*," I said painfully, my face reddening. "You're, um, my adviser now, remember?"

"Ah, yes," he responded slowly. "Of course."

"Should I come by during your office hours later this week?" I asked, tentatively.

He nodded and smiled wanly. I turned and headed to the door, glancing back as I exited. He had fixed his attention on his briefcase and was absentmindedly clicking its latch open and shut, over and over again.

A group of guys sat on the top steps outside the dorm, blocking the door. I walked purposely up the stairs, arms crossed, averting their gaze, and hoped they would move.

"Excuse me," I muttered.

"What's the magic word?" asked the one most in my way.

He had brown hair and looked like he was trying to grow a beard but not having much luck. I had the feeling that he was asking the same question of every girl who tried to pass. My face burned. I hated him for making me say it.

"Please."

He smiled and shifted to the left to create a space for me, and I let out a deep sigh as I pushed open the door. Sometimes I wished I'd been placed in a girls' dorm. But while some floors in McMahon were coed, at least I lived on a single-sex floor. I couldn't imagine having to see guys first thing in the morning on the way to the bathroom or after, say, squeezing blackheads until my nose glowed red. Likewise, I had no real interest in see-ing *them* engaging in the kind of infantile bathroom humor I had witnessed, by accident, on boys' floors . . . which also hap-pened to smell like dirty gym socks and soiled underwear. Of course, there were usually a few guys roaming my floor on any given day, but more often than not, they were there to visit a girl and quickly vanished behind a closed door.

In the foyer I made a beeline for the elevator, but Linda jumped out of the mailroom and accosted me. She was wear-ing a yellow coat with brown cords, and her curly hair was pulled into a ponytail.

"Hi!" she shouted as if we hadn't seen each other in weeks. "Where have you *been?*"

"Class," I said with some surprise. "Why? Have you been looking for me?"

She laughed as if I had said something funny, and then, as if to confirm this, she told me I was hilarious.

"You take everything so *literally!*" she yelled, following me into the elevator. "Asking you where you've been is just, I don't know, an *expression*."

I smiled, embarrassed. "Well, then, where the hell have *you* been?" I asked.

She then proceeded to tell me where she had been. First a sociology class, then the library, then lunch in the cafeteria, and now in the dorm, with me. She even included what she'd eaten for lunch: a grilled cheese and a bowl of tomato soup.

"By the way," she said, "remember Pete? My guy? Well, I was right. He's *totally* into me." Her voice dropped to a whisper: "We hooked up after the party last week."

I could never figure out what people meant by "hooking up." It seemed to cover everything from kissing to oral or straight-out sex. Part of me wanted to ask Linda what her hookup consisted of, but another part didn't really want to know.

"That's great," I said. "Are you guys, like, an item now?"

Something like uncertainty flashed across her eyes before she blinked it away. "I wouldn't say we're an *item*," she replied. "But I know he's into me. He was all over me at the party, and *in front of* his friends. He kept telling me I had the greatest tits he had ever seen."

I knew better than to ask if he had called her since.

"What are you going to do now?" she asked when we reached my room.

"I'm going to go for a jog," I said. "Want to come?"

She laughed and told me, again, that I was hilarious, before bounding down the hall toward a group of squealing girls. When Linda arrived, their glee notably shifted and their smiles faded. Inwardly I cringed. Why would anyone risk being made fun of or disliked for friendship? I changed into sweats and re-turned to the elevator. Gwen, the beautiful girl from the end of the hall, was waiting there, too—also in sweats and sneakers. She smiled at me and I smiled back. Gwen was a senior, like me, and had the kind of healthy, athletic look of a Nike ad: light honey-colored hair to her shoulders, ivory complexion, and deep, chocolate-brown eyes. She was tall and thin, but her at-tractiveness was in her energy, too, bright and infectious. She was rarely alone, but she also didn't seem to need lots of friends, and I could tell she avoided some of the more gossipy cliques. She just seemed so . . . normal. So when she spoke to me that day, at first I thought I had imagined it.

"Are you going running?" she asked.

"Oh," I said. "Yes. I am."

"Me, too."

The elevator arrived and we stepped in. "Do you . . . run on campus or off?" I stuttered.

"It depends on the weather," she said. "If it's bad, I stay; if it's good, I go. What about you?"

"Oh," I said, "I never run on campus."

We got off the elevator and went outside. The sky was darkening and it looked like it might rain. Bad weather. Now was the awkward part. We would each give a little wave and then run in opposite directions. Only she didn't move, and nei-ther did I.

"Would you mind if I ran with you?" she asked.

I glanced over my shoulder to see if she had asked someone else. "Oh, um, no, not at all. But . . . I run slowly. Really slowly. You probably run fast. I wouldn't want to hold you up."

She laughed. "I'm not exactly in training. I haven't gone running in, like, two months. Don't worry."

She led us to the left, which meant we would be running on campus, even though I had just told her I never did that. But the reason I never ran on campus was because it seemed like you should only do that with someone else. Also, I wasn't a pretty runner. I wanted to be able to run sloppily and unseen. Gwen, I could tell immediately, was not that kind of runner. I struggled to keep pace with her, but she never even broke a sweat, and she talked evenly without seeming to need a breath as we passed by the stadium, the library, the auditorium. I was relieved when she told me she had been a track star in high school, a hurdler, and I could picture her sailing over the hurdles as if they weren't there. She told me about her town (New Canaan), her last boyfriend (Sam), her major (psychology). I gasped out my own major, omitting to mention that I was a transfer. Then she shared a pretty innocuous piece of trivia she had learned that day: "Alfred Kinsey's sex research inspired Hugh Hefner to publish *Playboy*."

"Seriously?" I asked.

"Yeah," she continued. "And I'm pretty sure my professor would like to hand out copies of the magazine and have a big orgy. Whenever he talks about pornography the tips of his ears redden and his speech speeds up. I try not to make *any* eye contact."

I hesitated. It wasn't that I didn't *want* to talk about sex, but I felt unable to. I swallowed and wiped away the sweat on my forehead. Then I told her about a book on prerevolutionary Russia I was reading. In rural villages in the 1800s, things were so communal that when a marriage occurred, the groom screwed his bride in front of the whole village.

"No way!" she cried.

"And if he couldn't . . . get it up," I continued more brazenly, "another man stepped in to do the honors. And if *he* failed, the matchmaker was supposed to finger her."

She burst out laughing. "God," she said, "talk about performance anxiety. What kind of history book is this, anyway?"

I laughed, relieved my anecdote had gone over, but still wanted to move past the sex topic immediately. "I think I just felt a sprinkle," I said.

A crack of thunder boomed and the world seemed to shake. Rain spilled from the sky and within seconds we were soaked.

"Should we . . . take a shortcut back to the dorm?" I panted.

"Fuck that!" she laughed. "I *love* running in the rain. Isn't it wonderful?"

It was. Or, at least, it was wonderful running in the rain with someone who actually wanted to run in it with *me*. We ran the full circuit around campus, and until we got back to McMahon, drenched to the bone, for that brief period I felt young, happy, and unafraid.

*

three

The rain lasted for days, but it wasn't just rain—it was a torrential downpour. If we'd lived in the tropics it would have been a monsoon, only this was Connecticut, so it was *cold* rain. Umbrellas were useless, and when you got to class, your sopping pants and cuffs clung to your skin. What the weather meant for me, though, was that I didn't go to the library at night and couldn't search for my crush, Patrick, amid the stacks. Maybe, I'd think dreamily during study breaks, Patrick was returning to the same table on the fourth floor, night after night, in hopes of seeing me again. Maybe he was leaving notes for me in the carrel I always studied at. No, scratch that. Maybe . . . he'd forgotten the short blonde I'd seen him with and was leaving a single red rose at my carrel with *no* note.

Why not?

I bent over my desk, trying to study, but Faith was in the room, pacing from her desk to the window to blow out cigarette smoke—a small victory I had won in my goal to smell less like an ashtray, but in its own way just as irritating. And worse, our neighbor Sasha was blaring music.

Faith, wearing stonewashed black jeans, a clingy red sweater, and a pair of bright white Reebok sneakers, sat down and opened an engineering textbook. I tensed and waited for her to begin her most aggravating habit.

"Wow," she murmured, jumping straight into the routine, "how *fascinating*."

I kept silent, hoping she would leave it at that. I knew she wanted me to respond, "What's so fascinating?" but I wouldn't. Not now. Not ever.

"God," she continued, a bit louder, flipping a page, "can you *believe* that?"

Don't respond, I told myself, but the pressure to respond when spoken to—the pressure to be polite—overcame me.

"What?" I asked, defeated, hating myself.

Faith seized the opportunity to give me a full lecture on the mechanics of wheels. Instead of listening, I pondered the miracle of hairspray: Faith's blond bangs curled high above her head, frozen into a tidal-wave mold. The hair itself looked brittle. Dry. If I were to touch it, I wondered . . . would it crumble into dust? Behind her on the wall hung an eight-by-ten photo of Faith and her mother, a Caldor special: the blue sky, the fake wooden frame, the two blank stares with frozen smiles. Faith called her mother by her first name, Candace, and prided herself on their friendship rather than their mother-daughter relationship. She told me once that when she'd get home from school with her friends, Candace would hand out beers and joints. I studied Candace. She still wore her long blond hair hippie-fashion, circa the 1960s: straight, greasy, and parted down the middle. Her tanned face was lined, at odds with her youthful clothes. Her teeth flashed yellow, foreshadowing what Faith's would look like if she continued to smoke at her current maniacal rate.

"What are you making that face for?" Faith asked, interrupting my random thoughts and blowing smoke into my face. "You look like I just farted."

"Sorry," I laughed, "I was just thinking that I'm getting tired of our decor. We should get a tapestry or something."

She looked at me as if I were crazy. "Who gives a fuck about our 'decor'?" she asked. "In less than a year we're out of this hellhole. But if you want to spend *your* money fixing it up, go right ahead."

"Oh yeah," I replied, "money."

I had none. I treated myself to a few dollars a week from my paycheck—garnered from a pathetic work-study job I'd gotten sitting in the campus information booth. Everything else I earned went toward tuition, including whatever I took in during summer and winter breaks at a cable factory in my hometown. Factories pay better than minimum wage, and there were always a few of us college kids working alongside the regulars, feeling somewhat sheepish about our brief appearances. The rest was provided for through loans. Perkins. Stafford subsidized. Stafford unsubsidized. My parents couldn't understand why I would leave Eastern, with its cheap tuition, but I never considered asking them for help anyway. Even if they'd had the money, they didn't see the point of college unless you were taught a useful trade that paid big bucks, and since my interests followed the history of a place that was no more real to them than Oz, they openly decried my deepening debt. Besides which, they hadn't assisted my brothers. The fact that two of my older brothers, Mark and Phil, didn't graduate from high school, and that the other four—Bill, Adam, Jacob, and Danny—didn't *apply* to college was irrelevant.

It was 11:50, according to the clock situated on the bureau behind Faith's head, when the phone rang. It was late for someone to be calling, but I picked up, relieved to have a break from her monologue.

"Hi. Is this Natalie?"

"Yes."

"This is Patrick. We met last Friday . . . at the library?"

I thought I could feel my heart pressing against my rib cage. This wasn't supposed to happen. Even in teen movies like *Pretty in Pink* or *Sixteen Candles,* I always cringed a little when the unpopular girl finally got the hot, popular guy she'd been pining for. What on earth would they talk about after the credits rolled? I didn't want reality, I preferred the safety of fantasy. But it was *my* fault, I had told him my last name. All he had to do was look me up in the student directory, just as I had done him. "Hi," I replied, keeping my inflection low. Relaxed. "Just a second."

I cupped my palm over the earpiece. "Do you think you could go to the lounge for a while?" I whispered urgently, standing to usher Faith out.

She gave a surprised look, then shrugged and moved to leave, and I waited a beat before returning to my call.

"Let me guess," he said when I pressed the receiver back against my ear. "You're studying, right?"

"Yes . . . or, no, not exactly. I'm *trying* to study."

"Well, you can't be trying very hard if you're answering your phone."

I paused. I knew I should laugh, but I felt uncomfortable.

"Sooo," he continued, "aren't you going to ask me how I did on my makeup?"

"I wasn't planning on it," I replied, astonishing myself.

He laughed. "You're intimidating," he said, "but I guess you already know that."

I twirled a strand of hair around my finger, tightly, and prepared to deliver my trademark brush-off ("I have a boyfriend"), but something held me back. It was just a phone call. A harmless phone call. I could try. I could try to be someone different, if for only a few minutes.

"How do you figure?" I asked.

"Come on," he replied playfully. "You've mastered the 'studious, beautiful librarian' type perfectly. Men love that shit. You must get ten calls a day from guys."

I blushed. He was flirting and now it was supposed to be my turn. "Close," I kidded as my face twisted painfully with embarrassment. "More like twenty."

"Really?"

"*No.* Of course not," I replied. "You're the first guy who's called me this semester. Unless you count my dad."

"Really?"

I picked up a pen and began to draw shapes, methodically, on a yellow legal pad. "I have to thank you for calling," I said, searching for something to talk about. "My roommate was just haranguing me to death about wheels—how they work, how they were developed . . . that kind of thing. She inserts historical bits to interest me. Did you know the wheel was invented during the New Stone Age, in Mesopotamia?"

A slightly awkward silence ensued and, suddenly panicked, I asked him what he was majoring in.

"English. You?"

"History. Or, really, Russian history."

"Are you Russian?"

"No."

Pause.

"Do you know anyone who's Russian?"

"Not really," I replied, smiling in spite of myself.

"Are you planning to move to Russia?"

"I don't think so."

"Then why major in Russian history?"

"Because it's fascinating," I laughed, amused by his straight-forward questions. "Why major in English?"

"Because I want to be a writer. It has a purpose, in other words. What are you going to be? Can you become a Russian?"

I smiled. "Maybe I'll be a professor," I replied, "or go into law."

"Sounds like a lot of effort. A lot of repetition. I prefer creative subjects."

"Russian history is filled with stories that you'd be hard-pressed to ever make up, and is at least as absorbing as a lot of novels. It may not be 'creative,' in your sense of the word," I retorted, blithely, "but that doesn't mean it's not worthwhile and fulfilling."

"Okay," he replied after a lengthy pause, "but just tell me this. Since you're a Russian history major, does that mean you're a Communist?"

"No," I laughed. Then, more seriously: "Communism doesn't work. Or, at least, it hasn't worked, historically. But I like its ideals. Capitalism is pretty horrible."

"Oh, God," he sighed, "you're not one of those students who walks around handing out Socialist fliers, are you?"

"No," I replied, indignant but amused. "Why? Do you not *like* Socialists? Are they too kindhearted for your taste? Not greedy enough?"

"Ayn Rand is where it's at. I pledge allegiance to the individual and to my own happiness. Everything else is useless and ultimately weakens society."

Someone began to speak to him in the background and he asked me to hang on. I was glad for a reprieve but, to my amazement, found that I wasn't frazzled; I felt happy and charged by the conversation. Had I somehow changed? Was I suddenly ready to meet someone . . . or was it him? Was he different from the other guys who had occasionally called me? He just seemed so . . . *confident*, like he couldn't care less if I liked him or not and that, paradoxically, it was more about whether he might like me—and so far I wasn't entirely sure that he did. It made speaking to him easier somehow. Music drifted, faintly, into my ear, and I tried to guess what it was. The Smiths? Depeche Mode? Music wasn't something I invested a lot of time or money in.

"Sorry," Patrick said, returning, "I have to go."

"Sure," I replied, stunned by a pang of regret. "But, real quick . . . who *was* he?"

"Who?"

"Ayn . . . Rand?"

"*He?*" he said with a shocked laugh. "You're cute. Rand was a *she*. Gotta go."

I heard a click. I held the receiver in my hand, limply, and tried to quell my disappointment and newest embarrassment. Did he want to see me again? Talk to me? Who knew. I opened a world literature text I kept on my desk for reference and looked up Rand in the index, then flipped to the appropriate page. The weight of my error and lack of knowledge made my skin crawl. Ayn Rand, as it turned out, was a *she*.

I went over our brief conversation and convinced myself that I had sounded stupid during the entire thing. "Did you know the wheel was invented during the New Stone Age?" I recalled with horror. "Russian history is filled with stories that you'd be hard-pressed to ever make up." How could I have said that? And then, of course, there was the grand finale: "You're the *first* guy who's called me this semester! Oh, except for my *dad*." Why hadn't I just told him I was a virgin, too?

I sat on the windowsill. One lonely tree stood outside in the dim rays of the streetlamp, battered and bent by the wind. Sasha's music continued to blare, and suddenly it became the target of all my frustration and unhappiness. I paced the room, then grabbed a history book from my desk and walloped it against the pulsating wall. It made no dent in the stereo's volume. I slapped my hand against the wall, but that made even less noise. *That's it*, I thought, clenching my fists. I gripped the doorknob and thrust the door open. Sasha was someone girls generally avoided. She worked at a Hooters-style restaurant in Hartford called the Blue Lagoon, and in the dorm she wore things like high-heeled leather boots and shirts with plunging necklines, and she sashayed down the halls in a way that made you feel like she was doing you a favor by letting you get a glimpse of her. But that night, adrenaline racing, frustrated by my awkward conversation with Patrick, I rapped on her door.

Voices emanated from inside. Laughter. Then Sasha peeked out. "Hey, everybody," she yelled drunkenly, swinging the door open, "it's my neighbor, Natalie! Isn't she hot?"

Sasha stood in a nipple-baring lavender negligee top and blue jeans. Her black hair dropped to her shoulders in a straight bob with short bangs dangling over her forehead. I tried to keep my eyes locked on hers but kept crossing my arms as if the action might inspire Sasha to do the same. I felt overdressed but safe in my loose, long-sleeved black T-shirt and baggy jeans.

"She *is* hot," a male voice replied from within. "Ask her to come join the show."

I felt the blood drain from my face as Sasha placed an arm around me. Inside, several guys circled a pudgy redhead in a red lace bra and white pants. "My friend and I are giving a little lingerie show," she slurred into my ear. "So, do you need to borrow some sugar or something?"

"No," I said nervously. "It's just that it's midnight, and your music is, um, loud, and I was wondering if you would maybe lower it."

"Is that all? Hey—no problem!" she yelled, patting my back. "I'll turn it down *right away*. But why don't you come in for a drink first? Here we are, *neighbors*, and yet we've barely said two words to each other!"

With that, she grasped my hand, pulled me into the room, and slammed the door. A white shag rug covered the floor, posters of Janet Jackson and Mariah Carey draped the walls, and, much to my disgust, a tube of K-Y sat openly on a desk. I stood within the circle of guys, trying to figure out how best to leave, when a pockmarked man who looked too old to be in college put his arm around me. I wrenched myself away from him.

"Hey, little lady," he said, "I don't bite. Unless, of course, you want me to."

Sasha and her female friend burst out laughing.

"*Well*," Sasha said, finishing off her drink in one gulp, "looks like the 'little lady' isn't into you. She finds you *repulsive*. Right, Natalie?"

I gaped at her. What was I supposed to say?

Sasha laughed harder. "This is Brady," she said, resting a hand on his shoulder. "My brother. He's visiting from Pittsburgh for the week."

Her brother. There were *so many things* wrong with that statement.

"*What?*" she laughed. "We've grown up seeing each other's wing-wings. Seeing and touching are two different things."

"Yeah." Brady grinned, eyeing my chest, "but I prefer to see girls who are *not* my sister. How 'bout it?"

The nameless leeches surrounding us echoed his order: *Yeah, show us your tits. Give us some nipple.*

I started to perspire, but I couldn't make myself move. Sasha stepped in front of me and placed a hand on my shoulder. "*Jesus*," she said warily, "just go back to your room and keep studying." Turning to Brady, she sneered, "Natalie can't even deal with women seeing her tits in the bathroom, and I'd bet a million bucks she's still a virgin. Like she's going to show *you* her unmentionables."

The guys circling us laughed and whooped. I closed my eyes.

"Maybe she has a deformity," Brady suggested, now even more intrigued. "Or," he continued, stroking my arm, "maybe she just needs the right teacher."

This finally revolted me out of my stupor. I pushed him out of the way and yanked on the doorknob until it opened. As the door slammed shut I heard the laughter erupt on the other side. Laughter at my expense. I turned to open my own door, then heard another opening down the hall. Gwen was wearing over-sized flannel pajamas, and when she saw me she waved and began walking toward me. Before I knew it tears were falling down my face. I took a deep breath and wiped them away, but new tears fell in their place.

"Hey, are you okay?" she asked. "What's wrong?"

This only made me cry harder. When I couldn't speak, Gwen grabbed my hand and led me to the adjacent stairwell. It was cold sitting on the gray cement steps. "I'm sorry," I stammered, burying my face in my arms. "You must think I'm a total freak. I never cry like this. I swear. I don't know what's wrong with me."

"Really?" she asked. "Never? I cry like this at least once a month. PMS. Do you . . . want to talk about it?" she asked.

"You'll think I'm an even bigger freak."

"Yeah . . . you're probably right."

I smiled, then related the evening's occurrences, omitting my phone call with Patrick but divulging my most embarrassing secret: I was a virgin—a humiliating fact that, apparently, everyone suspected anyway.

"Look," Gwen said lightly, "Sasha is just jealous that you haven't been screwed by half the campus and come down with gonorrhea, like her. I mean, for God's sake, she's down the hall showing her 'wing-wings' to her *brother*? That's just fucking gross. And who cares if you're a virgin?" she asked loudly, her voice reverberating in the stairwell. We laughed as she dropped to a whisper: "There's *nothing wrong* with waiting."

"I bet you're not a virgin, so you can't talk," I replied.

"Oh, yeah, I slept with an asshole when I was seventeen. I peed, thinking I was coming, and the guy got grossed out and never talked to me again. But I *did* become a woman that day, so all was not a loss. Right? Aren't you envious?"

I smiled, but barely. "Really?" I asked more hopefully than I should have. "You've only . . . done it once?"

"Well, no," she replied, raising an eyebrow and crossing her arms, "but so what? I give myself more pleasure than any guy has ever been able to give me, though I'm hoping that won't *always* be the case. So, in the meantime, just get yourself off and remember that you're not really missing anything. Of course, if you *really* want to experience penetration, there's always cucumbers and bananas. Just start small, okay?"

I laughed, though appalled. "No *way*," I gasped. "With my luck, it would get stuck and I'd have to go to the emergency room—where someone I know would spot me. A girl in my high school put a frozen hot dog up herself and had to have surgery."

"That's an urban legend," she laughed. "Everyone knows of a frozen-hot-dog victim."

I grinned, realizing that *of course* it was a myth. How could I have ever thought otherwise? We brushed ourselves off and returned to the hallway.

"Want to go running tomorrow?" she asked.

"Oh. Yeah. That would be nice."

I let myself into my room, and Faith was already in bed, sleeping soundly, oblivious to the loud thudding music next door. Groping blindly, I located and turned on the night-light by my desk and began to change. I removed my ponytail elastic and let my hair fall, then pulled my shirt over my head and unsnapped my bra (turning my back to Faith, just in case). My breasts released. I caressed them, kneaded them, moved them in circles, wiggled my torso to make them shake. Alone, like that, I didn't mind my body. It was a feminine body, with curves and shadows and soft lines. Alone, in the mirror, I felt like someone else. Confident. If only I could be this person when I left the room, too.

I pulled on a T-shirt and climbed into bed, and as I settled under the covers I revisited Patrick's phone call. Maybe he had actually thought it *was* cute that I hadn't known Ayn Rand was a woman. I sighed. I began a new fantasy then, that the conversation had gone much better than I had first imagined. Relaxing, revising the conversation in my head, I stared into the blackness, searching it for signs of love.

four

I ran down the main hall of the history building as fast as I could, then took the stairs two at a time up to the third floor. The grades were taped up next to Anderson's office, and I traced the list of names until I located my own: 97. A private glee rose in my chest. With each A, I felt more like I belonged here, surer of myself and more distant from the failure I had always assumed would be mine. Sometimes I felt like returning to my town with my graded exams; I would find my former teachers and shove all my A's in their faces. *Yeah?* I would say to my high school guidance counselor. *Beauty school, huh? Thanks for the vote of confidence.* There was bitterness toward my parents, too, but it was more of a mild, lingering resentment. Blaming them for never attending a parent-teacher conference, for never asking to see a report card, felt like a waste of time. It was like complaining about the fact that I was born in Connecticut rather than sun-soaked Hawaii: It couldn't be helped.

As I stared at my A-plus, it felt similar to how I used to feel after doing penance: I was forgiven of some wrongdoing. I was a *better person*. I was cleansed.

I tore myself away from the grade list, letting out a happy sigh, and noticed a light on in Anderson's office. I focused on the sheet of paper pinned to the door: *DO **NOT** BOTHER ME OUTSIDE OF MY OFFICE HOURS*. I ignored it and knocked.

"Enter," Anderson called out, the door muffling the severity of his order.

I pushed the door ajar and poked my head in.

"May I come in?" I asked, smiling.

He was reading at his desk and reluctantly raised his eyes. He wore his standard suit and white shirt, and a navy tie with yellow and purple stripes. His ties were the only variation in his style. I dropped my bag and took a seat, enjoying the clutter around me. Books were scattered in piles on the floor, loaded into bookcases, and piled precariously on the desktop. He closed his book and I beamed at him, grinning ear to ear.

"I take it, Ms. Bloom," he said, "you've just seen your grade and couldn't resist coming here to tell me so. Why else would you disturb me outside of my office hours?"

"Thank you!" I exclaimed, unable to contain my joy a moment longer.

"You always seem so surprised," he replied, giving in to a small smile himself. "But why? You've never received less than an A-minus from me."

"You can never be sure," I answered.

Anderson studied me then. "You'd like to talk about your future," he declared in almost a challenge. "But how can I talk about your future when, really, I know nothing about you, other than the fact that you study well, write well and have a knack for memorization? If I'm to be your adviser, I need to know more. Start talking," he ordered.

I sat back in my chair. "Start talking?" I asked. "About what?"

"About yourself. Why are you here, for instance. Why history?"

I stared at my hands. "At first," I began as my palms moistened, "I chose history because I could gets A's in it. But then . . . I don't know . . . it started to seem important. It's like . . . some people deserve to be remembered."

"Some people 'deserve to be remembered'?" he laughed, with something close to disgust, "You may as well major in journalism and write obituaries for the local paper, Natalie."

I flinched. I had tried to answer him from the heart and he had mocked me. A lump formed in my throat. I couldn't locate words to express my convictions. I focused on the window behind Anderson; its black ebony borders, a smudge marking the glass. Bits of fallen leaves sat on the windowsill outside, gently moving with a breeze. I felt a need to go to the window, to wipe away the smudge.

"Natalie," Anderson said, snapping me out of my momentary freeze, "is our meeting over? Where are you?"

I looked at him. "I just . . . I like reading about foreign places and events. I don't know why."

Anderson sighed. "Natalie," he said, softer now, "as your adviser, I'm going to tell you something I have observed about you. Do you realize that whenever you speak in class, you end your sentences with 'I don't know,' or 'but I'm not sure,' or some other qualifier—which undermines whatever you have just said? I know this isn't you. I read your papers and essays and there are no weak statements. I see confidence and a woman who knows her own intelligence. Will you teach someday and end your lectures with 'but . . . maybe not'?"

"But . . . " I began, letting the sentence drift off as I started to cry. I placed my face in my hands, horrified. This was not what I had expected.

"Please," he said awkwardly, rummaging around his desk until he located a box of tissues. "Don't. I apologize if I was too brusque. What I'm *saying* is that you have talent, and it would be a shame if you failed to see this or allowed others to surpass you because of weaknesses that could have been controlled."

I swallowed and wiped my nose.

"What I would like is to see you go as far as you are able," he continued. "And from my viewpoint, that is very far indeed. History in itself isn't going to lead to any particular 'job' per se, but it will provide you with knowledge and discipline for whatever field you decide to pursue."

He rose then, heaving himself up with some exertion, and limped around the books on the floor until he reached the door. With his hand on the brass knob, his body framed by the rich cedarwood, he looked down at me. "Come back next week," he said in as nice a voice as he could muster. "I wish I had more time now, but I have a personal meeting I must attend to. But, really, I look forward to advising you, Natalie."

I slipped out, thanking him as I passed by, and walked

quickly out of the building. It was cold out, but bearable, with thick white clouds concealing any hint of color. Leaves, still the brilliant red and orange of early autumn, fell and scurried along the dying grass. I went to a small courtyard nearby and sat on its circular stone wall. In the center, a fountain bubbled, with one pool set high above another. A group of future freshmen walked past with a tour guide—a clean-cut guy sporting a UConn jacket and matching cap who, I suspected, volunteered his services in hopes of impressing the prettiest high school girls in the bunch. They stopped several feet away and the Husky-loving guide pointed to the humanities building, mentioning the high standing a liberal arts education from UConn was considered to have in the world of Life After College. I twisted my body in the opposite direction and looked at my reflection in the water. The way I was holding my head—my chin tucked into my neck—I looked as if I had a double chin, and I quickly jutted my chin back out. Then I poked a finger into the icy water, scattering my image in a thousand different directions.

I pulled my legs up onto the stone ledge and hugged them to my chest, then rubbed my temples where a headache was beginning. Suddenly a rock hit the water directly in front of me, splashing freezing droplets into my face and wetting my coat— brown corduroy with a large rip under the left arm exposing a red-and-white-plaid lining. I let out a small scream and jerked my head up in irritation to see who had thrown the missile. Patrick stood a few feet away, grinning. In the daylight he looked even taller and more attractive. He wore khakis with a royal-blue down jacket, and his hair was slightly redder than I'd recalled. A light breeze blew strands into his face, and he swept them aside. He was handsome, and at that moment, impish.

"Is that how you say hello?" I asked, wiping the drops of water from my face and drying my wet hands against my sleeves.

"Sorry," he replied, sitting beside me. "You just looked so lost in thought. So preoccupied. I couldn't resist the opportunity for surprise."

I smiled, reluctantly. "Your ambush succeeded."

There were fourteen thousand students on campus. How did he come to walk by at that particular moment, when I was so completely out of sorts? I wasn't ready to see him.

"I apologize for getting off the phone with you so quickly when I called last week," he said. "My dealer had just shown up with some pot. I had to pay him and—you know how it goes—when you buy it you have to then smoke some with the fuck. Protocol."

"No, I didn't know that," I replied, cataloguing this new information about him as I shifted an inch or two away. Not once had I ever fantasized about him doing bong hits. "I've never actually bought pot."

"Really?" he asked, sounding genuinely shocked. "I completely pegged you for a stoner."

I looked at him, offended. Because of my brothers, most of whom were avid pot smokers, I was wary of pot and of those who smoked it, and I had only recently tried it with Faith. The one time I had done it, it was fun, but all I could think, as Patrick sat staring at me, was that he could see through my conservative veneer to what lay beneath: white trash and low expectations.

"Are you serious?" I asked.

"No," he answered, straight-faced. He shrugged and smiled, then reached out and wiped away a drop of water from my cheek.

"Missed one," he said.

I averted my eyes, embarrassed by his touch, then I looked at my watch, purposefully. "I've got to get going," I said, trying to sound indifferent.

"Where to?" he asked with evident disappointment. "I was hoping you might want to grab some lunch with me. I was just on my way to the Student Union. I can tell you all I know about Ms. Ayn Rand."

I reddened at the reminder, but realized that I didn't want to leave.

"I guess I should eat." I shrugged.

Patrick laughed. "Wow. You 'guess you should eat.' I don't think anyone has ever sounded so thrilled to hang out with me."

I smiled as my blush deepened. He joined me and we began walking across the dried lawn toward the Student Union. Small groups of students clumped together here and there, leaning on elbows, squatting, sitting Indian-style while smoking or chatting or studying, and we weaved through them, giving each a wide berth. A guy trying to look like Kurt Cobain strummed on a guitar, humming a tune that I knew I should know but didn't. He was awful . . . and yet a gaggle of girls sat listening to him, nodding their heads along to the mellow beat, smiling too earnestly in their Doc Martens and self-made necklaces. I glanced at Patrick. Seeing him in the flesh made me realize how childish my fantasies had been—and yet I continued to have them even as we strolled along. For instance, when he rolled his eyes at me while nodding at the Kurt Cobain wanna-be, it proved, in some small way, that I was right in thinking that he was different and that, together, we could see things in the same way. I again had that fleeting feeling of being *known* even without having revealed a thing, and it made me breathe a little faster while smiling like a numskull. He was a full head taller and I saw that his shoes—a pair of standard brown loafers—were scuffed, the right one not even completely attached to the sole. I figured he was from the rich part of Connecticut, though I generally thought this of most students. Greenwich, perhaps, or maybe Fairfield. Was blue, the color of his coat, his favorite color? I was glad he dressed as he did, neither buying into Husky-mania nor the flannel-shirted grunge so popular at the time—but mainly because if he *had* been into grunge, he wouldn't have been interested in me. Grunge, goth, alt-rock, baseball-capped frat boys, and scrunchie-wearing sorority girls . . . it seemed like each clique erected an exclusive club based on fashion alone, and if you, yourself, didn't dress accordingly there was very little cross-mating. I stole a glance at Patrick's face, noticing light-blond stubble and tiny lines skirting his eyes. I usually fantasized about smoky, dark-haired, dark-eyed guys. Mediterranean looks. Patrick oozed English paleness, Irish freckles.

"Don't think I can't feel you staring at me," he said with a swift scoop of my hand into his. I resisted an impulse to snatch my hand away. The feel of his palm pressed against mine felt . . . nice, but I still wished he would release me. We weren't friends—we weren't *anything*—and I disliked this phony display.

"Look," I said, finding an excuse to withdraw my hand. I pointed at a Hare Krishna adherent handing out brochures on the Student Union's steps, his orange tuft of hair pointing skyward.

Patrick studied me for a minute before replying. "I'm thinking about joining their ranks. I like their message: tranquility and love. What more could one want?"

I smiled and lightly nudged his shoulder.

"You, apparently," he continued, holding his shoulder in mock pain, "prefer strife and violence. You'll never be accepted, so don't even try."

I smirked as we walked on. My gait felt off-kilter; my arms literally felt like they belonged on someone else as I swung them, crossed them, and kept them still.

"Can I ask you something?" Patrick asked, staring at me.

"Sure."

"Did it bother you when I held your hand just now?"

"Yeah, actually, it did," I replied, holding my head high.

"Why?"

"Because you don't know me, and I don't know you."

"Oh," he replied, sounding disappointed. "I thought we did know each other. I thought we even liked each other."

I stopped and he smiled, softly and with kindness, and almost shyly put his hands in his pockets as if unsure of what to do with them. The clouds broke, sending a flash of sunlight across his face. I was confused. I wanted to ask him what he meant by the word "like."

"No," I finally replied, "I can't stand you."

His mouth opened slightly and his eyes swelled. I pursed my lips, constraining the desire to grin, but it was too late. Patrick laughed. He mussed my hair and gave me a light squeeze. A gust of wind blew Patrick's hair back, exposing his high forehead. I momentarily thought of phrenology—if there was anything to it (which, of course, I doubted), Patrick's forehead would have to be a mark of intelligence.

"Oh, Natalie," he sighed, once again closing his hand around mine and leading me toward the Student Union, "where have you been?"

"Where have *you* been?" I responded in the same vein, sliding my hand out of his and offering him a gentle, but slightly sarcastic, smile.

Jonathan's was a generic fast-food place in the Student Union, and you could use some of the points on your food card to eat there. It was on the first floor, past the lobby and the hall filled with flyers and advertisements and the stage where students were allowed to preach to passersby. The students who were employed at Jonathan's always seemed to be having way too good a time as they dipped potato wedges into scalding animal fat. Other than a Husky paw print, the place itself had no theme—no Burger King crown or golden arches—but it featured the color blue in its accents. The name of the place was in neon blue, the menus used blue type, the clerks wore blue aprons, and the room overflowed with small formica tables that had bright blue seats attached to them.

I scanned the overhead menu, repeatedly, not sure of what to order. If I ordered the special, French onion soup, I would risk turning Patrick off with slurping sounds, not to mention unsavory breath. If I ordered a burger, there were always those awkward bites when the tomato squeezed out of the bun, dripping mayonnaise and grease all over your hands. Even the chicken nuggets seemed too risky, with their greasy fried shells.

"What do you want?" Patrick pressed as the throng of waiting customers glared.

"A baked potato," I blurted, judging it the most manageable choice.

"Anything on it?" the female clerk asked. "Cheddar cheese? Broccoli?"

"No," I replied, handing over my ID card to pay. "Plain. And I'll have a water. Tap, please."

We took our trays and found a table in the corner. En route, several guys who knew Patrick yelled out hellos. He casually replied "Hi" back. Passing one table of five guys, he flipped them off, whereupon the group broke into uncontrollable laughter.

"Losers," Patrick said, sliding into the seat across from me.

I smiled and split open my baked potato. Steam fled out, exposing an overcooked white interior, and I knew before tasting it that it would be as dry and crumbly as cardboard. I doused it with salt and a pinch of pepper and hoped for the best.

"What brought you to UConn?" I asked, spooning in a mouthful. Worse than I'd expected. It was so dry I wasn't sure if I'd be able to swallow. I took a swig of water to help push it down.

"Is this an interview?" he asked.

I blushed and picked at my potato. "Why *not* UConn?" he said. "It was easy. My parents have enough money to send me anywhere, but I didn't really have the grades. I also figured that, since I want to write, it didn't really matter where I went. I shouldn't have to go to school at all. But I don't mind it. My parents pay, I don't work, and I get to smoke a lot of pot. It's a good deal."

I took another overbaked bite and tried not to resent the way he so easily accepted his free ride, focusing instead on the implications of his words. He was rich. I was right. And again he was talking about pot.

"What about you?" he asked.

I shifted uncomfortably. Should I have told him I was a transfer student? I had grown used to the disrespect that an education from Eastern received at UConn. "You must really like pot," I said, sipping my water and changing the subject. "You mention it pretty often."

He leaned back in his blue plastic chair and finished chewing a bite of burger, his mouth swiveling in a circular motion that I found charming.

"I do like it," he finished, picking up his Coke. "It's probably my favorite thing in the whole world."

"Wow," I replied, wondering if perhaps I had underrated weed. His favorite thing in the whole world?

"I think it lets me see people as they really are."

"Is that a good thing?"

"Depends," he said, looking at me intently. "Sometimes it makes me feel a little crazy. Everyone seems affected. Fake. Ugly."

"You don't make it sound very fun," I laughed with some nervousness.

Patrick smiled. I felt his gaze scan, flitting from my hair to my face, zeroing in on individual features—my eyes, nose, and mouth. "You're cute," he said.

I avoided his eyes and tried not to smile, but the corners of my mouth tugged upwards. My palms grew damp and I feared wet rings would soon appear under my arms. Time to change the subject.

"How 'bout those Red Sox?" I joked, loathing myself for my obvious discomfort.

He continued to look at me, his look satisfied. Almost rapt.

"How 'bout the fact that my head is too large for my body?" he countered, deadpan.

I laughed. "No," I giggled, shaking my head back and forth. "It is not. It fits you. You're tall. If your head were any smaller it would look weird."

"I don't know that I agree with you. You know the McDonald's commercial where Mac Tonight sings at a piano? His head is giant and shaped like the moon? I think my head looks like that."

I covered my mouth to keep from spewing potato every-where. His comment was funny because it was true: I could see a resemblance to Mac Tonight, albeit a slight one.

"See?" he continued. "You think so, too, or you wouldn't be laughing so hard."

I grasped my water and took several gulps, trying to suppress the giggles that were spilling forth.

"Thirsty?" he asked.

His question made me laugh harder. I focused on my potato until my manic laughter slowed and finally ceased. Then, in as serious a tone as I could muster, I replied, "Yes, I am thirsty."

Then I began laughing again. Hysterically. Silently.

He leaned forward, breaking into laughter himself. "You're funny. Either you must really think I have the biggest head in the universe, or you don't get out enough."

"I can't help it," I whispered, the words squeaking out between soundless heaves. "I never laugh like this, I'm sorry."

I buried my face in my arms in deep embarrassment, abashed but still happy. I relaxed, my laughter died. I glanced up and gave him a tiny, shy smile. "I'm sorry," I whispered again.

"Don't be," he whispered back, placing his hand on my knee under the table, reiterating his earlier claim: "I like you."

I checked his expression for sarcasm, and, not seeing any, smiled what might have been my most honest smile ever. I felt absolved. A priest could wipe away sin, but Patrick, perhaps, could wipe away insecurity, and in a different way than earning A's could.

"You know," he then said, leaning back in his chair with his hands folded behind his head, "it's kind of weird that you *don't* know who Ayn Rand is. She was Russian. She denounced the Bolsheviks? Have you *never* heard of *Atlas Shrugged*?"

My honest smile wavered. I hadn't studied about this person . . . this person who was *Russian*. Russia and all things

Russian were supposed to be my specialty. The one field where my ignorance wasn't so obvious. I felt as if Patrick had just slapped me after handing me a flower. "Oh, yeah," I stammered guiltily, "I think I remember something about her now."

He eyed me, amused. "Was she a psychologist or a political figure?"

He was testing me, and I was about to fail. I stared at him, blankly, my smile weakening.

"She wrote *novels*," he said cheerfully, squeezing my knee again, forgiving my lack of knowledge with a dashing grin. "I'll lend you my copies, if you want."

My smile, my honest smile, returned, though with a bit more reserve. "Okay," I said quietly, nodding my head. "Thanks."

*

five

After a whole life spent avoiding boys and romantic realities, how do you embrace a real romance when it finally presents itself?

You don't, exactly. You continue to think in a puerile way, bestowing the idea of love with hearts and lots of XO's—even if that's not your personality.

Especially if it is not your personality.

The day after our chance encounter, I sat at my library carrel with a book on Lenin open before me, but all I could think about was Patrick. Words blurred and my mind drifted to bits of conversation and looks shared between us at our impromptu lunch. *Wow*, I thought with a mixture of worry and excitement, *not even Lenin can hold my attention*. General Brusilov or even Trotsky I could have understood. But Lenin? I giggled.

It was Patrick's history I wanted to memorize. My mind ran through some of the bio that he had shared, and what was most surprising was how closely it paralleled the fantasy-Patrick I'd been thinking about. In a way he personified what the university meant to me; he was worldly, intellectual, wealthy. He came from a background that was entirely different from my own blue-collar one. I imagined that in high school he would have been in the popular clique that dismissed girls like me. It made me feel as if I had fooled him somehow. This excited me, but it was intimidating, too.

Like me, Patrick was a senior, but unlike me he knew exactly what he wanted to do after graduation. He intended to move to New York City, a place he described as a shimmering island of glass and light, of culture and intellectual pursuit, whereas before I had always pictured slums, ghettos, crime. He thought he might find work in a book publishing house to start off—to earn money while he wrote his own novels and plays. His confidence was absolute. My own future was murky, but he would be an artist. Smart and refined. He could quote Shakespeare and passages from Chaucer's *Canterbury Tales*. He had favorite authors: Ernest Hemingway, Raymond Carver, Willa Cather, Paul Auster. I, myself, had only read Hemingway's *For Whom the Bell Tolls*, but that was in high school and I couldn't remember it at all. That I had read Gogol and Tolstoy meant nothing, because they had been *required* reading, whereas Patrick consumed books, mainly, it seemed to me, for *pleasure*. He had two younger sisters, Sherry and Belinda, and both—according to him—were more attractive and talented than he, assertions that only served to make him more appealing. I couldn't fathom a sibling bestowing genuine compliments on me or on anyone else. Sherry was a sophomore at Yale and wanted to be a doc-

tor; Belinda, a senior in high school, intended to study archi-
tecture at the Rhode Island School of Design. His parents, still
married, were, in his view, as annoying as a couple straight out
of *Leave It to Beaver,* only smarter. His father, a CEO for a
food company, enjoyed his success but felt unfulfilled. ("He's
always encouraged me to write," Patrick confided. "He doesn't
want me to end up doing something lame like him.") His
mother, on the other hand, was valedictorian of her high school
class but passed up college in favor of marriage, a decision he
clearly disapproved of. ("She could have done anything," he
scowled. "But instead she was a stay-at-home mom.") He liked
several bands, but none compared to Morrissey and the Smiths.
He worshipped Howard Stern, much to my chagrin. He liked
basketball, baseball, hockey, and football—a sports guy (definitely a negative, but bearable). He was self-effacing, funny, and
an atheist—a fact he reported with obvious certainty, like it
was the only rational conclusion out there. But, most importantly, he seemed to like me. *Me.* Even though I hadn't revealed
nearly as much about myself as he had, I felt certain that he
wasn't like the other guys who had hit on me over the years—
the ones who had clearly only done so because they liked something about the way that I looked. Patrick, I could tell, was
reacting to my personality.

I laid my head on my folded arms and went over, for the
thousandth time, the moment when he had asked me out:
Walking together out of the Student Union, he had brushed a
leaf off of my shoulder. "Where are you going now?" he then
asked, appearing despondent to part ways.

"Class," I replied, smiling.

"How about later?"

"I have to study," I answered.

"Well, what will you be doing at, say, two a.m.?"

I laughed. "Sleeping."

"I'm not having much luck here. Okay, let *me* tell *you* what you'll be doing on Friday night, then: dinner with me—someplace retro-stylish, like Friendly's. Afterwards, I'll escort you to a high-class, elegant, beer-guzzling party. Right?"

Enough nonsense, I commanded and pinched myself to control my excitement. I was terrified, though, at the prospect of going to a party with a guy. Would we guzzle alcohol, or would we actually talk? And if we *did* get drunk and make out, would we ever talk again afterwards? Of course, the dinner beforehand was an even more frightening prospect *because* there would be no alcohol. I sat upright and looked at my book, unconvinced, then looked at what I was wearing: blue jeans and an oversized gray sweatshirt. A new worry arose: *What am I going to wear?* Nothing I owned, *nothing*, would do. Jeans would have to suffice for my bottom half; I prayed Faith, or maybe even Gwen, might allow me to raid her closet for my top half.

In fits and starts I managed to finish reading the page I was on and flipped to the next. A photo of Lenin with type surrounding it spanned both pages. I traced my fingertip over his features: his shiny black eyes, sharp nose, and thin lips. He wore a fur cap in the shot, hiding his balding scalp, and appeared to be screaming at a crowd that would be forever cut from the frame. I read the caption beneath it, but the words didn't penetrate. Instead I pictured Patrick typing on a newsroom-style typewriter, the keys clicking and clacking as he wrote great, inspired things. Why had he waited to ask me out? Would we ever have spoken again had we not run into each other?

The library lights flicked on and off three times, alerting students to pack up as the library was about to close. I checked my watch and was astonished to see that it was ten to midnight. I placed my books into my green knapsack and made my way out slowly behind an attractive couple with arms draped around each other, blocking the aisle so that no one could pass. Some twenty people stood waiting for one of two elevators. Everyone seemed to have come in pairs. I watched the couples hug, the friends laugh, and tried to listen in on the conversations and the whispers. The elevator doors opened and everyone flowed in, cramming into the available space, then crammed some more until bodies pressed into one another as the elevator began its descent. I froze to keep inadvertent contact to a minimum.

"You're Natalie, right?"

I jerked my head to the left, stunned to hear my name. A familiar face—though I wasn't sure how—looked back at me. It was handsome, symmetrical.

"Yes," I replied, joining the crowd as it moved, en masse, into the lobby.

"I was in a history class with you last semester. Intro to Ancient Civilization? My name's Jack Auburn."

"Oh, okay," I replied, remembering and placing him: the sharp jawline, the friendly brown eyes and tan skin and perfectly placed features. The class had been huge, with at least two hundred students, housed in a giant lecture hall that had seats stretching arclike around the professor's dais, like a Greek amphitheater. How could he have noticed me? "I can't believe you remember my name!"

"I remember lots of things about you," he replied with a smile, casually placing his hands in the pockets of his jeans. His T-shirt, green with a blue-ridged collar, rode up, exposing tight stomach muscles. The way he held himself, the leather cuff at his wrist, the carefree attractiveness of his face, the waves in his hair, was, simply put, very cool. "You used to shake your hand out when class ended from taking notes so fast," he continued. "It was very impressive."

I tensed and looked at the floor. I thought he was making fun of me, but I decided to go along with it. "Yeah," I said, "I'm a geek."

"It wasn't geeky," he said, shaking his head. "It was awesome. I used to sit near you, hoping you'd notice me, but you never did. Then there was that fateful day when I asked if I could borrow your notes. You said no."

"I did?" I replied, reddening. "Sorry. It's . . . kind of a policy. I leant my notes once and never got them back. So, now I don't. Lend."

"That's legit," Jack said, "you're forgiven. But only if you notice me the next time I see you. Okay?"

"Okay." I laughed, made a goofy face, and said, "No problemo," in a guttural, inane voice.

Jack gave a half-smile, amused.

"Take it easy," he said, walking backward to join a group of friends standing by the elevator. "Peace."

I watched him put on his jacket—a red fleece pullover with a hood—and walk out. I cursed myself for my ridiculous "No problemo" and inched toward the exit to avoid catching up with Jack's entourage. Outside, the fog felt refreshing. I smiled and laughed at myself for my nerdy behavior, even as I argued with myself that Jack was not my type. Anyone who said good-bye with the word "Peace," I thought, was probably not someone I would enjoy spending time with. I liked "cool" people from afar but often cringed when they started speaking. Patrick, on the other hand, was a different kind of cool in my mind. A genuine cool achieved through intelligence and wit, not gimmicks and name brands. He might not have possessed Jack's exceptional good looks, but he was far cooler than Jack because he didn't care what people thought. He didn't *try*, and it was this, his *not trying*, that impressed me most of all.

When I got back to McMahon, Linda was sitting in the main lounge, alone, writing in a notebook. I considered sneaking past on my way to the elevator, but decided against it.

"Hi," I said, sitting on the generic beige sofa beside her. She was wearing a black turtleneck and black slacks that made her look trimmer than usual.

"Natalie!" she said. "I'm so happy to see you! I was just thinking I needed a study break."

I settled in a bit more, pulling my feet up onto the couch. Her skin glittered and appeared smooth as porcelain, and I wondered if I should borrow her powder for my date. "Any news about Pete?" I asked hopefully.

Her smile vanished. "You know what?" she said, some-what aggressively. "I'm over him. I thought he was cute, but he's a jerk."

I didn't want to know why Pete was a jerk, but Linda leaned in close: "He told my friend Ian we had *sex*. Can you believe that?"

I wasn't sure what to believe. "And you . . . didn't?"

"*No.* My God, Natalie! I don't just put out like that! And what a creep for saying it, either way!"

"Oh—I didn't mean . . . anything," I said nervously, trip-ping over my words. "I mean, I didn't think that you *had* had sex."

Her buoyant smile returned. "No biggie," she said. "And anyway, I'm pretty sure Ian told me because he has a crush on me. He probably wanted to make sure that I hadn't slept with such an *asshole*. Do you know Ian? He lives on the second floor . . . he lives with Robbie?"

I nodded, even though I had no idea who Ian was.

"Ian and I have been friends for, like, two years, and I wouldn't want to jeopardize our friendship by having a fling with him. I mean, he's been *kind of* with this girl Samantha for a few months, but it's definitely not going anywhere. I shouldn't say this, because *she's* my friend, too, but she's kind of an airhead. She majors in *Sports and Recreation*. Can you be-lieve that's a major?"

Linda laughed, and I laughed along, but I felt terribly un-comfortable, and at that moment I didn't pity Linda but I did rather despise her. I got up to leave.

"Natalie?" she said as I bid her good-bye, a desperate ping

in her voice. "You won't tell anyone what I said? About Ian, and Samantha? I shouldn't say mean things."

I stopped. I wondered if Linda had any idea of the things that were said about her, but I didn't think she had a clue. "Don't worry," I said. "I don't know who Ian is, and I don't know who Samantha is, either. In fact, I really don't know *anyone*, Linda, so who do you think I would tell?"

Her shoulders relaxed and she laughed. "Oh Natalie," she said, "you're so funny."

I wanted to shake her. I wanted to tell her that I highly doubted that Ian liked her romantically and that it was strange of her to assume such an improbable thing, especially since it sounded like he had a girlfriend. A few months with one person in college was a major commitment. But Linda was erecting all sorts of façades around herself—maybe to protect her ego, or maybe just to feel likable, and that I could understand. I just couldn't understand how *often* she lied to herself. It made her seem slightly crazy, and it was clearly why she was so roundly disliked.

"I'm *not* funny," I said, wanting to burst at least one of her bubbles. "And I really have no idea why you keep saying that I am."

"You just don't see it," she said, returning to her notebook with a giggle, "but you are."

And that, there, is the kicker. How other people see us, I was learning, is not necessarily how we see ourselves.

I went upstairs and got ready for bed, but I couldn't go to sleep until I had imagined Patrick's first kiss, repeatedly. It would happen after our dinner at Friendly's but before we got to the party, and it would accompany a simple, direct line from him, like, "I like you," or "Can I kiss you?" I hoped, though, that he wouldn't ask and would just *do it*, even if it took me by surprise . . . because if he asked me for a kiss, I knew that I just might say no.

*

six

The period before the first date is vitally important, in the same way that Christmas Eve is just as—no more—thrilling than Christmas Day. The anticipation, the fear, the hope, the adrenaline buzz, until you are dizzy with exhaustion . . . who doesn't recall this as well as any date? But how you behave—how you *think*—during this important period can explain so much of what happens to you after.

Sunlight flooded in through the library's giant square windows, warming my back as I read for an hour or more at a stretch, taking breaks only to use the water fountain or the bathroom. Not that I was getting any real work done. I closed my book and leaned back. In less than twenty-four hours, I would be going on my first official date. What would Patrick think if he knew he was the first to take me out? Would he be intrigued? Dismayed? Terrified? Would he assume all was not well in the hardwiring of my brain?

Twenty years old. That was how old my brother Jacob had been when he killed himself. Ever since my birthday last December I had been aware of this commonality with my dead brother. I pulled at the skin on my face and felt the taut flesh. Jacob had always seemed generally happy to me. To everyone. His first suicide attempt, of course, woke us all up to the fact that he *wasn't* happy, but even after that it was easy to forget— probably because we never, ever, talked about it. Life went on. Jacob's life went on, too.

I redid my sagging ponytail, packed up, and returned to the dorm, not entirely aware of walking across campus. I stopped off in the mailroom when I reached McMahon, but as usual there was nothing in my box except for junk mail and a notice concerning new safety precautions on campus, all of which I tossed. I took the elevator and moved down the hall, murmuring required hellos. All up and down the hall, doors were left open to encourage visitors and also to advertise the personalities of those within. Some blared the poppy Spin Doctors or Hootie and the Blowfish and screamed "I'm fun!"; others advertised allegiance to the Velvet Underground, the Grateful Dead, or Phish and a propensity for drugs. And then, of course, there were the classic-rock-themed rooms, with continuous play of Hendrix, the Eagles, Steve Miller, and the Doors. My door, of course, was closed tight. I unlocked it and shoved it open, but then . . . oh . . . no.

Faith and her boyfriend, Keith, were nude, their bodies entwined on Faith's narrow bed.

I clamped my eyes shut, but it was too late. I had seen it all: the in-and-out motion, the boobs, pubic hair, and flesh.

"What the fuck!" Faith screamed.

I squinted my eyes open and was relieved that they were already hidden beneath her pink comforter. Keith, who always seemed untrustworthy, smiled and allowed her to cover his bared torso, which, I noticed, was hairy and obscenely muscular. His dark brown hair was tousled, his cheeks pink with exertion. A bland-looking guy, made blander by his utter lack of interest in anything other than himself. He was crude, belligerent, arrogant. He was a high school dropout, but this had never daunted him, and, if anything, fueled his sense of oafish superiority. He didn't need to shell out thousands of bucks to earn a degree that wouldn't necessarily lead to a better-paying job, and his current job—as a croupier at the Foxwoods casino—provided him with a decent income *and* health benefits. This, of course, didn't inhibit his blatantly racist comments, and he slurred the casino's Indian operators every chance he could get. I couldn't stand him. He knew it, I knew it, and Faith knew it. She tried to limit his visits to when I had class, but the overlaps were inevitable, and I couldn't stop myself from haranguing her: What kind of twenty-eight-year-old hangs out at a college dorm? What kind of a jerk leaves his stuff in the middle of the floor? It was this—his frequent visits, his overnight stays—that affected *me*. *I* had to listen to his inane lectures about Life, to his prejudiced philosophies, to his chauvinistic comments, to his jokes that were never funny. *I* had to endure his Public Displays of Affection—groping Faith and slobbering all over her face. But at that moment he wasn't Keith. He was just a naked guy in my room.

I spun around, aghast.

"Sorry," I muttered inaudibly, "I thought you had class now." I slipped out, shutting the door on Faith's continuing cries of grievance. Once in the hall, I stood motionless. My thoughts were stuck on the thrusting motion I had briefly witnessed, and the image made me sick with embarrassment. I felt as if I had viewed them doing something disgusting, like vomiting. Was it the nudity, the grinding of flesh against flesh? Or did it just strike me as wrong, like a grotesque, rippling fart that makes you either laugh or run away as fast as you can?

I ducked into the women's bathroom and locked myself in a stall the color of a rotten peach. Scrapes of paint flaked away, exposing a black base. The metal was etched with graffiti and drawings of dicks and pussies, thus labeled, and I realized with a kind of doomed anxiety that looking at cock drawings on toilet stalls was my only real knowledge of what a penis even *looked* like. So what if I grew up with six brothers? Unlike Sasha, I never, *never*, saw their *things,* or wing-wings or whatever one called them. God, no. And they never, *never*, saw my things. God, *no*! And sex, the idea of it, the word itself, was never mentioned. My parents had a smorgasbord of children, clearly the result of fluid passing between them, but as far as I was concerned, my parents' marriage was one where sex was limited to the goal of procreation. If a couple kissed on TV, I was told to leave the room. If a couple kissed in the movie theater, I was instructed to use the lavatory. There was, of course, the one "essential" conversation. My mother's classic birds-and-bees speech. It went something like this:

"Natalie, there's something you should know."

"What?"

"Someday blood will come out of your . . . you know, down *there*, and it's okay."

End of discussion.

Later, when my breasts were two tiny triangles, I had nervously asked her to buy me a bra, but she said there was no need for one, and, ashamed, I was afraid to ask again when I truly did need one. I briefly wrapped tape around my upper torso in an effort to disguise their development, but the tape loosened by midday, and besides, it was very uncomfortable. I grew to loathe my breasts, especially in the company of boys. I mean, no wonder they had ogled me back then. My boobs had jiggled much more than other girls', leaving much less to the imagination.

I grimaced. It had been far worse with my brothers. Having breasts around them just seemed . . . *wrong*.

I glanced down at where my breasts should have been, but they were hidden by the looseness of my heavy gray sweatshirt. Two girls entered the bathroom and I tensed, preparing to leave, but they were just checking themselves. "Yeah, he's pretty good in bed, I guess," a bored voice sighed. "Really?" her companion asked. "He seems like the selfish type."

Sluts, I thought, in complete jealousy.

After they departed, I grabbed the neck of my sweatshirt and peered down at my full breasts, held poised in a white lace bra, and they looked . . . pretty. I closed my eyes and imagined Patrick standing before me, reaching out and lightly running his hands over them. The thought thrilled me, frightened me, sent strange sensations fluttering through my body, ultimately focusing, well, down *there*, which suddenly felt moist and hot and aching for physical contact. I tentatively touched myself through my jeans, tingling at the slight pressure that pleaded for more. But then the shame set in—the shock at what I was doing, at what I was considering. I yanked my hand away and flushed the toilet in case I had company. Then I took the stairs to avoid meeting anyone in the elevator, because I felt like anyone who saw me would suddenly possess ESP and know what lurid thoughts were passing through my brain. Outside, it was thirty degrees, and made worse by a biting windchill. It amazed me how quickly the weather could change here. I pulled the cuffs of my sweatshirt down over my fingers and willed my legs forward.

The campus was in a desolate phase and resembled an abandoned factory mill. Ugly brick buildings, yellowed grass, trees that were balding and surrounded by dead brown leaves. Students walked briskly, forgetting sidewalks and traipsing across lawns, taking every shortcut possible in order to reach a place of warmth quickly. I began a light jog toward the off-campus bus stop with the goal of finding something sexy to wear in the decrepit town of Willimantic. Or, if not exactly "sexy," something more appealing than what I then owned. Something that wasn't two or three sizes too large. A bus neared and I sprinted as my knapsack swung wildly. I flailed my arms to attract the driver's attention and leapt onto the bus a second before it pulled away from the curb.

"A buck," the obese driver ordered. I dug into my coin purse and dropped four quarters into the feeder, then chose a seat and rested my head against the window, savoring the heat blowing out of the vents. Landscape zipped by, increasingly tinged with poverty as the bus neared Willimantic. Trash lined the road. Ugly. I tensed, as I usually did when nearing my hometown, although the bus would deliver me before I actually reached it. I took out a textbook, but before I knew it the bus jerked to a vicious stop. My bag fell and slid several rows ahead and I quickly jumped up to retrieve it, but by the time I reached the end of the aisle, the driver was already closing the doors.

"Hey!" I yelled. "This is my stop."

The driver looked at me, and with what seemed like the greatest of frustrations swung the doors open again—his body language implying he was not just reopening a door but being asked to shovel shit. I could almost read his thoughts: *Fuck you, college bitch, fuck you right to hell. You're no better than me.*

"Sorry," I murmured, and hopped off.

West End Mall. Shaped like the letter "T" and carrying several chain stores, it was the down-market version of the universal American Mall, with fewer options and bare of any sprightly fountains or gardens. I walked quickly, taking a quick survey of each store before deciding on the Weathervane. The sale rack, where I headed first, was filled with orange turtleneck sweaters and puke-green pants. Not what I had in mind. I turned next to a table offering scoop-neck sweaters in an array of colors. I chose two—one a heather gray, the other a soft violet—and asked for a fitting room.

"Of course," the salesgirl replied, blond hair flowing and a frozen, lipsticked smile on her face. "But would you mind first storing your bag at the front desk?"

I handed over my backpack and took a stub with the letter "A" on it in return, annoyed. When I was a kid, store clerks had always watched me and my brothers like hawks, assuming our ratty clothing meant shoplifter.

"Now be sure to let me know if there's anything I can do to help," she purred. "My name is Brianna."

I muttered "Thanks," slammed the door, and tried on one of the tops. The fit was snug. Its material lightly cupped my breasts but was still loose enough to not make me feel completely exposed and self-conscious.

"How was everything?" Brianna fake-smiled when I exited. "Do you need a different size?"

I shook my head and stopped to look through an earring rack. I chose a set of silver hoops and held them up to my ear in the miniature mirror. Next, I fingered a silver necklace with a tear-shaped turquoise stone.

"Some of our jewelry is fifteen percent off," Brianna interrupted, startling me. "But unfortunately," she went on, deliberately eyeing the necklace, "not that."

My cheeks reddened. "I don't like the necklace," I said defensively, "but are these . . . earrings on sale?"

"Yes!" she exclaimed exuberantly, as if someone had just asked her if she'd like a million dollars.

I smiled curtly and strolled over to the cashier—*See, Brianna?* I thought, suddenly more like my bus driver than I'd expected. *I am buying these things. I can afford them . . . I can afford anything I damn well please, so why don't you go screw yourself*—and laid down the sweaters and earrings in a heap. A middle-aged woman asked me how I was doing in the flattest voice I had ever heard, a voice that said she hated herself and the world but was too entirely bored to do anything about it. She looked past my head as she snatched my five-hundred-dollar limit credit card.

"Did anyone help you?" she asked.

Brianna hovered beside me, pretending to refold already perfectly folded scarves. She looked at me and smiled deeply.

"Brianna," I answered reluctantly. I signed the sales slip quickly. I hated using my credit card. *I shouldn't be here*, I thought, *I should never have come. I should be at the library, studying*. I grabbed my parcel and fled before I could change my mind, convincing myself that each step away would lessen the urge to return my purchases.

"Hey, you!" Brianna called out, forcing me to look back. I half-expected an accusation, but instead my bag lay across her outstretched arms. "Silly," she scolded, "you almost forgot this."

Slipping it back over my shoulders, I was relieved to feel the pressure of my books against my back. I dug in my pocket and handed over the stub with the letter "A" on it. "Thank you," I said to Brianna, meaning it with my whole heart. "Thank you so much."

When I reached my room there was a note taped to the door. "Come see me when you get this. Gwen."

I removed the note with something like pride and walked down the hall. *I won't stay long*, I thought, knocking lightly. Gwen opened and waved me in. The top bed, I noticed, was stripped. Her roommate, I knew, had essentially moved in with her boyfriend off campus. Gwen, though, was elated to have the room to herself. I sat on the floor and crossed my legs, Indian-style. "Got your note," I said, smiling. "What's up?"

"I should be asking *you* that," she said, joining me on the carpet. "Has Sasha bothered you again?"

I shook my head, happy to be sharing this subject with her. "No, although yesterday she called me 'Sandra Dee.' But I don't think with too much malevolence."

Gwen laughed and then, without pause, launched into a monologue about a guy she liked in one of her classes, confiding all the stats she had so far uncovered about him.

"What about you?" she finished. "Anyone 'interesting' in your life?"

I tucked my hair behind my ears. "I don't know," I laughed nervously, "although I have a date tomorrow."

"A date?" she asked with genuine confusion. "What do you mean, a 'date'?"

I slumped my body to the ground. "I don't know," I whined, then reported what Patrick had said: "He's taking me to Friendly's, and then to a party."

"Wow! I don't know anyone who's actually 'dating'! That is so . . . weird! I thought couples only met here when they were too drunk to remember their names. No one told me there were men who actually take women out to *dinner*! Where did you find him?"

"I don't know," I said, clearly determined to preface all of my statements in this annoying way. "At the library."

"Okay, that is just too crazy. I now officially hate you."

"Don't," I said, laughing for the first time all day. "This will make you very happy that you're *not* me: I walked in on my roommate and her boyfriend *doing it* today."

Gwen made a retching noise. "Seriously?" she groaned. "Gross. That's gotta be on par with catching your parents. I've seen that guy, he's nasty."

"The thing is," I continued, seriously, "it made me feel so weird. It made me think about why I'm so freaked about sex."

"How so?" she asked, a little too eagerly.

Instead of replying, I crossed my fingers, lifting my ring and pinky fingers over my already-crossed middle and index. A nervous habit from childhood. As soon as all of my digits were crossed, I splayed them apart and began the process anew. I was shocked that I had led our conversation from its initial light tone to this. I considered telling her about my "sex" revelations—my hatred of my breasts, my embarrassment at going through puberty surrounded by so many older males—but I didn't feel like it meant much suddenly. So I crossed and uncrossed, and crossed again. I pretended that crossing my fingers and not answering Gwen was the most ordinary thing in the world. Pretended that, in a way, I wasn't even there.

Gwen waited a beat, then spoke: "Earth to Natalie . . . anybody home?"

I looked at her. She seemed so nice, so interested. I had a sudden urge to tell her that I'd grown up with six brothers, not the five I'd told her about during our first run. I always felt bad when I told people I only had five brothers. It made me feel like a liar.

"Never mind," I finally replied, annoyed with my wandering mind, "it's nothing."

"Nothing?"

"Yes," I smiled, standing and picking up my bag. "Nothing."

"Please sit," she pleaded. "You can't expect me to just *drop* such a juicy subject."

I slowly sank to the floor again and laughed with nervousness. My cheeks grew hot under her watchful gaze. "I'm sure I'm just freaked because I have *zero* experience," I giggled, crossing my arms. "You got any pointers?"

She studied me for a long moment, and I felt myself starting to sweat. "You'll be surprised," she said sincerely. "It'll all come to you naturally."

I nodded stupidly. I was relieved she hadn't taken me literally and told me about foreplay, but it also embarrassed me that her reply seemed heartfelt. I would have felt more comfortable if she had fake-gagged or rolled her eyes. I stood and picked up my bag. "I'm sorry," I said brightly, dropping the subject altogether, "but I *have* to study."

"Wait," she said, then went to her desk and picked up a tube of lipstick. "Wear this tomorrow," she ordered lightly, handing it to me. "The color will look good on you."

I nodded thankfully and left with it clenched tightly in my fist.

Faith was hunched over her desk, engrossed in a book, when I slowly pushed the door open. I dropped my bag, sat down, and, after an unbearably long minute, whispered the never-fail greeting, "Hi."

"Hi," she answered steadily. Another minute passed, and she spoke again: "Don't worry about this morning. No big deal, okay? I just don't want to talk about it. Like, ever."

"Neither do I," I replied. "I am sorry, though," I continued, flipping through a notebook. "I've learned my lesson and I'll knock from here on out. Always."

"You didn't knock just now," she reminded, then crumpled a piece of paper and tossed it at me, grazing my ear. I spun around and was relieved that she was smiling.

"How are things, anyway?" I asked.

"What do you mean?" she countered guardedly.

"I mean, with you and Keith. No more fights? No more jealousy?"

She reached for her cigarettes, taking her time to fish one out and light it. Her hands were shaking a bit and she looked, in general, vulnerable. Most telling of all, her bangs lay somewhat flattened on her scalp.

"I don't know," she replied, inhaling deeply. "Same old same old."

"Meaning?"

"He thinks I flirt with guys here, he accuses me of sleeping around, he threatens to break up with me on a regular basis. I tell him he's crazy, I tell him I love him, I apologize over and over again for nothing. Same old same old."

I sighed. Why did she stay with him? I wondered if you could be in love with someone who habitually made you feel bad.

Faith went back to her book. I looked at the pile of texts on my desk and felt exhausted. I wasn't really behind in my studies, and, after my date, I would have the entire weekend to immerse myself in Russian history, Russian language, Russian literature. I changed and climbed into my bunk, rolling onto my side to sleep, but before I did, I told Faith that I hated Keith.

"I do," I said to the wall unapologetically. "I hate him."

Faith climbed into her own bed and clicked off the light. "Suit yourself," she said warily, "I won't stop you."

seven

I was watching *The Love Boat* when I heard that Jacob was dead, and I didn't know what to do with the news. And so, after my parents told me, I wanted to finish the *Love Boat* episode, but I knew that I couldn't. I would never find out if Doc got the girl, and it felt somewhat like an inconvenience. Instead, I joined my family in the dining room and watched them all cry and scream in disbelief, and it was such a horrible and confusing sight that I ran to my room, picked up a copy of *Black Beauty* and began reading, without pause. I was into horses. I wanted to be a veterinarian, like every other little girl. Black Beauty, I remember, was the ideal horse, the horse I dreamed about, and I pictured him—sleek, running wild, rejecting his captors, beautiful and courageous and noble in the face of constant adversity. But when my brother Adam came looking for me and discovered me reading the book, he grabbed it and hissed, angrily, *"How can you read at a time like this?"*

And that was when I started to cry.

Why this story, here? Because I wasn't ready. I wasn't ready for Patrick to become real in the same way that I wasn't ready for my brother to be dead. "Real" didn't mean true, and it definitely didn't have to mean good. It could mean other things, too, and I had learned that fantasy worlds were sometimes (often) preferable to reality. And just as frightening as the prospect of a "real" Patrick was a "real" me. What *real* disappointments would Patrick experience while getting to know the *real* me? The hours upon hours I'd spent thinking about our pending date and our brief encounters in the library and at the Student Union had puffed me up with swollen, pink-perfumed love. Now, as I was about to face him, the air that had been holding me afloat was deflating, fast, leaving me wilted and afraid.

The morning had passed quickly. So, too, had the afternoon. Too quickly. I attended classes, ate breakfast and then lunch, and studied as best I could, but my stomach was upset and my head ached and I thought I was developing a twitch in my left eye.

The time had finally arrived for me to go outside and wait.

I whined as I looked at myself in the mirror. A large pimple had formed on my chin over the course of the day, the kind that couldn't be popped and was painful even when left untouched. I pressed the inflamed skin gently, wishing the pus back into my body.

"It's not that bad," Faith piped up from her desk. "With makeup he won't even notice."

"That's like saying you wouldn't notice Mount Everest next to the rest of the Himalayas."

"Well, maybe you wouldn't if it was foggy enough."

"I'm canceling."

"No," she ordered. "You're not. It's about fucking time you went on a date. If you want, I can do your hair."

I glanced at her, noting that with the new day her hair had returned to its frozen tidal-wave mold, then I picked up a tube of concealer and dabbed it over the pimple, gently rubbing it in. The end result was barely better, and possibly even worse. But I felt better for at least having tried.

The sky was settling into darkness, but a deep streak of pink sunset spread for what seemed like a mile. I waited on the corner, glancing nervously at my watch. I was ten minutes early. Despite the cold, my hands were warm and sticky with perspiration and I kept drying them off on my brown corduroy jacket. Mostly, I tried to ignore the throbbing pain on my chin. I had a strong urge to touch the giant zit but feared I would remove the makeup I had so carefully applied. I glanced toward the library and could just make out students reading in the lit windows. Was my carrel empty? What would the other regulars think when I didn't turn up?

"Natalie?"

I turned and saw Jack. The Jack from the library, from my Ancient Civilization class. Cute Jack. He was approaching at a light jog, his dark hair pushed back, his olive skin smooth and definitely acne-free. Seeing him brought me out of my anxiety about the date and into the present, and for a brief moment it felt as if I could relax. It was only Jack—an acquaintance I would greet and then take leave of. No harm, no foul.

"What's up?" he asked, a little breathless. "Why are you standing on the corner?"

"I don't know," I said. "I thought I'd give prostitution a try."

Jack laughed as I proceeded to turn bright red. I couldn't believe I had said that. I didn't say things like that, ever. It just seemed like the kind of thing you were supposed to say when someone asked you why you were standing on a corner.

"Um, actually, I'm just waiting for . . . a friend. He's picking me up here."

"Lucky him," Jack replied, smiling and giving me a wink. I grinned, embarrassed but flattered, then remembered my blemished chin and turned my face away from his, hoping to put it at an angle where the pimple would be less noticeable.

"Hey," he continued, slipping the tips of his fingers into his jean pockets, "my brothers and I are having a party tonight. At Delta Chi. You guys should stop by."

I frowned at the word "brothers." A frat guy. I shouldn't have been surprised, but it was still disappointing. "Sorry," I said shyly, with confusion, "I don't . . . go to frat parties."

Jack smiled and said "Ouch" while shaking his hand as if I had just slapped it. "Why? Have you ever been to one?" he asked.

"Yes. Sorry, but most frat guys seem pretty lecherous."

"Well, we're not *all* like that. It surprises me that you're so judgmental."

I shoved my hands into my pockets. I tried to think of how to respond, but all I could come up with was: "I'm sorry."

Jack looked let down. "Hey," he said, raising his eyebrows, "no need to be sorry. Everyone's entitled to an opinion, right? Guess I'll catcha later. Peace."

He turned and began walking in the direction he'd come from. I felt wretched. The fact that I flinched when he offered his trademark "Peace" made me feel even worse. He was right: I was judgmental. And he, despite his carefully put-together look—Adidas sneakers, faded Levis, beaded *necklace*—was not, if only because he had now approached me twice, openly and genially. That never happened. People just didn't acknowledge others they recognized from class or the dorm. It wasn't a universal shyness, or even snobbery, I don't think, but more a basic social insecurity. People didn't go around saying "What's up?" all the time, as Jack just had, because it was risky, the words could be interpreted in too many ways (Was that a come-on? Does she think we're friends?). And to move beyond "hello" with those you barely knew was almost unthinkable without alcohol: only a crazy person like Linda did that. But then there were those like Jack and Gwen, who managed to speak to their fellow humans in a relaxed, straightforward way as if it were no big deal.

A brand-new-looking black Saab halted in front of me and my panic returned. Patrick leaned into the passenger side and waved me in. He had the radio tuned to an alternative rock station, and the new Beck song about being a loser played softly. I pulled on my safety belt, fingers shaking, as Patrick slipped the car into second gear. His hand rested lightly on the stick shift, ready to slow down or speed up—casual but alert. A safe driver. He wore a white oxford with an unbuttoned black wool coat and tan khakis.

"Your car," I began, inspecting the interior. "Wow. That's all I can say. Did your parents buy it for you?"

He paused at a stop sign and studied me, his gaze traveling over my body and settling, finally, on my face. "You look nice," he said matter-of-factly.

I blushed and looked out the window. "So do you," I forced myself to answer, feeling giddy, as if in the midst of a make-believe game.

"Why is it, again, that you don't like compliments?" he asked, staring ahead at the road, slowing down for yet another campus stop sign.

My heartbeat quickened into a potential youthful heart at-tack. It was feasible. I had just read of a twenty-two-year-old woman who had died of one in Montana. I wondered if sweaty palms and armpits were symptoms, because both, on me, were drenched.

"I do like them," I answered weakly after a minute.

Patrick arched an eyebrow at me.

"Okay," I smiled, crossing my arms over my breasts, "maybe I don't love them, but I'd rather get a compliment than an insult."

"Hallelujah," he replied, pulling into the Friendly's parking lot, just on the outskirts of campus. He turned off the stereo and without the distraction of the music I quickly became even more anxious. "Can I ask you something?" he said then, his eyes scanning over me a bit critically. "Why do girls always wear their hair down?"

My hand flew up to my scalp and I pushed my fingers through my hair—which was clean and silky smooth. I had spent an entire hour blow-drying it so that it would feel extra soft. "What do you mean?" I asked, shooting a glance his way.

"Nothing, really," he replied with a smile. "I'm just making an observation."

I smiled back awkwardly and opened my door, relieved to step outside. Was he trying to belittle me? I couldn't imagine any other guy saying something like that. It made him seem eccentric, enlightened, even. As we climbed the stairs to the restaurant, a strong breeze sent my loose hair flying every which way. He was right: I should have worn it up.

"Are you trying to say," I asked, "that you would have liked my hair better back?"

"Oh, no," he said, stopping and placing his hands on my shoulders. "Really. I just mean, most girls wear their hair down, right? If anything, you're lucky because you have a pretty face, so you shouldn't hide it."

"So then you *don't* like my hair down."

Patrick smiled and looked up at the night sky. He was lit with a red glow from the neon Friendly's sign and his expression seemed joyful.

"Listen." He grinned. "You know how some guys are into legs, while others are into, I don't know . . . butts? I'm kind of a ponytail guy. I just think they're really cute."

I smiled foolishly and tucked my hair behind my ears so that it no longer covered any part of my face. This meant that my gigantic zit gained prominence on the white canvas of my face, but I wanted him to find me attractive. "Girls wear their hair down," I said, shrugging, "because, um, they think they look better that way."

"I know," he stated. "But *why* do they think that?"

I felt as if I were suddenly in an anthropology class. Or was Patrick a feminist?

"You *know* why," I laughed nervously. "They think that *men* prefer it that way."

He nodded as if he had led me to a great insight that had, until now, been hidden from me. It was as if I had admitted to a personal weakness that extended to my entire gender. I wasn't sure if I should be annoyed or inspired, but after my brush with Jack I decided to withhold judgment. Inside, fluorescent lighting bore down, and I shrank under its glare. Seated in a red-vinyl booth, I immediately cupped my chin in my hand.

"Would you mind if I sat next to you?" he asked after a moment.

I shrugged, wishing he would remain on his side of the table, but he moved in beside me and took my hand in his. My wet, sticky hand.

"Sorry," I said, sliding my palm out of his, "I guess I'm kind of nervous."

"I like that," he replied.

I arched my eyebrows.

"I mean, I think it's sweet," he said, taking hold of it again. "I like how it's warm. Slightly wet."

Oh my God, I thought. "Um, can we . . . just not hold hands right now?"

"Of course," he answered, placing my hand gently on my lap. "I'm sorry. I didn't mean to make you uncomfortable."

I looked over his head, glaring at a waiter in hopes of bringing him over, but the waiter breezed past.

"So, how are your classes?" I asked, attempting to change the subject.

"My classes are fine," he replied in a robotic voice. "How are yours?"

I laughed, accepting his teasing. "Well, since you're such an expert conversationalist, why don't *you* say something, then."

"Let me think," he pondered, looking up at the ceiling. "What would I like to know about you, Natalie Bloom?"

I rolled my eyes and gave him a friendly shove.

"Seriously," he continued, smiling, "what do you think I should know?"

My face tensed. I didn't know what he should know about me. I didn't know where to start, or if there was any point in starting.

"What about your family?" he suggested.

I looked over his head, again trying to attract a waiter, to no avail. "I have five brothers." I shrugged, striking Jacob from the final count.

"Older or younger?"

"Older."

"Should I be scared?"

I looked at him directly and recalled, briefly, my brothers' bulk and brutality. "No," I replied, leaving off the rest of the sentence: *Because you'll never meet them.*

"How many boyfriends have you had?"

I felt sucker-punched. I stared at the table and felt myself perspire. "I don't know what to tell you," I finally sighed, angry to have to reveal my inexperience so soon. "None. What do you think of that? Impressive?"

"So what?" He shrugged. "It's just surprising."

I didn't know what to say to that. I occupied myself with neatening the sugar packets as my heart pounded.

"I've only had one girlfriend," he confessed then. "And anyway, you just haven't had a boyfriend *yet*. You will. Unless, of course, you prefer women."

I didn't acknowledge his attempt at humor and refocused my attention on the ketchup bottle, feeling shamed and wishing, in a way, that I did prefer girls. At least then I would know what to expect when the clothes came off.

"Who knows?" he continued. "Maybe *I'll* be your boyfriend. I would think you were crazy, because you're clearly out of my league. You're like an eight or a nine, whereas I'm like a six, or *maybe* a seven on a good day."

I smirked, but still didn't look at him.

"You're right," he nodded, as if I had just objected. "I'm probably more of a five; maybe even a four after I've worked out. Some guys look great after working out, with their muscles hard and sweaty—you know what I'm talking about—but I just look like, well, like a sweaty Bugs Bunny. A six-five, skinny guy with a sweaty back is not very pretty."

I laughed and again pushed him as my tensions subsided. He

clearly wasn't put off by my boyfriendless past; maybe it was better to have that confession out of the way. My voice came out softly, almost in a whisper: "I've just never met anyone that I wanted as a boyfriend."

Patrick smiled and leaned in close, his breath warming my earlobe. "I'll tell you a secret," he joked, "I've never met anyone that *I* wanted as a boyfriend, either."

After dinner we arrived at the keg party, a few doors down from where Patrick lived. It was typical off-campus housing. Each side of the street was lined with ratty, two-story buildings. Patches of lawn, the grass bleached and dead, stretched out before each unit, meeting the cement sidewalk with apparent indifference. Pitiful trees sprouted here and there, neglected and sickly, with brittle leaves clinking in the wind. I climbed out of Patrick's sparkling car and forced myself to walk beside him.

The front door was open and music blared—the Beastie Boys' "Brass Monkey"—along with the unintelligible hum of dozens of people talking loudly. A young blond girl vomited into a large garbage can that was placed outside for, I guessed, this exact purpose. We elbowed our way through the entrance, passing a sea of heads: a mix of men and women, faces flushed from liquor. The buzz of conversation and peals of laughter swarmed around me. I felt claustrophobic and dizzy and nudged Patrick, hoping he would find a place less crowded. He seemed to understand—or maybe he felt the same way?—and led me by the hand to a comparably spacious corner. I leaned against the wall, took a deep breath, and scanned the room, when

Patrick suddenly put his arm around me, surveying the scene with me. His arm, weighted across my shoulders, felt possessive. I ignored my instinct to shake free of his grasp. Here was the guy I'd been fantasizing about, doing *exactly* the kind of thing I wanted him to do in my daydreams. He looked down at me, and I smiled before quickly looking away again, desperately searching the crowd for a familiar female face, like Gwen's, or even Linda's. And that was when I spotted Jack and, simultaneously, was spotted *by* Jack. I smiled a goofy smile and watched him excuse himself from a conversation with two girls obviously flirting with him to make his way in our direction, stalled by the packed bodies. When he arrived beside us, Patrick's grip on my exposed arm tightened.

"I thought you had your frat party tonight," I said to Jack, goofy smile still pasted on. I wanted, desperately, for Patrick to release me. It embarrassed me to have him holding on to my arm. Still, I gave Patrick a twitchy smile, as if I owed him an explanation for the attentions of such a good-looking guy. Would he be surprised that I could know someone like Jack? He was looking Jack up and down and seemed generally displeased.

"I'm going there soon, but, well, I don't know. You know how lecherous frat parties are. A party like this, on the other hand, is far less seedy and more, well, intellectual, wouldn't you say?"

I blushed, noting several couples nearby grinding into each other, humping through their clothes.

Jack held out his hand to Patrick and introduced himself. Patrick, in turn, barely looked at Jack and tugged at my sleeve. "Let's go in the other room," he whispered.

"Sorry," I said to Jack. "I've got to go."

"No need to apologize," Jack replied with a smile. "Really." Instead of saying "Peace," he flashed a "V" with two fingers.

I returned his smile and turned, somewhat reluctantly, to leave. I felt safer with a third person around, and I wanted to clarify and tell him that, ordinarily, I didn't go to parties like *this*, either, but in an instant he was swallowed up by the dancing crowd.

We found the keg line and waited, and when we reached the guy in charge, Patrick paid and filled up two large red plastic cups with piss-colored beer. I took mine, thanking him as I did, and proceeded to gulp down half of it, hoping it would numb my nerves and get me through the rest of the evening.

"Impressive," he said when I came up for air.

"I could drink you under the table," I kidded, immediately regretting my joke. I thought he had looked at me mockingly, but it quickly morphed into acceptance.

"You probably could," he replied. "Especially since I don't drink much. Pot is better. It doesn't make you act like an imbecile."

I rolled my eyes. "Yeah," I said, taking another sip, "so you've said."

He tucked some loose strands of hair behind my ear. "Who was that guy?"

"No one. We were in a class together last semester."

"Oh. Some people might consider him attractive," he said, deadpan. "Can you *believe* that? But not you. You're into freaky tall guys with bad posture . . . and, really, who can blame you?"

I laughed but avoided his eyes. I knew I should run with the joke or talk about his preference for girls with bushy eyebrows, but I didn't know how to, so I let my laughter trail away into a silence that seemed to amuse him. He reached into his coat and pulled out a plastic bag filled with marijuana, along with rolling papers. "What do you say?" he asked.

I paused, then nodded and followed him outside, where we walked to the side of the building. Several clusters of smokers stood huddling in circles, the scent of marijuana wafting through the air, smoky trails forming small milky clouds. Patrick squatted and expertly rolled a medium-sized joint. I watched him flick the thin paper with his tongue and refocused, quickly, on a pack of nearby smokers laughing wildly. I didn't want to smoke pot. Why had I so readily agreed to do something I didn't want to do? I took a swig of beer and wished that Faith were there.

"Here, you first," he said, offering up the joint.

I held it between my pointer and thumb and raised my eyebrows to let him know I was ready. He flicked a silver Zippo and I inhaled too deeply; the smoke hit my throat hard and made me gag and cough uncontrollably. I grasped my neck and hacked away with abandon. My lungs felt bruised, as if they would never receive oxygen in the same way again. I finished off my beer and refused to look at him as I regained control of my body. When it finally stopped contorting, I saw that Patrick wasn't paying me any attention anyway. I watched him take small hits off the joint in rapid succession while staring at three girls smoking a bowl next to us. They wore tight white long-sleeved T-shirts with red tie-dyed bandannas wrapped around their blond heads. They looked expert, smoking from their little brown pipe; they held their puffs in and let the smoke seep out for maximum effect, and they remained somewhat calm instead of giggling . . . which is what I wanted to do.

The drug was hitting me. Party sounds drifted into my ears yet sounded light years away. Snippets of conversation, of laughter, of yelling and music—all there, but muted. People, too, looked different, even the three girls beside us. They still looked intimidating, but, I thought, seeing everything in slow-mo, *so what?* I glanced at Patrick, and all I could think of was how big his head truly was.

"Hey, Mac Tonight!" I yelled, slapping my hand over my mouth a second later in astonishment. I was horrified by my words, but Patrick laughed. He took another hit and handed me the joint.

"Be careful this time," he warned playfully, "or I'll have to charge you for any pot that doesn't actually reach your lungs."

I took it and inhaled, slowly, allowing it to slink into my throat. The drug was making me feel loose, happy, uninhibited. I realized I was grinning like a court jester. If I let myself start giggling, would I ever stop? I focused, hard, trying to stay present and engaged. It seemed vital that I not give in to the laughter bubbling up inside of me. "What were you thinking just now," I asked boldly, "when you were ogling those girls beside us?"

"Was I?" he asked, a chagrined smile tugging at his lips. "I was just in a daze."

I crossed my arms and stared at him with amusement.

"Okay," he nodded, "I was just thinking about how manufactured their whole look is. How they *look* really cool but, come *on* . . . matching fucking bandannas?"

I laughed, relieved that we were on the same wavelength, and nodded my head vigorously in agreement.

"But because they're hot," he finished, glancing at them once more, "they can do anything they damn well please, I guess."

My momentary relief fled. I remembered my pimple and awkwardly cupped my hand over my chin.

"What are you doing?" he asked.

I dropped my hand and turned away from him, trying to maneuver my face so the zit would disappear from his sight. Then I noticed how baggy my new sweater looked under my unbuttoned coat. How boring, really, my outfit was. Why hadn't I dressed more hiply and worn a tie-dyed bandanna in imitation, or a tight T-shirt with some cool logo on it? Maybe a gas-station logo—those seemed more and more popular. I began to take off my coat, then decided against it and began to button it instead. Patrick reached out and cradled my face in his hand, unwittingly pressing his palm against my bubbling pimple, and, no doubt, removing the makeup covering it. I was mortified, but before I could do anything about this, I felt his lips press against mine, felt his tongue part my lips, felt it slip into my mouth, felt it dart, felt it push, pushing, pushed.

I tore myself away and stumbled backwards.

"What's wrong?" he asked, looking around as if he expected a police raid.

"Nothing," I said, laughing nervously. "It's just that, I'm really messed up. I need to go home."

"Why?" he asked with irritation. "Do you have a curfew?"

"I told you," I replied, my nervous laughter increasing in scale. "I just feel *really* messed up. Thanks for tonight, though. Really."

"Wait a minute," he said, reaching me in a single stride. "I don't want you to go."

I said it then, before I could stop myself: "It's just that I have this really hideous zit on my chin, and it's driving me insane. Literally, insane."

"What, this?" he said, smiling, touching the pimple without an ounce of disgust. "I think it's cute how you've been trying to hide it all night."

I reddened.

"Come on," he said, caressing my face, "I'm *into* you. Is it because I said those girls are hot? I'm honest with people I respect. Saying that they're hot is the same as saying that it's nighttime. It means *nothing*, it's just a fact. Now will you stay?"

I looked at him and considered a further exchange of arid kisses.

"I'm sorry," I said, looking at the ground, "but I have to go."

He shrugged, ran his fingers through his hair and carefully extinguished the joint, replacing the roach back in the plastic bag. He dug into his pocket and brought out his car keys, looking at me as if I were an extremely heavy load he was now cursed to carry, and we walked together to the parking lot. Patrick climbed into the Saab, leaned across the passenger seat, and unlocked my door. I felt like a child who has misbehaved in public and now has to deal with the wrath of her parents on the ride home. "I really am sorry," I said, pulling the seat-belt strap over my body, securing the buckle. I couldn't believe this was how the night was ending. I was disgusted with myself.

Patrick glanced at me and smiled. It was a slight smile but a smile nonetheless. As the car went into reverse, I saw that Jack was still there, talking to a group of people on the front lawn. He saw me, looked straight at me, and smiled, again flashing a sign of peace. I gave it back, first making sure that Patrick wouldn't notice, but my return gesture was so furtive that I doubted Jack saw it, either.

I had managed to blow my first date.

I pretended to be half-asleep with my head resting against the window. The car smelled of him, of Patrick, and I breathed in deeply since I was certain I would never smell it again. Part of me was relieved. The pressure to be with someone could be placed on hold now indefinitely. It would be better to wait until I was completely finished with college, which, really, would occur in less than a year.

The car slowed and I straightened and smiled for no apparent reason. As he pulled into the dorm parking lot, I unbuckled my seat belt and kept my hand on the door handle—ready to leap as soon as the car paused, which I did—opening the door and swinging out my legs.

"Hold on," he said, annoyed. "What the hell happened tonight?"

I stopped and leaned back, my legs still dangling outside.

"I'm sorry," I replied.

He put the car into park and looked straight ahead, then laughed—a laugh that sounded tired but bemused. "I'll give you one thing," he said. "You're really a mystery."

"I'm not," I shot back, exiting and looking in at him with the door still open. "I told you, I just feel messed up. I'm not used to it . . . feeling this way."

"Is it that you've never been with a guy, either?"

"No!" I yelled, louder than I'd meant to.

"I mean," he continued, as if I hadn't said a thing, "if you want to get technical, besides my girlfriend in high school, there's been no one else, although of course I've *been* with other girls. But have you? Been with guys, I mean?"

I looked at him, tried to study his eyes, tried to figure out how he felt—right then—about me. But I couldn't tell, and I supposed it didn't really matter if he cared about me or not. He could care about me in my fantasies, instead. "Guess," I said with finality, shrugging and staring at the ground.

"Are you doing anything tomorrow night?" he asked a moment later.

I looked at him, surprised by the question. I shrugged again and told him I'd made tentative plans with a friend, though in reality I planned on going to the library to study.

"I'll call," he said.

He drove off and I ran inside. He would call me. He would call me and this—whatever it was—would continue. Any reservations I may have had about Patrick that night vanished and were replaced with fresh hope and ardor. Now I was safe and alone and free to fantasize about him on my own terms again.

I was ecstatic.

I raced up the fire-escape stairs, fueled by excitement, my skin tingling with adrenaline and goose bumps, but I was also still high from the pot I had smoked. Linda was leaving the bathroom in a pair of pink pajamas covered with teddy bears when I got to my floor. She waved, and I, unable to contain my joy in my high state, ran up to her, laughing.

"What's this?" she asked. "You look *far* too happy. Was there a hot party at the library?"

"I didn't go to the library tonight," I beamed. "I went out with . . . someone."

"You *did?*" she shouted, bouncing up and down, toothbrush in hand. "And I take it this *someone* was a *guy?*" She followed with a barrage of questions: "Do I know him? Where does he live? Is he cute?" Then, suddenly, she came close and sniffed, scowling at the scent of marijuana on me. "Natalie," she chided, "smoking pot is so . . . *uncool.*"

I blushed at her pronouncement but tried to shrug it off. After all, for some people smoking pot was about as cool as you could get. So what if I, myself, had been in Linda's camp just a few days ago? I had changed. I was *changing*. And I wasn't about to let Linda spoil my high. I allowed the airy feeling that seemed to carry me down the hall to lift me higher and higher in spirit—and, anyway, Linda quickly forgot her interest in my date and my new extracurricular activity and began gushing about Ian's continuing pursuit of her . . . and for once I chose to believe her.

*

eight

The first lesson I would learn about love is that it is filled with disappointment.

The second thing I would learn is that the search for a cure almost invariably ends up being self-destructive.

I sat at my desk, flipped open an art-history textbook, and stared at the page distractedly. He'd *said* he would call. Why would he say that and then not follow through? Was it to be deliberately mean? Or was it that he thought he would call but after giving it some extra thought realized I wasn't worth the effort? I frowned and picked up a yellow highlighter. At first I had tried to tell myself that his silence was a blessing—I didn't feel equipped to meet the demands of dating—but as the days passed it felt more like a judgment, and a slight. Not only did I want him to call, so I could hear his voice; I felt humiliated that he hadn't. Why couldn't he forgive my novice behavior? Why? Why? *Why?*

Faith was smoking on the windowsill, carefully exhaling outside. I shocked myself by joining her and asked for a cigarette.

"You're kidding," she said.

"I'm not," I replied, picking up the pack of Newport Lights and extracting one.

She looked at me as if I had lost my mind. I smiled at her and smelled the cigarette. It had a chemical scent, overlaid with mint and tar.

"Natalie, I don't know how to tell you this, but you would look ridiculous smoking. You're like . . . straitlaced. You look like the girl next door, you know?"

"Come on," I sighed impatiently, "just give me a light."

I placed the cigarette in my mouth and waited for Faith to light me up. Instead, she crossed the room to her desk and sat down with her back to me. "No way," she said. "I won't have you someday accuse me of getting you hooked. You can light your own damn cigarette."

"Fine," I sighed, flicking the lighter for a flame. I inhaled gently and blew out. There was a sweet aftertaste of menthol. It was early afternoon, and the quad's leafless tree swayed with a gust of wind as I smoked in silence and studied the cigarette dangling in my fingers. In the window I could just make out my blurred reflection, and I focused on my features rather than on the drab scene outside. Faith was right: I looked like the girl next door . . . but I wanted to be someone else. The problem was, who? I glanced at my roommate. She was hunched over her desk, and I was relieved that she wasn't watching. The more puffs I took the more I felt sickened, and I was sure I looked silly each time I brought the cigarette to my lips—but I was determined to smoke it down to the spongy filter anyway.

Two crows landed in the tree, perching on the same branch. One squawked, then the other. A bird conversation. I envied how nature had programmed their lives. If hungry, hunt. If tired, rest. The human species was so much more complex, and I felt I lacked some of the instincts others took for granted. Would I ever be able to figure things out on my own? And would anyone ever have the patience to teach me?

Patrick's failure to call had inflamed all my insecurities. First there was my appearance for me to rip apart. Then there was my personality. Finally, I'd begun obsessing over how differently we had been raised. My brothers thought me pompous just for using three-syllable words, where Patrick's family would probably mock me for the occasional mispronunciation. I winced. Would I ever meet his family? I pictured his home in Madison—a majestic two-story with a lush yard, maybe a brick courtyard out front—but I quickly backed off of the fantasy. Even if Patrick *did* decide to call me again and by some magical aligning of the stars became my first boyfriend, the idea of meeting his parents just seemed like a bad idea. They would ask seemingly innocuous questions, like, "What field is your father in?" I would reply, "He's a retired mechanic," and they would uncomfortably profess an admiration for anyone who knew how to hold a hammer correctly. I thought of the ways Patrick communicated his background: He spoke of his travels to places like Paris and Madrid, of Christmases spent skiing in Aspen and summers spent on Block Island. I, on the other hand, had never gone beyond the tristate area, and spent my summers swimming illegally in the local reservoir—when I wasn't working.

I hugged my knees to my chest. Could something have come up to explain Patrick's silence, some kind of family emergency? Maybe he'd had to go home for some reason . . . or maybe he'd gotten a nasty flu? My spirits rose. I was good at lying to myself, and had been ever since Jacob's suicide. In the days after his death, when classmates asked me if it was true that my brother was dead, I looked them straight in the face and said, "No." Making things up is kind of par for the course for a ten-year-old . . . but part of me had truly *believed* that Jacob wasn't, in fact, dead—that he had staged the whole suicide thing and had actually skipped town. I hadn't gone to his wake or his funeral (my parents thought I was too young), so I hadn't seen one thing, really, to prove to me that he *was* dead. There were my mother's tears, but without a dead body to see . . . how could I be *sure*? So, when pressed by my nosy peers, I reported that he'd moved to Florida, a place I myself had never been but always wished I could visit. Jacob, I lied, was in this place, in this child's utopia. He was living on the beach and working at (of course!) Disney World. But everyone knew I was lying. They knew because Todd Trudeau bragged to my classmates that Jacob had shot himself at the end of *his* street, and that it was *his* father who had called the police. But I stuck to my story. What did I care if no one else believed it? They didn't *need* to believe it.

I did.

The cigarette burned lower until I was about to smoke the filter, achieving my goal. I rubbed the yellow-stained butt into the ashtray, a purple drugstore freebie. My head felt light, and I had to grab onto the bed frame as I stood. The nicotine had left me nauseous. I sniffed my fingertips and was surprised by how potent they smelled.

"So? Did you like it?" Faith asked.

"Yes," I lied.

"Bullshit."

I grabbed my bag and left for Anderson's class, first blowing Faith a kiss.

The sky was a thick gray as students milled about in groups of two or more, with singletons sprinkled in like salt, all bulked up in coats, hats, and gloves. I wrapped my scarf around my neck and fished my notebook out of my bag, opening it to the previous day's lecture in a last-ditch effort to cram. I had only studied for two hours the previous night instead of my usual six. I had told myself it was justified—everyone needed pampering now and then—but aimlessly lying about while thinking of Patrick, our date, and my errors, had hardly been a worthwhile indulgence.

My bared fingers were soon ice-cold. I felt ridiculous walking and reading at the same time, and, as if willing myself an accident, I tripped on the jagged sidewalk, falling to my knees and skidding my palms, hard.

"Ouch!" I screamed. My palms were cut and embedded with gravel, and my jeans had ripped, exposing my scraped knees. My one good pair of jeans, ruined. I found some Kleenex in my bag and gently wiped away the dirt. As I hoisted myself off the ground, two girls walked past, engaged in deep conversation, oblivious to my embarrassment. I studied my torn jeans and filthy hands one last time, slung my bag over my shoulder, and forged on toward the history building. In the classroom I took my usual seat near the door, third row from the front. Professor Anderson was writing in a leather engagement book at the lectern. The room's stark lighting brought out the deep lines in his face. When he stopped writing, he looked at me but offered no smile before he spoke.

"Rasputin. Someone talk about him for, let's say, three minutes. Anyone here willing to try? Let's keep it limited to a discussion of how his life affected the fall of the Russian Empire. Come on, this is an easy one. Volunteers?"

I hunkered down and moved my head so he wouldn't be able to see it behind the head of the girl in front of me.

"No volunteers?" he asked, sounding cheerily disappointed. Then he did it. He called on me. "Natalie Bloom. Why don't you give it a try, please."

I sat up straight and raised my hand tentatively.

"It's all right," he prodded, "I've already called on you."

"No," I said quietly, cringing at the sound of my voice. "I'd rather not. If it's all right with you."

Anderson walked to the head of my row. "Three minutes," he demanded. "And please stand."

I rose slowly, feeling faint under the gaze of all of the eyes turned in my direction. It didn't matter that Rasputin was a figure I had studied and knew; in an instant I questioned all of my knowledge. "I don't know," I blurted lamely. "The tsar, Nicholas, was wishy-washy. And his wife, Alexandra, controlled him—his decisions, his way of viewing the empire. I guess, um, when their son Alexis was found to be a hemophiliac, they tried everything to save him, but only when they hired Rasputin did Alexis seem to get any better. Eventually they started to listen to Rasputin on public policy, on foreign affairs, on all the different levels of government. Even, um, when it was clearly to the detriment of the empire. And, well, that's what it was. Detrimental."

I shrank back into my seat. Anderson paced back and forth at the front of the room. Once, twice, then once again.

"Interesting," he said, pausing mid-step. "Not three minutes, but then, who's counting? I hope, however, that if you ever plan to go into the teaching profession you learn to clarify your points. For instance, you say the tsar and his wife 'started to listen to Rasputin.' Did they merely 'listen' or did they actually effect policy based on their consultations with the man? Word choice is vitally important, Natalie. So, now I'd like to give you another chance. Please say a few words on why Rasputin had little or *no* effect on the downfall of the Romanovs. And stand up."

I did as I was told, rising and looking at him in disbelief, my cheeks colored and hot. "I . . . can't," I stuttered. "I . . . think he did contribute to the fall of the empire."

"I'm not asking you what you believe," Anderson pushed with irritation, "I'm asking you to give me a different version. Historians have to look at every angle, at every possibility— or they need to at least be aware of competing theories."

I swallowed and glanced nervously at the class. "Well," I began, not sure of what to say, and immobilized by fear of choosing the wrong words again, "I guess, um, it's probably somewhat hyperbolic to think that one person, any person, affects the course of history, but, I don't know. I personally think individuals do affect history, but . . ."

"Natalie," he interrupted, "I'm not asking what *you* believe."

"Right," I nodded, gripping my scraped palms together. "Then, as I was saying, it's unlikely that Rasputin singlehandedly caused the downfall of the empire, because I guess it was Nicholas's deplorable government that triggered it; it was the tide of popular opinion and the brewing discontent. The Russian population was tiring of the aristocracy, of the tsar's inability to help the masses, of poverty and unemployment. I guess, um, if Rasputin had a role, it was probably in further antagonizing the masses against the rich and the tsar and his wife. The downfall, in that case," I concluded, my voice rising pathetically, "was a result of . . . popular revolt?"

A guy at the back of the class clapped and gave a sarcastic whistle; I turned and smiled with embarrassment before slinking back into my desk. Anderson shrugged his shoulders as if to say, "An okay response. Definitely not great, but okay."

The lecture began then, and I jotted down half-finished words and abbreviated sentences, glad to focus on something other than my performance, although it was difficult not to replay my words over and over again in my head. I paused in my note taking and lingered on my two versions of Rasputin, seeing Anderson in front of the blackboard but no longer hearing him, his voice droning in the background like white noise. I scanned the students seated near me. There was Rick, a beefy ROTC arch-conservative guy with a blond brush cut. There was Cara, a five-foot-tall Korean-American with jet black eyes and hair who always wore tight, flattering clothes. Then there was Joe, an economics major and the kind of guy you could spend years going to classes with yet never really know much about. Average height, average build, brown hair, brown eyes, silver-rimmed glasses, and an unmemorable face. Was I any different? Would *I* ever affect the course of history in any way, shape, or form? No. I frowned at the sight of my torn jeans. I was wearing a black, long-sleeved T-shirt and black loafers; I felt my earlobes and remembered I had worn my fake diamond studs. Cubic zirconia. My hair was yanked back in a tight pony-tail, and I wore a white-faced Timex with black roman numerals. An unobtrusive, sensible outfit. Not unlike Joe. I, too, might be considered nondescript. Unmemorable. I imagined Rick and Cara laughing together, joking about how Joe and I should go out and have boring, frigid sex between study breaks.

Joe caught my stare. He shuffled his feet and slipped me a smile, then turned back to the lecture and his notebook, slouching over it and writing fast.

"Next class," Anderson said loudly, snapping me out of my daze, "you will be quizzed on today's material. I hope you all had the foresight to take good notes. Oh, and your midterm will be next Friday, as it states on the syllabus. Everything we have studied from the very first day of class will be up for grabs. There will only be *two* essay questions. Worth, obviously, fifty points each. Good day." He replaced his papers and engagement book in his briefcase and snapped it shut.

Blood drained from my face. I sent a pleading gaze Anderson's way as I pushed my notebook into my bag and hurried out of my seat, eager to plead my case.

"Professor?" I interrupted as he made for the door. "May I speak with you?"

He paused in the hall and glanced at his watch with irritation.

"I . . . I didn't take the best notes today."

"So?" he replied flatly.

"So . . . I'm sorry, but would you, please, go over the material with me later today?"

His brow arched. "You cannot be serious, Natalie. Borrow someone else's notes, and never, *ever*, expect me to repeat a lecture I've already given."

He turned and walked away, leaving me standing alone in the hall. I leaned against the wall and closed my eyes in order to feel my mortification more fully. What was happening to me?

I walked outside, buttoning my coat as I walked, and sat on a bench in front of the building. Several large oaks skirted the area and from their branches a few crows cawed. Joe walked out of the building. I was desperate. I stood and frantically waved him over.

"Hey," he said, gripping his black backpack tightly. Short stubble poked out in uneven pockets on his chin and upper lip. His glasses slipped down his nose and he pushed them back to position.

"Hi," I replied a little too loudly. "I was wondering if you might want to study for the quiz together later."

Joe looked around as if I had just offered to sell him dope. "What do you mean?" he asked.

I crossed my arms and smiled, trying to appear relaxed. "I mean, do you want to study together?"

Joe stared straight into my eyes with suspicion.

"Why?"

"Um, I guess I thought it could be helpful."

"Thanks, but I study alone."

He moved to leave. "Wait! Please, Joe," I said, cringing. "Just this once? I hate studying with people, too, so I promise not to bother you. However you want to do it is fine with me."

"Sorry," he insisted.

"Listen," I confessed, "I didn't take good notes today, okay? Can you help me out just this once?"

"I'm really sorry," he said, seeming relieved to finally understand my motive, "but maybe you'll take better notes next time."

With that, he walked off, offering a "wish I could help" smile.

My hands balled into fists and my nails nearly punctured my palms. I walked back to my dorm as fast as I could. My panic was turning to fury. When I reached my room, Faith was sitting at her desk. "Are you happy?" I shouted, unleashing my anger on her. "I *knocked* before entering."

Faith barely gave me a glance. "Yes," she answered vaguely, "I am."

I paced the floor and finally settled on the windowsill.

"What's up your ass?" she asked, still reading her book.

"I'm just ruined," I whined, unwilling to elaborate. "But can I have a cigarette?"

"Help yourself," she replied. "Always happy to encourage a cancer wish. By the way, that guy Patrick called while you were at class."

I almost dropped the lighter. "He did?"

"Yeah," Faith said. "And I think he was hitting on me. He was definitely flirting."

"What?" I cried. "What on earth makes you think that?"

"He was just being all, 'what's your name, how old are you, you have a nice voice' shit. I told him I wasn't interested in making any new friends today and hung up."

"I . . . I don't think that necessarily means he was *flirting*."

"Whatever."

I grimaced, cracked the window, and inhaled on the cigarette, feeling nauseous all over again, and watched the smoky tendrils curl past my face and outside. Still, something about it made me feel . . . better. I studied the filter: What had begun as a tiny yellow spot had now widened to cover the entire base. The menthol burned my throat and I wondered if regular cigarettes might be better than Faith's Newports. I decided to buy a pack to try, later. I looked at Faith. I wanted to drill her further on the phone call. But even if Patrick *was* flirtatious with her, I hardly had any right to be upset after just one date. Maybe he was naturally flirty. I saw the way some girls perched themselves on guy friends' laps, and how they patted each others' rears. Just because *I* wasn't like that didn't mean other people had to be as uptight as me. Maybe what Faith had perceived as flirting would be called *charisma* by others.

I went to my desk and retrieved Patrick's number, which I had carefully written on an index card and placed in the back of the top drawer, then I dragged the phone into the hall. It never even occurred to me to hold off returning his call or to make him wait as he had made me wait. That he had finally reached out to me again was like hearing I had won the lottery. I punched the buttons quickly, and Patrick picked up right away.

"Hi," I said, "it's me. Um, Natalie. My roommate told me you called."

"You mean the girl with no sense of humor?"

"Yeah," I laughed nervously, "I hear you're a big flirt." I wrapped a strand of hair tightly around my finger, then released it to begin anew.

"No. I've just been socialized among civilized persons, which your roommate clearly has not."

I laughed. "You'll get no argument from me."

"So," he went on, "I was calling to see if you might want to come over tonight. I've got a six-pack with *your* name on it. Any interest? Please?"

I pulled the strand of hair until it cut off circulation and my fingertip turned purple. I thought of mentioning his failure to call since our date. Part of me understood his delay wasn't related to any flu or a sister in the hospital—but what would be the point in finding out that he just hadn't gotten around to it? I would only seem uncool or, worse, needy. And anyway, didn't I know, from the moment Faith told me he'd called, that I would agree to anything he requested? He was giving me another chance. "Sure," I said, heart pounding, "I guess that could be fun."

"I really wish you would stop qualifying your sentences. It makes me feel like leftover macaroni and cheese. The kind you make out of a box that becomes hard and crusty after the first ten minutes."

I giggled. "I happen to love Kraft mac-and-cheese, just so you know."

"Um, are you telling me that you love me?"

"Be quiet," I said, laughing harder but also blushing at the word "love." "What time should I come by?"

"How about seven?"

Anderson arose in my head. I needed to study, and if I were to go at seven, I would barely have any time.

"Okay," I replied quickly. "See you then."

After applying nearly an entire stick of antiperspirant and checking myself in the mirror seventy times, I set off for Patrick's, glad to be wearing my winter coat to hide what was beneath: a tight-fitting white top (Faith's) that gripped my body and its contours like a coat of paint.

The last trace of light in the sky vanished into blackness as a persistent wind pushed against me on the long walk. When I finally reached Patrick's apartment complex, I saw his black Saab parked in front, shinier and more impressive than all of the cars around it. Holding my breath, I knocked and finally exhaled when he didn't answer after what seemed like several minutes, then knocked a second time.

"Just a sec!" he hollered from within.

When he pulled the door open I took a step backwards. A towel was knotted around his waist and his torso was bare and virtually hairless. "Come on in," he said casually. "Make yourself at home. I'll just be another minute."

He ran up a staircase and disappeared. The living room was spare; there were no photos or posters on the white walls, and the furniture was functional but little else. I don't know what I had expected, but with the presumption of his wealth, it was *more*, in general. Butterflies churned in my stomach, as if I were about to compete in a race. The TV was on and I sat down in front of it—not taking off my coat, not even unbuttoning it—and watched the show *Cops* until Patrick returned, wearing khakis and an oversized blue denim shirt. Its largeness made me feel ridiculous in my skin-tight top, still buried beneath my coat.

"Can I ask you something?" he asked in his usual opening line.

"Sure."

"Why do you have your coat on? We have heat."

I smiled and reluctantly began unbuttoning. I paused at the third button and asked if I could have some water. He smiled, impishly, and rose to fetch some. "You know," he called out from the kitchen, "if you don't want to draw attention to something you should act quickly. Slowness leads to anticipation, and anticipation leads to, well, eagerness."

"Or disappointment," I let slip before I could stop myself.

I winced and quickly undid the last three buttons and shrugged the coat off. I looked down and was amazed by my popped-out cleavage, the sight of which made me feel ashamed. I crossed my arms in a straitjacket mold, then crossed my legs, too.

Patrick walked back into the room carrying a six-pack in one hand and my water in the other, and I saw his eyes drop to my breasts, saw them open just a bit wider with . . . what? Joy? Stupor? Disapproval? I couldn't tell. I expected him to acknowledge my new look, but instead he just sat down on the couch, set the drinks on the coffee table, dug in the cushions for the remote, and zapped off the TV. I, in turn, forgot the water and snatched a beer, cracking it open and taking deep gulps, thinking that a bit of intoxication was just what I needed.

"Did you notice your name?" Patrick asked.

"What?"

"I mean, remember how I said I had a six-pack with *your* name on it?"

I looked at my beer and saw that masking tape had been stuck on top of the brand name to make it read "Natalie Light." I smirked and exhaled, then took several more sips. Patrick patted the empty square beside him and smiled. "I have a great idea," he said, patting harder. "Why don't you sit here? I have a secret to tell you."

"But we're the only ones here," I answered, not allowing my eyes to meet his, "so, really, you can just say it. You could probably scream it and no one would hear."

"Perhaps, but part of the fun of a secret is whispering it into someone's ear. And since you're the only one here, and a guest, no less, I think you should humor me."

I stood and self-consciously adjusted my top, clutching the material near my neck. I kept several inches between us when I sat down and tucked my arms at my sides. The excessive antiperspirant hadn't helped and I was horrified as two wet drops of sweat dripped from my armpit.

"What's the secret?" I asked, fiddling with a pulled string sticking out of the cushion.

"Oh. I don't actually have one."

He leaned in, and I expected a kiss, but instead he traced my lips with his thumb, finally inserting it into my mouth. He moved it slowly back and forth, never taking his eyes off of the movement. I felt giddy, but I used all of my effort to keep a straight face, and before long I gave in to his prodding and began to suck on it, feeling strange and awkward yet paralyzed by his seriousness. He had never seemed that serious before, and I thought that if I were to upset things with a laugh he might never forgive me. Heat rose to my face, and with something between terror and joy I realized I was getting aroused.

My inexperience suddenly didn't seem to matter so much. Gwen had been right about that.

"Come on," he commanded, his voice thick, "follow me."

He walked up the stairs and I obediently followed, feeling fear but curiosity, too. I went into his darkened bedroom and allowed him to press me onto the bed. Moonlight streamed in through the window as he undressed me, alternating between removing my clothing and his own. His bared skin looked almost iridescent in the light. I reached out and timidly stroked his chest, his back, and was amazed by how smooth his skin felt, like it had been dusted with talcum powder. We kissed—long, deep kisses that never quite ended. Soft, measured, flowing, they were unlike any kisses I'd ever had before, and being sober, I realized, made them even better. The kisses, coupled with hands gliding over soft skin, made me finally understand the notion of ecstasy. He pressed himself on top of me and I felt something firm and solid push between my thighs, and this, too, I allowed, much to my surprise. But when he moved to take off his underwear I gripped his hand hard.

"I'm sorry," I whispered.

"You're sure?" he asked, his voice disbelieving.

"I'm sorry," I nodded.

"But I've got, you know, protection. I want you. I want to feel you. Look at yourself."

I reddened in the dark. I was completely naked, save for a pair of dark green panties. I was so exposed. So *naked*.

And that's when I panicked.

I stood and struggled to get the tight white shirt back on. He flicked the light switch, blinding me and flooding me in light before I could get dressed.

"No!" I shouted. Then, more softly: "Could you please put the light off?"

Before darkness shrouded us once more, I caught the expression on his face. He was looking at me as if I had lost my mind, and that look upset me even more than the possibility of his naked penis.

"Can I put the light on now?" he asked, annoyed.

"Yes. Sure."

Again, illuminated. He stood and pulled on his khakis as he did. He rubbed his eyes and then smiled. A resigned, tired smile.

"I'm sorry," I said again, backing through the doorway and starting down the stairs, trying for a joke, "but at least I'll understand if you don't call this time."

Patrick followed in silence and opened the door for me to leave. He looked more handsome than ever, and I regretted everything.

"You're okay walking home alone?" he asked.

I nodded.

He gently glided his palm over the top of my head, then pulled me to him and kissed me, delicately, on the lips. His arms around me felt strong and secure. "Be careful," he whispered.

And then he closed the door.

*

nine

Climbing is a slow, purposeful effort.

The descent is always faster.

When Anderson handed back the quizzes at the end of class, my shame prevented me from looking at him as I grabbed mine from his outstretched hand. I stuffed it into my backpack and fled, then waited to look at it until I was back in my room, alone.

The first page had a red-penned "X" over it, and as I scanned the others I read little notes, like "B.S." for "bullshit" and "WHAT????" On the final page, a lengthier note outlined all I had gotten wrong and stressed that it appeared I hadn't studied at all. There were no personal remarks, no offer of a makeup. Only the final remark: "48/100," or, in other words, I had gotten my first F.

I closed the essay book and buried it under a mound of textbooks, wishing it out of existence. But it did exist, and I knew that this little quiz would pull down my GPA, pull down my grade in my best-loved subject. I was no longer the "perfect student." Worse still, Anderson was disappointed in me. My stomach felt queasy, and I held it, doubled over on my chair. *Oh my God*, I thought, and it became a kind of mantra: *Oh my God oh my God oh my God.* Clearly, this was to be my punishment for almost having sex with Patrick. For letting him undress me, distract me, and fill my mind with fantasies. Clearly all my angst at being a virgin had been misplaced; purity had felt much better than *this*.

The phone rang and I answered in a daze.

"Hey. It's Patrick. The guy you're clearly not interested in."

I pressed the phone to my ear hard, and before I could stop myself, I started speaking: "Patrick. Look. About the other night . . . that can't happen again."

"What can't happen?" he asked innocently.

"You know."

"No, I really don't."

"In your bedroom."

"You mean, the kissing and touching part?"

"Yes."

"Why? I thought it went pretty well, until you ran out the door, that is. But it's fine if you want to wait a while."

"No, that's just it. I don't want to wait. I just don't want to do it at all. Anything."

"Why?"

"Well . . . I . . . I don't know. I can't explain it."

Patrick paused. "Natalie, do you not want to see me again?"

I hesitated. I wanted to be near him all the time, and that was what terrified me.

"I'm sorry," I whispered, hating myself. "But I think that would be best."

"Wow. Okay. Well, bye."

I heard the farewell click but continued to press the receiver into my ear, and when I took it away my ear ached. My stomach rolled, worse than before, and I rocked back and forth, grasping it. This didn't help, and I lay down, curled up on the cream-colored carpet. When Gwen knocked and poked her head in ten minutes later, I was still on the floor, and seeing her, I burst into tears.

"What's wrong?" She dropped her backpack and kneeled beside me. "It can't be that bad, can it?"

I looked at her, speechless, and nodded. Then I tugged out my failed quiz from under the pile of books and handed it to her, breaking out into even louder sobs as she flipped through the pages, pausing on the last one to read Anderson's remarks. I rubbed my eyes and blew my nose, then walked over to Faith's desk for a cigarette.

"Okay," Gwen said. "Where is Natalie . . . the girl I go running with?"

I ignored her, cracked the window, and exhaled a puff of smoke.

"How long have you been a smoker?"

"Since the other day. I like it."

She sat opposite me on the sill. Her hair fell loosely on her shoulders and gloss brightened her lips. I started to tell her all about my recent trials—of my evening at Patrick's, of my slacking off in my studies. Gwen listened and followed the cigarette I was holding as it rose, then lowered, then rose again.

"I'm sorry about your test," she said, reaching out to take my cigarette away and stub it out, "but it was just a quiz and it won't affect your grade all that much. As for this guy Patrick . . . if you really like him, why should dating him put your grades at risk? One shouldn't exclude the other. You just have to learn how to balance the two. As for smoking, please don't do it around me. My dad has emphysema."

I looked down at my lap. Her mention of her dad's illness made my problems seem petty. I wasn't sure what to say. Her father's illness made me think of my own family, of my brother Jacob, and I felt more alone than ever. "I'm not sure I want to be alone tonight," I admitted, lifting my head but cringing at how I sounded. "Do you, maybe, want to study together?"

She gave a rueful smile. "Sorry," she replied, walking over to admire herself in the mirror. "I finally got that guy I told you about to notice me. He's coming over tonight to 'study.' Hope that's not all we'll be doing."

"Ha," I forced a laugh, wiping my face and turning back toward the window. "Okay. That's great. Have a good time."

"Thanks," she said, opening the door. "And good luck with . . . everything."

"Wait," I said quickly. "Why, um, why did you stop by just now?"

Gwen shrugged. "Just felt like it," she replied. "See ya."

The sky was a dark blue with a line of orange at the horizon as I headed out to the library. The carefully spaced benches sat empty in the cold until a couple walking ahead of me, arm in arm, suddenly fell onto one. As I passed, their voices dropped to private whispers and I looked elsewhere—anywhere but at them.

The day before, work crews had removed the plastic sheeting from one side of the library building. It looked more solid and imposing without that fluttering bubble, but I missed it. Soon it would just be another imposing building, like any other. Two guys were sitting outside on the steps with matching Mets baseball caps, and as I climbed past they made a show of yelling "Hell-o!" but I walked on, pretending I hadn't heard.

"Hey," one snapped, "we said 'hello,' not 'fuck me.' "

His friend burst out laughing as I pushed through the revolving door, my heart racing. Assholes. Dicks. The things guys could say with confidence as long as a pal was there to bolster them amazed me, but it also made me ache for my own pal, to soften bullshit like this. Patrick would never participate in that kind of taunting behavior, I thought, but then willed my thoughts not to go there.

Settled in at my fourth-floor carrel with relief, I debated which subjects to study and arranged my books in the proper order to reflect my decisions. But when I uncapped a yellow highlighter and opened a Russian lit text to begin reading Chekhov's play *Uncle Vanya*, my thoughts returned again to my brother Jacob. I was here in college to study about all these generations of dead historical figures, but Jacob's life and death were subjects I still didn't understand. More and more he'd been creeping into my thoughts lately. When I catalogued what I knew of him, what I remembered, I realized that my "memories" had probably never actually happened. After he was gone, and I had relocated him to Disney World instead of the grave, I imagined that we had done all sorts of fun things together and that he was my "favorite" brother; I recalled him reading stories to me, I remembered him taking me to the local fair, and to the zoo—things he had never actually done.

But there were also those events that refuse to be altered. Like the day, shortly after Jacob's first failed suicide attempt, when I was on my way into the kitchen to grab a snack and overheard my mother telling him that she loved him. *I love you, Jacob.* I had never heard her say those words before, and it was almost like hearing her say pornographic words like "cum" or "cunt." And later the same day, she asked me to tell Jacob that *I* loved him, which, very reluctantly, I did. And his smiling response: "You don't have to love me, Natalie." These words made me cry, though I wasn't sure why, and I surprised myself and asked him if he loved me—a question I had never posed to anyone before. "I don't know," he'd replied truthfully, "I'm not sure that I know what love is." So, I then said what any hurt ten-year-old might say in that situation. I told him I loved Biffo, our dog, more than I loved him.

I love Biffo. I love him more than you!

Yes. This I remember clearly.

But back to Chekhov. I read his play without pause and then moved on to other subjects. I had to read a chapter on medieval art for an art history class, and then I began writing a paper on Aristotelian logic for my law class. I worked steadily until the library lights blinked three times, and then I walked home.

*

ten

When midterm exams rolled around, I was usually all business. There was a competitiveness in the campus air. You could see the confidence—or sense of doom—in students' faces as they walked to class before being tested, again and again. They emerged from their rooms in the morning looking haggard and weary. Girls went without makeup and hairspray; guys sprouted facial hair. Bottles of No-Doz and Vivarin littered desktops, and the aroma of strong coffee filled the halls—which were far quieter than normal. RAs enforced curfews and cracked down on those who saw no difference between midterm week and any other week. Study lounges were suddenly actually used for studying. The library, usually packed with empty tables and carrels, was filled to bursting—and my carrel was suddenly occupied, every day, by someone else. All in all, though, I *lived* for exams, because with each one I aced I could feel just that much better about myself. I even relished the queasy jitters I'd get right before a test, and the way it felt like my whole life depended on how I fared. But something was different this time around. I was distracted.

Thoughts of Patrick surfaced every time I cracked a book open, and now I didn't even fight them. I *wanted* to think about him, and I wanted to think about him *instead of my studies*. It didn't matter that I had blown it. Every night, and periodically throughout each day, I reenacted the evening when we had almost "done it," but in my mind we actually "did it," and in my mind I was sexy and sure, not fleeing the scene like a frightened child. At the library, I *tried* to stay true to my studious self: I would read a paragraph and *then* think of Patrick. And so on and so on, ad nauseam. You can imagine how effective it was.

I ate a quick lunch, memorizing, between bites, the correct order of the amendments to the Constitution for my law class. For once there was a relative silence in the cavernous cafeteria, everyone buried in books, readying for their own imminent exams. When I was done eating, I packed up my things to go, but as I stood I noticed Jack in the hot-food line. He was alone, and I considered going up to him to say hello. Instead, I hurried to drop off my tray and slip out of the room. Just as I pushed open the door, though, he shouted out my name.

"SHHHH!" several people shot back, and he apologized while jogging over to where I stood, frozen. He was wearing a dark-green Henley with faded jeans, and looked far cooler than I, in a pair of old jeans and a baggy blue sweater. "Why are you here?" I said robotically, forgetting to say hello first.

He shrugged. "I figured it would be easier to study in this cafeteria than my own, where everyone would bug me."

"Oh," I replied.

He smiled. "I guess you've already eaten, huh?"

"Yup," I said. "I have."

"Too bad," he said.

My face heated and I pushed the door open a bit wider. "I should . . . go," I stuttered, "but . . . it was nice to see you."

"Yeah," he nodded. "It's always nice to see you. Good luck with your exams. Peace."

"Thanks," I sputtered, realizing as I did that a drop of my spit had landed on my chin. I wiped it away and laughed with embarrassment, and then I let the door close in his smiling, cute face.

Jesus! I swore as I took the stairs up to my floor. *Why am I such a moron?* My heart was still racing and my skin bright pink when I entered my room, which was a mess because neither Faith nor I ever took the time to put things away during exams. Clothes lay on the floor, and our desks couldn't be seen beneath all of the junk thrown on top of them. Faith's stress level was evident just in the objects surrounding her: a gigantic Styrofoam cup of steaming coffee; a bottle of ginseng; a stack of books and yellow stickies; an ashtray filled with a pile of butts, and a carton of cigarettes within easy reach. Her normally carefully coifed hair was wilted, and she glowered at me as I entered. Faith had taken her most important midterm that morning, and since she had barely slept in forty-eight hours, I thought it best to go to the library to do my own studying. I started gathering what I needed, sifting through papers and books.

"*Shhhhhhh,*" Faith hissed, nose still buried in her book. "Be *quiet.*"

"How was your exam this morning?" I whispered.

"I don't want to talk about it," she replied tersely. "And I don't have *time* to talk about it even if I wanted to. I have another exam tomorrow."

"I hope you're not planning to stay up all night again," I said. "You haven't slept for two nights already."

"I slept for two hours after my test," she sighed. "That'll have to be enough."

"Faith," I said, "I'm all for all-nighters, but this is ridiculous."

Faith buried her head in her arms and began weeping. "You don't understand," she cried. "I'm not going to make it. I'm barely passing my classes."

I sat down, speechless, and dug in my bag until my fingers located the box of cigarettes I had bought the day before: Camel Lights, the cellophane still unbroken, crisp. I lit up and realized the whole smoking thing got easier and more natural with every puff. I watched my roommate cry—a rare occurrence that I didn't feel equipped for. I couldn't rub her back or offer comfort in any other physical way because we didn't do that kind of thing. I'd had no idea that her grades were in trouble. I wasn't sure what to say.

Faith blew her nose and took a few deep breaths. Then she faced me, her mascara smeared down her pale face. I tried to offer a gentle smile and told her to try not to worry.

"Easy for you to say," she said. "You'll probably get straight A's. I, on the other hand, am thinking about dropping out."

"What?" I yelled. "You're kidding, right? You're in your last year . . . how can you even *think* of dropping out?"

"Because I *hate* it," she said, her eyes welling over. "I fucking *hate it here*. I'm not smart enough. I'm positive I flunked today."

With that, she began to cry again.

"Come on," I said, "you're just overtired. Why don't you tell me about the material on your test tomorrow? That always helps you."

She looked at me and wiped the tears from her face. "Really?" she asked. "You have time?"

No, I needed to reply, *I don't*. "Sure," I said brightly. "But you have to promise me you'll sleep for at least a few hours tonight."

"Okay." She smiled. "I promise."

For the next hour, I nodded and cooed intermittently as Faith explained thermodynamics. It gave me a chance to forget about my own exam worries and to think, instead, about more trivial concerns. I cringed as my embarrassing moment earlier with Jack popped in my head, and then moved on to Patrick. What was he doing now?

"Natalie!" Gwen shouted from down the hall, sprinting toward me with a grin. I smiled and jogged down the hallway to meet her, then slowed when a guy exited her room behind her. He was broad shouldered, and pulling on a baseball cap over what appeared to be just-slept-on dirty-blond hair.

"I want you to meet someone," she sang, grabbing my hand and leading me back toward the guy in her doorway. "This is Noah."

"Hi," I said, imitating what I hoped was a smile. He nodded in reply and I watched as they fell into an embrace.

"We're going down to grab lunch," Gwen said. "Want to come?"

"Oh," I said, cheeks afire as I backed up toward the elevator, "um, no, thanks. I . . . I'm going to the library. To study."

"Wait," she said, following. "We'll go down with you."

"Oh. No. I have to use the bathroom first. Bye!"

"Okay," she replied, sounding disappointed. "Bye, then."

I waved and ducked into the safety of the girls' bathroom and locked myself in a stall. I wasn't jealous, exactly. I just felt *lame* in the face of their happiness. I counted to twenty and then took the stairs down. It was sunny out, and the open air refreshed me. I had an hour before I had to be at my law class, and I looked around furtively, extracted a cigarette from my bag, and sat on the curb to smoke it. I felt too conspicuous there, however, and moved to a section shrouded by bushes. Then I flicked my new Bic lighter and inhaled until a clear, red ember was aglow. I smiled, feeling less like myself. No one would ever guess that Natalie Bloom was a smoker. Just as Faith had said. I inhaled more deeply, and only halfway through decided I would smoke another as soon as I finished the one in my mouth.

"Natalie?"

I twisted, my heart dropping into my stomach, and saw Professor Anderson approach from the parking lot behind me. I dropped the cigarette as if I'd been caught watching porn by my father. My face blanched. My tongue felt tattooed with tar. "I'm sorry," I croaked.

He studied me, frowning, for a long minute. "I'd like to speak with you," he finally said, averting his eyes. "Follow me."

Sun rays filtered through the bare tree limbs above, dotting the ground in a multitude of spotlights. We found an empty bench, and Anderson made a grunting noise as he sat, lowering himself slowly and with effort.

"I don't smoke," I blurted, feeling frantic and soiled and wanting forgiveness. "I was just trying it. I'm not going to do it again."

"That isn't what I want to speak with you about," he said. "Smoke if you want to. It's no one's business but your own."

I sat silently beside him, disappointed in myself for not hiding better.

"What's going on?" he asked then, facing me.

"What do you mean?" I asked.

His eyes narrowed and he looked away. "Well," he sighed, sitting forward in preparation to leave. "Okay."

"Wait," I pleaded. "I just don't know what to say."

He leaned back again and stared at me. "I thought you were supposed to visit me yesterday. Or am I no longer your adviser?"

I slapped a hand across my mouth. I had forgotten our appointment. "I'm *so sorry*. I went to the library . . . like I usually do. I forgot."

"It wouldn't have been worth noting," he continued, "except for your performance on the quiz."

I squeezed my hands together as a new rush of shame flooded in. When I remained silent, Anderson sighed. "This is your last year," he said, a warning creeping into his tone. "Don't get distracted."

I looked at him, afraid. "But what if I am?" I admitted. "What if I can't help it?"

"We all have things that distract us, Natalie," he replied. "You have to compartmentalize the distractions. Otherwise, how would anyone ever achieve success? We'd *all* be wallowing in our own personal morasses if we couldn't cope."

"But sometimes," I began, steadying my voice, "it all feels like too much."

"Is it a boyfriend?" he asked, sparing me a tone of playfulness.

"No," I replied quickly.

Anderson leaned back against the bench and reached into his coat for a handkerchief. He blew his nose, coughing afterwards for a solid minute. "You're smart," he stated when he finished, looking up at the trees overhead. "But you're fragile, too. If you're not careful I'm afraid you'll break, Natalie."

What's that supposed to mean? I felt like screaming. Instead, I nodded, tucked my hair behind my ears, and waited for more. I looked up at the craggy lines of his face, the puffiness around his eyes, the salt-and-pepper stubble, and then realized it was he who wanted me to speak. To fill in the blanks surrounding my performance in class and on the quiz. I tried to find my tongue but couldn't make it articulate words. Anderson waited patiently for a minute or two, then heaved himself off of the bench.

"Until Thursday, then," he said, barely looking at me. "I hope you study well for the exam."

I started to stand up, intending to stop him, but then I sat back down and watched him move away. "Study, Natalie," he said, bequeathing one last piece of advice. "Other things can wait."

I stayed on the bench a little longer, waiting for my queasiness to pass.

*

eleven

A text lay open in my lap as I sat in the window, an ashtray on top of it, and I ran my fingers over the part of the page that was still visible, caressing the silky paper. Faith was out, and I wanted to take the opportunity to study in my own room. It was a gray day, but occasionally a burst of sunlight would fracture the clouds, briefly lighting the room. I looked at the sky, inhaling on my cigarette, then looked down at the ground, seven stories below. *It would be so easy*, I thought, *to fall*. I shuddered and moved off the ledge to sit on the edge of Faith's bed. In the instant that the thought had entered my head I had visualized the whole scene: me, falling headfirst. Me, hitting the ground, my head splattering upon impact.

Adrenaline raced through my body. Pins and needles prickled my spine, and I grabbed a blanket and wrapped it around my shoulders, holding the cigarette between my teeth as my thoughts turned to Jacob. How many times must he have visualized his demise before finally pulling it off? On some level I suspected it was natural to imagine your death, but because of Jacob it freaked me out. Did my DNA predispose me to make bad thoughts come to pass? I tried to think about Patrick instead, but the image wouldn't fade: I still saw myself dead, on the quad, students gathering to stare in horror at my bloodied corpse.

A knock startled me out of my stupor. I crushed my cigarette and waved my hands at the residual smoke, then cracked the window before opening up.

"Hey," Gwen said, pushing past me and scowling. "My *God*. It *reeks* in here."

I reddened, sat on Faith's bed and shrugged. Gwen eyed me, awaiting a response, but after a moment she sat on the floor. "You don't look so good," she said.

"Thanks." I grimaced. "You, on the other hand, look amazing."

And she did. Her hair bounced, her skin shone. The white T-shirt she wore with her jeans clung just enough to give her breasts a delicate outline.

"So," I asked more cheerily, "are you and that guy I met . . . going out? It seems like you're always together lately."

"You mean are we 'boyfriend and girlfriend'?" she replied, then seemed to think it over. "Yes," she concluded. "I mean, we haven't used those explicit words yet, but I know if I saw him with someone else I'd have to kill him."

I laughed, but with the bitterness I had tried to shelve. She was so happy, and I couldn't help wanting to spoil it, just a bit. "That was fast," I said. "Really, really fast."

"Well," she said, a wrinkle marking her forehead, "sometimes these things *do* happen fast. Are you, like, upset about this?"

I walked to the window. "No, no. Absolutely not. I'm happy for you. Although I guess I do miss having a running partner."

"Yeah," Gwen agreed mischievously. "But I'm getting other kinds of exercise."

I resisted an urge to roll my eyes and smiled.

"I love him," she revealed, sitting up excitedly. "He's the nicest, most amazing guy I've *ever* been with. I could die today in happiness, Natalie—I mean it! He's considerate, he's sweet, he's smart, and, well, he's amazing in bed. I mean *amazing*."

She grinned and looked at me, noticing my awkward smile. "I guess you don't want to hear about *that*," she giggled. "But I'm telling you: You should wait for a guy like Noah. I wish he was my first! Now I get what all the fuss is about. I can't get enough!"

I laughed a little, in spite of myself. "Spoken by someone who has the *ability* to compare."

She leaned back on her elbows. "What was your guy's name . . . Patrick?"

I nodded. I hadn't told her the specifics of what happened the night I fled from Patrick's apartment. I worried that if I told her the story, Gwen would think Patrick had only invited me over for sex. Though on some level, I knew that *was* why he had invited me over. He had been in a hurry to move things along, to move me, specifically, into his bedroom. And even when he'd called me afterwards, hadn't our conversation been all about sex? *It's okay if you want to wait a while.* But I didn't want Gwen or anyone else weighing in on the matter. It hardly seemed fair to blame him. Patrick wasn't the problem. I was the problem.

"So, what do you think of Noah?" Gwen asked.

I tightened my ponytail and sank to the floor. "I don't know him," I said, conjuring up Noah's angelic face in my head. "But he's cute. No question."

She sighed and closed her eyes, envisioning, no doubt, the cute face itself. I watched her and thought of Jack, who had the same good looks as Noah. I glanced at Gwen. "Is he a *frat* guy?" I asked teasingly.

"Watch it," she laughed. The conversation then shifted to a debate over frat guys versus off-campus guys, and as Gwen listed what she felt to be a few decent attributes of Noah's fraternity, I imagined her and Noah having sex until I had to look away, embarrassed.

I needed to go running. My books beckoned, my midterms with Anderson and another in international relations the next day nagged, but what was one more hour? I wanted to feel some physical pain; I wanted my throat to burn with each gulp of icy air. I laced my sneakers and slipped on a heavy gray sweatshirt and my only clean sweatpants, a pair of white UConn leggings with blue paw prints climbing up the front of the left leg—a gift from an aunt that I loathed.

My dorm was on the edge of campus, so instead of turning left and encountering the masses I went right toward the streets of Colonial-style homes and white picket fences. When I reached the bottom of a long, steep hill, a hill that I usually avoided, I planned to turn around. But Patrick and Gwen and Noah and sex were still swirling through my brain, and suddenly the memory of Patrick seeing me naked was all the inspiration I needed. I hated my soft curves; I wanted my body to be toned and sleek. At the summit I turned around and descended, and then scaled the hill four more times until my knees throbbed and my chest ached. But when I returned, finally, to level ground, I experienced a runner's high that left me newly energized. I picked up my pace and even sprinted in short bursts, vowing now to forsake cigarettes. Being healthy was too good a feeling. A couple of cars drove past, but the second moved slowly . . . deliberately. I squinted at it up ahead and froze when I identified it as a black Saab. Patrick. The car pulled over, and I watched with dismay as he stepped out.

"Hey," Patrick yelled semi-urgently, waving frantically as I forced my legs to move in his direction, "why are you running?"

"Um, what do you mean?"

"I mean, is someone chasing you? Because there's no other reason I can think of why someone would willingly run. Should I call the police?"

I grinned and crossed my arms. "Thanks," I said, "but I think I lost him a ways back."

"Phew," he breathed, smiling and melting me right there: I was forgiven. I felt as if I'd been tickled. He wore his bright-blue coat and khakis, and his hair was a mess, like he'd just climbed out of bed. I stopped when I was about twenty feet away and smiled shyly, unsure of whether to bring up our last encounter, or the phone call where I'd "ended it." I hoped he would fully absolve me and ask me to join him for lunch. We could start over again, from scratch. We'd meet, initially, during the daytime, when kissing and touching wasn't necessarily expected, and then graduate to nighttime dates. Or maybe I could try to be more normal this time around and just go with the flow.

"C'mon, Patrick," a female voice chided sweetly from inside the car, "we're going to be *late*."

Of course. Who was I kidding? I hoped that the girl inside would at least spare me actually having to view her ravishing beauty. I could just make out her profile, but the Saab's tinted windows didn't give much away, except that her long hair was pulled back in a ponytail—Patrick's favorite look. He glanced into the car and shrugged. "Want a lift?" he asked.

I said no and somehow managed a feeble smile. "I better keep running though," I said, cringing at my joke but unable to stop it once started. "That . . . guy might catch up with me again."

Patrick waited a second before smiling—but I was sure it was at my lack of cool. At how off my timing could be, and not just in his bedroom. He waved and climbed back into his Saab, revving up and disappearing around the corner. I stood there in a stupor, no longer in any mood to run. I wished I could crawl. I moved forward numbly until I could see campus a half-mile ahead. Then I pushed my legs into another sprint, hard and fast. Cold air whipped against me, and I imagined my arms and legs slicing through something solid instead of empty air. I was a blender, cutting through ice, breaking cubes down into chips, the chips into slush. A huge red SUV turned onto the street, going too fast. I could hear its engine roar, I could see it buckle slightly as it shifted gears. I imagined myself leaping out in front of it, imagined my body flattened and bloody on the black tar. Imagined myself dead, for the second time that day.

My long hair was still soaking wet from my shower, but I didn't have the energy to blow-dry it. I rubbed it with the towel and pulled it back. *This is good,* I thought as I packed up my bag for the library. *I'm glad Patrick's with someone else. I'm glad Gwen is with Noah and Faith is with Keith. Now I can focus on what's important: my studies.* I sighed and went to get my keys, but when I couldn't find them I decided it was fate ordering me to smoke before my study session, and I cracked the window, taking in the fading sunset of violet and pink. Faith was passed out on her bed, the result of extreme sleep deprivation. She'd probably even sleep through a fire alarm, should there be one tonight; false alarms were pretty common during midterms.

I breathed in the cigarette and succumbed to picturing Patrick and his invisible date on their drive to . . . where? Friendly's? Then they would return to his apartment, where Patrick would undress her and lick her . . . well, lick her everywhere. In all the right (*the wrong!*) spots. She would have flowing blond hair and big breasts, not unlike Barbie herself. Or, worse, she would look just like Gwen—smart, athletic, glowing.

I finished my smoke and noticed my keys plopped dead center on my desk. I stuffed them into my coat pocket and opened the door, coming face to face with Linda.

"That is so funny!" she squealed. "I was just about to knock!"

"Hi," I said. "I'm just on my way to the library."

"That's why I was coming to see you. I'm going to the library myself."

My spirits sank a tiny bit lower. I wanted to tell her that I wasn't much in the mood for company, but I just smiled and walked with her to the elevator. When the doors opened, two guys were inside.

"That is so funny!" Linda squealed again. "This is Ian and Robbie, Natalie. Today must be my lucky day, because I keep running into the people I want to see!"

Ian, the guy who Linda believed was secretly in love with her, nudged his roommate and gave Linda a withering look. Robbie, in turn, grinned knowingly, and it annoyed me; I felt defensive for Linda. But then Linda started to giggle, and as she did she looked at me expectantly. She wanted me to giggle, too. She wanted Ian and Robbie to think that we, too, were sharing a secret that they were not privy to. The few seconds that passed before the elevator delivered us to the main floor felt interminable.

"Catcha later," Ian said, and as he and Robbie walked out ahead of us they high-fived as soon as they went through the doors.

"What was *that* all about?" I asked Linda.

"How should I know?" she replied somewhat coyly before dissolving into laughter. "Let's just say . . . Ian and I spent some time together the other night."

I frowned. "No," I said. "Tell me you didn't."

"We each had a little too much to drink, but don't worry, we didn't do it. I just, um, gave him a little . . . happiness."

I did not want to know whether "happiness" meant hand-job or blow-job, but even in my inexperience I knew it had to be one of them.

"What about his girlfriend?" I asked.

"What?" she replied somewhat defensively. "Is it *my* fault that he fooled around? He doesn't even like her. He told me he wants to break it off, but he doesn't want to hurt her. I'm telling you, he's into *me*. We hung out together for *hours* the other night, and most of the time we were talking."

"Linda," I said, not knowing how to put it delicately, "it didn't seem, just now, like Ian, um, likes you all that much."

"Well, what do you expect? Robbie was with him. Robbie doesn't know about us, and he's also friends with Samantha, Ian's pseudo-girlfriend. Ian's just scared. He'll probably come to my room tonight, and I hope he does. I think I'm falling for him."

We climbed a flight of steps and went into the library, where Linda spotted a guy she knew and ran over to join him. She waved me over, but I pointed to my watch with feigned disappointment. Then I went to the fourth floor and my carrel. I rummaged through my bag and took out texts and notebooks, then stared at them. I was frozen. I couldn't study. I had several midterms to face, in constitutional law, international relations, Russian history, the Russian language, and art history, but I couldn't concentrate. I counted to ten, then twenty, then thirty, until I finally grabbed a Russian history text and flipped the pages without aim. I came to a photo of Rasputin and stopped. I already knew everything I needed to know about Rasputin, but there was something about the man that suddenly made me think of Patrick. I lightly tapped a pencil against the desk and turned the page, encountering a photo of a grim, unsmiling Alexandra, the tsarina. Suddenly it hit me: *I* was like Alexandra, the woman who idolized Rasputin, who needed him to help make sense of her world and awarded him talents completely out of synch with reality. I smiled, happy to engage my mind like this, and outlined the comparisons in my notebook: Alexandra believed Rasputin possessed unearthly, mystical powers and championed him. I, in turn, barely knew Patrick and yet had already ascertained that he was too good for me because of his . . . what? Wealth? Intelligence? Sophistication and humor? Wasn't *that* why I had really put a stop to the relationship? It had been too daunting to be near him, too intimidating. I leaned back in my chair. Alexandra meant little to Rasputin personally, but she derived what she needed from him. A chill ran up my spine and I breathed in, slowly. Just because Patrick didn't need *me* didn't negate my need for *him* . . .

And it was thus that I spent several more hours in the library, the night before my most important exam.

*

twelve

I went through my morning ritual in a dreamlike haze. I stood under the shower, letting the water pound my body, but it felt as if I had a second, thicker layer of skin zipped up over my flesh. I brushed my teeth and massaged my gums with the bristles, but after I rinsed, my mouth was still stale. Anderson's exam loomed, yet I couldn't focus.

Usually I was a pro at all-nighters. Motivated by the importance of earning an A, I was disciplined and able to stay awake. But last night my focus had been fitful; it was as if I felt compelled to do badly. Not just my self-discipline but my confidence, too, was gone. Now I was sleep-deprived *and* unprepared.

I stepped outside and stood still, hoping the piercing cold would wake up my ambition, as well as my body. When nothing happened, I ordered my legs to move in the direction of the history building, and I barely glanced up when I heard my name called. I felt a tap on my shoulder and turned to see Jack walking beside me.

"Hey," he said, stuffing his hands into his pockets. "Where you off to?"

"Exam," I replied stiffly, then said the only thought that came to me: "It's weird how we keep running into each other."

"It's not that weird," he smiled. "My dorm's basically adjacent to yours. I live in Brock."

I said, "Oh," and we continued walking in a heavy silence. I itched to be rid of him; I needed to think about my pending test. The more I thought about this the more frustrated I became, until I finally stopped and asked, "Is there anything I can help you with?"

Jack's eyebrows rose in surprise as he took a step away. He smiled and replied, "Um, yes, miss . . . can you tell me what aisle the toothpaste is in?"

I softened and apologized, explaining that I was under a lot of stress, explaining that it was vital that I do well on my exam.

"Do you really doubt that you'll ace it?" he asked. "Isn't that a given?"

"No," I answered, "it's not."

"I don't believe you," he said. "You're too smart."

"How would you know?" I snapped. "And, anyway, being smart has *nothing* to do with it. Either you've memorized the material or you haven't. And I haven't. That's why I'm a history major—you don't *have* to be smart, you just have to memorize your lines. And apparently I can't even do that anymore."

"Okay, okay," he said, nodding his head. "Sorry. I didn't mean to upset you."

I fiddled with a tissue in my coat pocket. "Just because you were in a class with me once doesn't prove that I'm 'smart,' " I said softly. "*Anyone* can get good grades. It doesn't take a genius. Trust me."

"Well, I certainly don't get the best grades, and I know that I try to."

I found that hard to believe. "Effort is all relative," I said. "Do you spend every free moment at the library?"

"Come on . . . do you really believe that anyone who wanted to could get straight A's? What if someone doesn't have the ability to digest what he reads . . . what if someone can't write for shit?"

"Then they can get straight B's. Or maybe even B-pluses. Regardless, they'll still be considered 'smart.' Which, of course, doesn't mean that they are."

The history building blocked out the blue sky, and I glanced at him. "Sorry," I said, "I guess when I don't sleep, I'll say anything."

"Maybe you should sleep less," he suggested. "That's more than you've said to me in all our conversations combined. But—just for the record—I *still* think you're smart."

I sighed audibly and lifted my arms, defeated.

"Hey," Jack called out as I climbed the stairs, "how'd your date go with that guy . . . the tall guy?"

My smile vanished momentarily until I forced it back on my face. "It went great," I replied brightly, then disappeared behind the wooden doors.

. . .

I took my seat and searched in vain for a pen, horrified that I could have forgotten the only thing I really needed for the exam. This was a forecast for disaster. I eyed the students seated near me and plaintively begged for a pen or a pencil, but no one had an extra. Anderson was already passing out the blue essay books, and I emptied my bag on the floor, letting papers and books fall in a single burst, but there was nothing, not even a pencil stub. Before the questions were passed back, my anxiety rose to panic and I suddenly found myself shouting, loudly, "Does ANYONE have a pen I can borrow?"

The gentle hum of pre-exam voices ceased and all eyes turned to me, including Anderson's. "*Excuse me*, Miss Bloom," he said severely. "It is not the duty of your classmates to supply you with a pen. It is *your* duty to come to class prepared. Be seated."

"Yes sir," I whispered. The girl sitting behind me tapped my shoulder and slipped me a blue ball-point, which I snatched with sick relief.

The xeroxed questions delivered, I paused before reading them. If only I'd had this motivating terror the night before.

"One hour," Anderson announced, looking at his watch, "starting . . . *now*."

I positioned my pen. The first question was general enough—I could bullshit my way to a good answer, but the second posed more of a problem. It involved Anderson's last two lectures, neither of which I had listened to carefully. I glanced at Joe—boring Joe, who was already writing madly—and sent invisible daggers into his neck, then I pushed the nib of my pen against the blue-lined paper: I wrote the numeral "1," placing a dark, circular period beside it. Then I made my hand move, made my mind form sentences and hoped and prayed that they made sense.

Forty minutes, gone. I glanced at the clock in disbelief. I knew I had spent too much time on the first question. But why not? It was the only one I could answer well. How was I supposed to come up with something decent in just twenty minutes? I reread the question, trying to envision a loophole, trying to make it ask a different question—a question I knew something about. I considered this strategy, seriously: If I were to write about Lenin's October takeover, maybe adding the peasants' viewpoint, could Anderson really not give me *any* credit? It wasn't the subject the question asked about, but some credit was better than no credit. *I'm going to do it*, I thought, and set my pen to paper, writing frenetically until Anderson ordered me to stop.

A group of students sat on the yellowed ground in a circle just outside of the history building, notebooks opened on their laps. I watched them as I passed, three girls and four guys, and overheard them testing each other for what sounded like an anthropology class. One of the girls was smoking and overweight, one was skinny and blond, like a cheerleader, and the last was pretty and intellectual with a pair of silver-framed glasses perched on her nose. The guys wore baseball caps, jeans, sneakers, warm jackets. They were sharing a large bag of Fritos and drinking

Cokes, and their heads were bent over their notes as they asked questions and tossed ideas back and forth.

"When women paint their fingernails red," the cheerleader asked, "what are they trying to convey?"

"Their status," the smoking girl replied. "They want everyone to see that they don't have to use their hands for manual labor."

"Okay," a guy with long hair piped up, "but what about when they paint their lips red?"

"That's easy," an athletic-looking guy with a baseball cap on backwards grinned. "Sex. Who said that—Desmond Morris? Didn't he equate it with the swollen, engorged lips of a . . ."

"Don't even *say* it," the girl with glasses laughed, and then all of them were laughing.

I picked up my pace, leaving the group behind. A sick malaise settled over me. I pictured Anderson reading my second essay, drawing expansive red X's over each futile page until he could print a large red F at the end of the answer. He would then transfer my score into his leatherbound grade book, disgusted. I stopped in my tracks, horrified, and retraced my steps. It couldn't hurt to explain myself before he graded the exams. I could make myself pitiable, a sympathetic character worthy of special consideration. I jogged down the long hall and up to the third floor, my fists clenched, afraid that if I paused I would chicken out. When I reached his office, I rapped in a burst of three precise knocks.

"Enter!"

I swung the door open and positioned myself before Anderson, who was reading a book at his desk. He scanned the person before him, starting with my feet and finally resting his eyes on my face. His look was worn and grave.

"What is it," he asked without the intonation of a question. "Be quick."

"Professor Anderson," I began, confession-style, panting, "I think you should know that I just did something I shouldn't have. I answered a different question than the one asked. I'm appealing to you to let me take a makeup exam. Please."

Anderson slowly closed his book, expressionless.

"I'm sorry," I continued, my voice beginning to shake. "I don't know what's wrong with me. I just can't bear to do badly on an exam, particularly *this* exam, and I know you don't do makeups but I'm hoping you might reconsider just this once. I promise never to do this again. Please, I—"

"Natalie," Anderson interrupted. "Stop."

I swallowed and gripped my hands together, awaiting the executioner's verdict.

"If you know that I don't give makeups," he said slowly, "then I have to ask you: Why are you here?"

"Because you know how much I care about my grades," I replied quickly.

"Maybe I should rephrase my question. Why are you wasting my time?"

I bit my bottom lip to keep it from quivering. Desperate tears demanded release. "Can't someone make a mistake?" I asked feebly, almost in a whisper.

"Someone *can* make a mistake," he replied, a bit softer. "And someone can pay for a mistake, too. Hopefully someone can learn from a mistake."

"I *have* learned," I pleaded. "I just need a little help. Maybe you could cut twenty points on the makeup, so that the highest grade I could get is an eighty. Or—"

"No," Anderson cut in, "I'm afraid I can't help you."

"Maybe I could do some extra credit?" I pressed on, tugging at a loose strand of hair. "I could write a term paper on whatever topic you choose."

"Natalie," he said sternly, "no."

"But what about me taking the initiative?" I began to whimper. "I'm trying to do right. Isn't that worth . . . something? If I fail this exam I . . . I don't know what I'll do."

"What you are *doing*," he asserted, "is being a self-serving student who expects favoritism. You may go now."

He turned back to his book as if I had already left the room, as if my despair meant nothing. I noticed a photo tossed casually on his desk, of him and a woman I presumed was his wife. Mrs. Harold Anderson. He was smiling in the photo and wore a simple short-sleeved oxford and a pair of khakis. His wife had white hair and high cheekbones, and wore a checkered dress. The sun draped their weathered bodies. Their eyes squinted. They were holding hands. He looked kind, warm, generous.

"I'm sorry," I said as I left, "for wasting your time."

I sat on a bench and cried bitter, fearful tears. It was easier to blame Anderson than myself, and so I did. *I was just asking for help this once,* I repeated mindlessly.

When I returned to my room, Faith was sitting at the window, smoking, her forehead pressed against her knees, wearing one of Keith's oversized white T-shirts that draped her tiny body like a tent. I grabbed a cigarette from my desk drawer and joined her, and the two of us inhaled and exhaled in silence.

"I'm finished," Faith said harshly, crushing the butt into her purple ashtray.

"Me, too," I agreed.

"I'm serious," she said angrily. "I'm quitting."

"Look," I replied, trying to be hopeful, for Faith's sake, "it'll get better. I just flunked *my* most important exam, too!"

"Congratulations," she said sarcastically. "You're really changing for the better, Natalie. Now you're a smoker *and* a loser, just like me. Do you feel cooler?"

"*Jesus*," I breathed, "I was trying to make you *feel better*."

Faith lit another cigarette and tried to run her fingers through her hair—quickly giving up when she encountered a wall of hairspray—then coughed and held her throat. "Sorry," she said when the hacking subsided, "I'm just totally fucked. I could stay here, but I'd have to repeat this year because I've done so badly. Or, I could transfer back to a community college and change my major. Do something with computers, I don't know. Who the fuck cares."

Keith knocked, then entered and strode over to Faith, whereupon he picked up her petite body, threw her over his shoulder, and spanked her rear end with too much force.

"Put me *down*," she screamed, "or I'll cut your fucking balls off!"

He set her on the floor, laughing. "Easy, girl," he said. "You don't want me to get rough."

I grimaced and turned away.

"Hello, Natalie," he said sweetly. "And how are you today?"

"Fine," I sighed. "Are you staying here tonight?"

"Yep," he said happily.

I studied him for a second. He seemed distinctly more cheerful than usual, and I wondered if he was glad Faith was thinking about dropping out. I nodded silently and grabbed my keys, jacket, and book bag before leaving.

When I finally returned at midnight, Keith and Faith were lying in bed in the dark, spooning in order to fit. Faith groaned and got up to use the bathroom, and I set my things down and sifted through the bottom dresser drawer for a pair of shorts and a T-shirt to wear to bed. As I was bent over, my rump jutting out, hands caressed my sides and I let out a shocked whimper. I spun around to see a boxered Keith standing in front of me with a finger pressed against his lips, a small, sick smile on his face. He jumped back into bed, and a moment later Faith returned, yawned, and joined him.

My heart pounded. Keith had never done anything like that before, and even though I suspected him of cheating on Faith, never in a million years would I have thought he would try anything on *me*. But in the moment I felt more afraid than angry. His touch had been sexual, and my mind was focused on the sensation rather than on who had touched me. I glanced at Keith, who winked while licking his top, narrow lip. Disgusted but silenced by Faith's return, I scowled and rushed out of the room.

How dare he?

I sat on the edge of a toilet, collecting myself. I contemplated bursting in and telling Faith, in front of Keith, what had happened . . . but what good would it have done? If Faith could date someone like Keith, she surely knew of his shortcomings.

I lifted my sweater over my head and unsnapped my bra, slipping on a green T-shirt over my head. I felt angry. Violated. But did I also feel a slight, albeit involuntary, excitement? What would it be like to be taken unawares—even by someone as vile as Keith? What if *that* was my "first time"? Then I felt ashamed—appalled—and left the stall.

I squeezed a long line of toothpaste onto my toothbrush and brushed in rough, circular motions. With the foam building in my mouth, I looked like a rabid dog. I closed my eyes tightly and tried to think about neutral subjects, about which artists represented the Renaissance and which the Romantic period for my art history exam—-but instead I imagined Keith edging up behind me and running his hands along the length of my body. I imagined him bending down close to my ear until his hot breath tickled my skin. I imagined him saying, *Don't worry, Natalie. I know you're a virgin, and I'm just fucking with you. I don't want you at all. Who would?*

thirteen

My palms were sweating and I held my breath as I checked my grade. I ran my finger down the row of names until I found "Bloom" and then traced the numerical grade written in blue beside it: 67. A D-plus. The lowest grade I had ever received on a big exam. I exhaled and breathed in, echoing all the while the grade in my mind as I backed against the far wall. There was despair, but there was something else, too, oozing through my body. It was relief. Not relief that I hadn't failed, but relief at having earned a low grade, fair and square. My lips skirted into a smile and I walked back to the sheet, quickly scanning the other grades. Joe had gotten the highest mark, a 98; the girl who had lent me the pen received an 85. The other grades ranged; most fell in the C-plus to B-minus category, with a few D's and only one F.

I pinched my cheeks as I absorbed the fact that I had gotten *the fourth-lowest grade.* This didn't make me more human. It just made me more stupid than other humans.

I hurried out of the building. The sky was the color of slate. Even bright-red backpacks looked muted. Back in my room, Faith was in bed, asleep, and I placed my things down softly. Keith, thankfully, had left early for work. I sat at my desk and clicked on a lamp and stared ahead at the concrete wall. I was losing what I'd worked so hard for. I was forsaking myself willingly. I felt self-destructive, and one thought kept reasserting itself: *Is this how Jacob felt?*

"Want to go out tonight?" Faith asked sleepily, startling me. When I faced her she was already lighting a cigarette.

"What do you mean?" I asked, my voice sounding thick and different.

"I mean," she said, inhaling deeply, "want to get trashed? We can go to Husky's."

I swallowed, pushing back the lump in my throat. Faith and I had never gone out together, not even once. We didn't even go to the cafeteria at the same time. I had taken it as a given that our relationship was limited to our room and nowhere else.

"There's a first time for everything, right?" she asked. "And, besides, you won't be seeing me for too much longer. I wasn't kidding yesterday. I'm quitting."

"When?"

"I'm not sure. But soon. So, how 'bout it?"

"Okay," I agreed. "It might be just what I need."

I opened my top drawer and extracted my last cigarette from its box. I lit up and tried not to notice that my hands were trembling. I inhaled too strongly and coughed, and I eyed the cigarette with something like anger. I shouldn't have agreed to go out. I should have told Faith that I needed to prepare for my Russian language exam, for my international relations exam. But with my 67, it seemed impossible to get good grades; it seemed as if studying was no longer the key.

To cheer Faith up, and because it was our last chance to act like roommates, I agreed to let her do my makeup for the evening. Now I sat patiently on the bathroom sink as my face was colored in with black liquid eyeliner, black mascara, silver eye shadow, mauve blush, fire-engine-red lipstick, and a dusting of powder. When I was finally allowed to look at myself in the mirror, I saw someone who wasn't quite me. Someone uglier, in a way, yet sexier, too. I had been transformed into a whore, and if only it were Halloween I wouldn't have batted an eyelash at my cheapened image.

"*Whoa*," Sasha said, entering the bathroom in a low-cut red T-shirt and tight jeans. "Who the fuck is *that*? Not *Natalie*."

"Be quiet," Faith snapped. "Not one more word."

"Why?" Sasha asked innocently. "She looks *amazing*. Natalie, if I'd known what a hottie you are, I'd have recruited you to work at the Blue Lagoon."

My face burned, turning me into a turnip under my caked blush. "We're just fooling around," I laughed. "I'm going to wash it off."

"Fuck that," Faith said. "Every guy at that bar is going to be drooling over you."

"You guys are going out?" Sasha asked, looping a strand of her black hair around her finger. "Can I join you?"

Faith and I stared at her in disbelief. "Why would you want to go out with us?" Faith asked suspiciously.

"Why not? We can do girl talk! We'll talk about how to give good blow-jobs and fake orgasms . . . right, Natalie?"

I bristled and turned on the faucet to wash my face, but Faith was quick to twist it off. Sasha laughed. "I'm just messing with you. Don't take everything so seriously. Hey! If Faith gets to do your makeup, I want to dress you! Okay?"

Faith squealed with delight, and before I could protest, she grabbed my hand and we followed Sasha back to her room. It was a mess. A ton of clothes towered on the back of her desk chair, threatening to topple over at the slightest touch. Makeup littered her desktop. She flipped her closet curtain aside and began to grab at tops, skirts, and even a pair of black leather pants, which I shook my head at vehemently. She modeled a gold-sequined top that looked skimpier than most of my bathing suits, then offered a red velvet minidress that, as mini as it was, actually had a slit that must have traveled above the waistline. I scowled. Sasha then stared, pointedly, at my outfit—a navy T-shirt that billowed and a pair of jeans that sagged away from my butt, and I found myself laughing. If I was going to go out with Faith's caked makeup, why *not* dress up, too? Why not pretend it really *was* Halloween? Maybe it would be fun. I looked back at Sasha's closet and spotted something that looked black and clingy. Something that I would never in a million years wear in real life. I held it up against my torso, and after Sasha and Faith nodded approvingly, I decided to try it on.

"Could you guys, um, turn around for a second?" I asked.

Sasha laughed. "I've seen tits before, Natalie. Mine, for instance."

"Just humor her," Faith giggled.

I squeezed into the top with its plunging neckline, and when Sasha and Faith looked they both whistled. Sasha then pushed past me and pulled more clothes out of her closet until she found what she wanted: a short black skirt, tailored from the exact same material, which must have been predominantly spandex. I struggled to get it over my hips.

"I don't know," I grimaced once it was in place. "Don't I look like a slut?"

"A little sluttiness never hurt anyone," Sasha smiled. "Trust me."

Before they would allow me to look in the mirror, they added some final touches to my ensemble. A pair of black heels soon propped my body skyward, and a pair of fishnets coated my legs; a gigantic pair of silver hoop earrings drooped from my lobes; silver bangles jiggled on my wrists. Sasha then covered my eyes with her hands as Faith guided us in front of the full-length mirror behind the door.

"Voilà!" Sasha said.

I stared at my reflection in the glass, trying to admire the girl looking back. I didn't recognize myself at all, which made it all seem doable. I began to laugh.

"That's it," Sasha declared. "We're done! Let's go."

. . .

Music boomed as we climbed the stairs to the bar. The bouncer checked Faith's legitimate ID and then barely glanced at the fake IDs Sasha and I flashed. I was Trista Gold, one of Sasha's coworkers at the Blue Lagoon, and she was Molly Spears, age thirty-seven. Neither of us looked anything like the women in the photos, but the bouncer didn't seem to care and instead looked more closely at the trio of cleavages, and I, in my costume, refrained from crossing my arms. We pushed past the crowd of people plugging the doorway and headed for the bar, where we ordered tequila shots and nabbed the last free stools. And then: "Natalie?"

I turned to see Patrick, towering above me. In my surprise my stool tipped a bit and I grabbed at the counter.

"Hi," he said, smiling. "You look . . . you look . . . sensational. Wow."

I blushed. This time I couldn't help but cross my arms. "This is my roommate, Faith, and our neighbor, Sasha."

He shook their hands and scanned their bodies. "Jesus," he said, "you guys look like Charlie's Angels. Hot."

Sasha and Faith burst out laughing.

"Listen," he said, "my friends and I have a table in back. Why don't you guys join us? Beer's on us."

Sasha and Faith readily agreed, and Patrick smiled at me in a way that made all the hairs on my arms stand on end. I was elated to be in his presence and proud that he could see me out with friends, but also a bit panicked at being caught in this outfit. We downed our shots and followed him through the mob of drunken students to his table. There were five guys seated, and Patrick took my hand to seat me beside him. My heart raced. Faith sat between two guys who looked like twins except that one had severe acne, and Sasha perched atop the lap of a chiseled, muscular guy with a brush cut. Patrick was dressed preppily, as usual, in khakis and a green T-shirt, but his friends wore more typical university garb: spring-break tees, jeans, and sneakers. Beers were quickly poured, and I clung to my plastic blue cup, gulping down the liquid. Patrick traced my shoulders with his fingertip, sending flutters down my spine. "God," he said, "you look gorgeous tonight."

A buzz had already formed, and I willed it to come on stronger. Patrick began talking to his friends, but kept his hand on my knee, rubbing it lightly. His touch reminded me of the night in his apartment. I looked down at my bulging breasts. My skirt was hiked so high. Of all people, I, Natalie Bloom, was pretending to be *sexy*. My cheeks fired up, recalling the way I'd screamed at Patrick to turn off the lights as I dressed. I yanked at my skirt, forcing it to cover a bit more thigh. But then I took a deep breath. Here he was. Here he *was*. Patrick. Patrick! I wanted him. I wanted him to want me.

Didn't I?

The song "What I Am" boomed from the speakers, and to make conversation, in the same way one says "The weather is great today," I blurted, "I love Edie Brickell," only the way I pronounced the songstress's name was entirely incorrect, more like Eddie Brickel, as in rhymes with "nickel." Everyone at the table stopped talking and looked at me, and I, guessing the blunder I had just committed was a big one—on the scale of declaring Ayn Rand to be a man—blinked back stupidly. Thankfully, Sasha and Faith laughed uproariously and clued me in to my error. But Patrick didn't laugh. He gave a half-smile, and then he recited the lyrics of the song in a deadpan voice, as if he were delivering a staid lecture: "I'm not aware of too many things. I know what I know, if you know what I mean."

His friends, as if given permission, then joined Sasha and Faith in sidesplitting laughter. To say that my face burned doesn't even hint at the ridicule I felt. Patrick, though, sensing his teasing had gone over the edge, leaned in and kissed my cheek, then mussed my hair playfully.

"Excuse me," I smiled weakly, "I have to, um, use the bathroom."

I stood, abruptly, and made my way through the crowd. A long line trailed outside of the women's lavatory, and I guessed it would be a ten- or fifteen-minute wait, a lucky reprieve. Away from the table I could return to being anonymous. Someone other than myself. Then I heard someone utter the word "fishnet" followed by laughter. I glanced back and saw three normal-looking college girls dressed the way I usually dressed: baggy clothes, sensible shoes, comfortable. They immediately looked away when they saw me, suppressing renewed laughter. I, in turn, pulled my hair forward, hiding my face.

After I used the toilet, I took a paper towel and rubbed my cheeks, my lips, as hard as I could, trying to erase some of the unnatural color from my skin, but Faith had done too good a job; I succeeded only in muting my ghastly red lips, my abnormally pink cheeks. Bodies pressed into me as I moved back into the bar, and I felt someone's hand pat my rear. When I finally spotted the table, spotted Patrick, I saw that Faith was making out with the acne-free twin to her right. Sasha was cradling her guy's face with her hand, oblivious to his hand resting between her thighs. An exit sign glowed through the darkness, invitingly, but I ignored it and retook my seat. I needed to see the night through.

"Hey, Eddie Brickel," Patrick said, pouring me a fresh cup of beer. "Want to get out of here soon? We can go back to my place and smoke a joint. If you want, of course."

I did want to. And if there was that tiny hesitation lodged in the back of my throat? Well, it could just stay there.

"Okay," I smiled robotically, "sounds good."

He grinned and ran his fingers through my hair. Then he turned back to his friends and resumed a conversation about basketball.

It was two in the morning when we reached his apartment. I was drunk. I followed him inside and took a seat on the couch while he rolled a joint. I was afraid if I took a hit I would pass out; as it was, I was having a hard time keeping my eyes open. But Patrick, thankfully, didn't offer it to me. He took a few quick hits, then sat beside me and planted his arm around me, his lips on my lips. We stayed that way for just a few moments before he explored my body, caressing my breasts and between my thighs. I still had an urge to push his hands away, but with the help of my complete inebriation I ignored it and allowed him free rein over my body. Then he undid his belt, pushed his pants and underwear down to his ankles and pointed at his semihard penis. I looked at it and laughed, burying my face in my hands.

"Come on," he laughed, slightly irritable. "Would you mind? It would really help me to get in the mood."

I uncovered my eyes and focused on his face. "Excuse me?" I asked.

"You know," he suggested, "it'd be great if you could . . . put it in your mouth."

My smile vanished. I think I had actually thought that we would simply make out for a while before I trailed home. Even through my drunkenness I suddenly realized how naïve that was.

"I'm sorry," I said, edging away from him. "I can't do that. I've . . . never done that."

"You've got to try it sometime," he said lightly.

I allowed myself to glance down again at his penis, and then I shook my head no, apologetically.

"Please?" he asked.

I was sobering up, rapidly. It was just a blow-job. How hard could it be? I'd spent so many hours thinking about this guy and daydreaming about what might happen between us, and, granted, blowing him was never in the forefront of my mind, but it would show him something. It would show him how much I cared. It could be the start of something bigger. And it would show him that I was no longer afraid, that I was ready to take the next step. But how did he feel? I wanted to ask him if he thought about me the way that I thought about him; I wanted to know if he ever considered being with me . . . as a girlfriend. If he genuinely liked me. If he . . . if he . . . might save me.

Instead I smiled at him and sank to my knees by the couch, taking him in my mouth.

"Slowly," he ordered, his eyes closed. "You don't have to bob your head so much. Good."

*

fourteen

I sat up in bed, hungover, and pressed my fingers against my throbbing temples as the prior evening came back to me. I lowered myself to the floor, gulped down a stagnant glass of water that had been on my desk, and rolled the cool glass over my cheek.

At least I was still a virgin.

I closed my eyes and remembered the thickened, slightly salty, purplish penis. I had licked it and sucked until my neck and jaw cramped with my efforts, and all for naught: It had shrunken and gone flaccid, a floppy stub of its former self. Patrick had finally told me to stop, and, while embarrassed, I was relieved that he had.

No, I was *overjoyed* that he had.

I hurried to bathe, soaping my body without looking at it. It was my last day of midterms. Afterwards many students would go home for a break, but I had signed on to work the information booth during the holiday. When I got out of the shower, Sasha was brushing her teeth in a tank and a pair of pink panties. I reddened at seeing a witness from last night and forced a smile.

"What a fucking night," Sasha said, rinsing. "*You* had a good time, eh, sweetie?"

I nodded and reached for the door. "I'll have your clothes washed today."

"No rush," she replied. "Maybe you want to hang on to them. They got you lucky, didn't they?"

I shuffled quickly back to my room. Faith was just waking up; mascara was smeared around her eyes and her molded hair was split straight down the middle of her scalp. I heard her light a cigarette as I dressed behind the closet curtain.

"Don't tell Keith," she muttered hoarsely. "I've never cheated before. I was just blowing off steam. And I only made out with the guy, I didn't have sex. Got it?"

"Yeah," I replied, appearing from behind the curtain. "Got it."

"So," she asked, a bit more cheerily, "did you . . . you know . . . do it?"

"NO," I snapped. "And I don't want to talk about it. Ever."

"Good," Faith nodded. "It's a deal."

I brushed my hair and felt relieved to see my look returned to its sensible, natural state. Then I threw on a coat, took two Tylenol, and left to take another exam.

Katya Abromovich, a Russian-language TA, never spoke in English, at least not in class. She dressed in outfits that showed off her long, sleek legs, often pairing fitted black pants with sparkly tops that recalled Christmas and cocktail parties. But she never looked cheap, or not in the way that I had the night before; she looked womanly. Her skin was pale and creamy, and her short hair was dyed platinum blond. She spoke in a high, feminine voice made husky by her Slavic accent, and exuded confidence. That day Katya wore a bright-red trench coat tied tightly at the waist because the heat in the building wasn't working properly. It was cold, but not too cold to cancel class.

After noting that I was the last person to arrive, Katya announced that she would therefore begin with me. I kept my coat on, too, and took the chair opposite her, my hands folded on my lap, my head swimming in pain. Language, thankfully, came fairly easily to me, and so I wasn't exactly nervous, but I guessed—based on my current track record—that nothing was guaranteed. I briefly went over basic conjugations, past tense (my most challenging category), and vocabulary, then carefully kept my gaze locked on my teacher's face so as to avoid looking at the roomful of eyes focused on me.

"How are you today?" Katya began without looking at me, instead making notes on a yellow legal pad propped on her lap.

"Fine," I replied. "Really well."

"What would you like to talk about?"

I shifted in my seat. "Anything," I replied with a polite smile.

"But that is up to *you*," Katya said, a little less kindly. "You do realize you were supposed to prepare a topic for discussion?"

Nyet, I thought in horror. Instead, I nodded and decided to talk about my family. I had a mother and a father, a lot of brothers, and a dog named Biffo. I would omit Jacob from the speech and keep it limited to simple statements, like what each person did for a living. The only problem was, I was having a hard time remembering vital vocabulary, like the word for "brother." I couldn't even remember the word for "dog." Katya began clicking her heel impatiently as I struggled to recall these most elementary of words. I blushed and pressed my fingers against my forehead, hoping the pressure would help reconnect the wires in my brain.

"Natalie," Katya interrupted, dashing off notes, "that's enough. Thank you."

"I'm sorry," I squeaked in English, "I'm really sorry."

She gave me a somewhat sympathetic smile and called on the next person, a blond girl wearing UConn sweats, her hair pulled back in a black scrunchie, who began to speak flawlessly on the American political system. I skulked to the back of the class. *This is what you get*, I thought dejectedly, holding back tears, *for going out last night, for being with Patrick, for doing what you did*.

I missed the old Natalie. The one who would have been prepared for this exam. I thought about all of the new "friends" I'd made lately. Why was it that the more people I connected with, the more it felt like I was disappearing?

"That guy Patrick called," Faith said when I returned to the room. "He wants you to call him back."

I dropped my things and sat down, then lit a cigarette from

the new pack I'd just bought. "What . . . what did his voice sound like?" I asked anxiously.

Faith shrugged and continued to look at the magazine spread across her lap. "How the hell should I know?"

I puffed on the cigarette until it felt like my innards were absorbed by a dense cloud of smoke, then dragged the phone into the hall and sat down on the cold floor. Patrick picked up after the third ring. "My roommate said you called," I reported, heart pounding, "so I'm calling you back."

"Well," he said, "it's Friday, and I thought we might pick up where we left off last night. Sorry I, you know, had a 'problem.' A little too much to drink."

He was taking the blame. Thank God. I laughed. "The thing is," I said, attempting to steady my voice, "I . . . I can't do what we did last night again."

"Uh-oh," he kidded with a sigh. "Are you dumping me *again*? I'm going to develop a complex. I kiss you and you run for the hills."

"No," I said and took a deep breath. "What time?"

I tried to empty my mind as I prepared to meet Patrick. I dug through Faith's makeup kit until I found a tube of mascara and applied it so that my lashes curled back and left little black dots on my eyelids. I reddened my pink cheeks and glided mauve lipstick over my lips. Then I pulled on my jeans and chose one of Faith's tight-fitting sweaters in a turquoise shade. I didn't cringe as usual or think *this isn't me*; I tried not to think at all.

I walked to Patrick's at a steady pace, and when I got there

I rapped—not too loud, but loud enough to be heard, and he invited me in. I moved through the foyer and took a seat on the couch with my legs crossed and my hands placed loosely on my lap. He asked me what I would like to drink, and I told him I would drink whatever he was having. He brought me a Heineken in its dark-green bottle, the red star on the label, and sat beside me. I didn't shy away or shift. I drank from the bottle, placed it on the coffee table, then picked it up and drank some more. He was talking, he was saying things to me, he was being witty, and I smiled. I smiled because he was trying, he was making an effort instead of just bedding me. I smiled because he felt there was a need, when, in reality, I had already made up my mind: I would lose my virginity. I would let events unfold without trying to control them. I could become someone else. Someone who wasn't me.

We had each finished two beers when his roommate, a short guy named Ryan, shook my hand and announced his departure for the entire night—an announcement he declared a little too deliberately—and then we were alone. Patrick kissed me. He laid me back on the couch and let his hands find my breasts, which he then squeezed. We moved up to his room, and I stayed the course, I let it happen, I let him do what, I thought, needed to be done. Except for when he tried to touch me . . . *down there*. That was one thing that didn't need to be done. Things were happening in the nether region that were unfamiliar: Fluids were involved, and it seemed I had no control over their emission. He stopped and rolled on a condom and then the sudden, stabbing pain in my groin made me yelp; I made a fist and bit on it to keep from crying out again. There was pressure, there was pain, there was hardened flesh pressing into softened flesh, there was a whispered sentence: *Your cunt feels incredible*. There was rocking until there was stillness. And then there was blood. On his navy-striped cotton sheets. I felt the warm liquid ooze between my legs, my thighs, and I jumped up to use the bathroom, grabbing my black panties from the floor and pressing them against my crotch, catching the red droplets before they had a chance to hit the carpet. "I'm so sorry," I called as I closed the door, "I'll clean your sheets in a minute." I flicked on the light and didn't move for minutes. I wiped the blood away with dampened Kleenex and waited until there was no more blood, until it was safe to return to Patrick. I pulled on my soiled panties and looked at myself in the mirror. My mascara, on my left eye, had run. I cleaned away the black ink, using outward strokes until my temple was clear, pale flesh.

He asked me if I felt okay, and I told him I did. He told me to get back into bed with him, but I just stood there and laughed. My nervous laugh was already returning. The event had taken place, the event I had been thinking of for such a long time, and it seemed strange now to be with him, naked, even in the dark. He tossed me the sheet and I returned to the bathroom and rubbed the quarter-sized spot under water with a bar of Ivory soap. It paled to a pink, but it refused to disappear. This seemed like an unforgivable offense, so unforgivable that I could feel myself starting to sweat. It was proof of something awful.

"It wouldn't come off," I said quietly, ashamedly, when I came out of the bathroom. "Maybe with bleach? Do you have any?"

"Don't worry about it," he replied, lying down on the bare mattress and closing his eyes. "I'll just throw it away."

I left the sheet on the floor and pulled on my jeans and sweater. He didn't stop me. He didn't ask me where I was going in such a hurry. He continued to sleep, or he continued to pretend he was asleep, and I knew I should leave. I should leave quickly.

I stepped gingerly toward the door and opened it a crack, letting the light from the hall drift into the chamber, and I glanced back at him. I hoped he would smile or offer some last acknowledgment, but he continued to lie perfectly still, his head turned ever so slightly toward the wall, cradled in his pillow. "I'll buy you a new sheet," I blurted, my voice ringing into the stillness like an irritating alarm. "I'm sorry."

He jerked his head up. "I said don't worry about it," he repeated. "It's just a fucking sheet. I have more. Jesus."

The *fucking* word hit hard; it punctured my heart, splitting it in two.

"I'm leaving for Thanksgiving break tomorrow," he said more kindly, laying his head back on his pillow. "I'll call you when I get back."

I nodded, thankfully, and slipped out, closing the door quietly behind me, and was blinded by the hall light, caught in its glaring teeth. I gripped the banister as I went down the stairs, feeling dizzy, like I might fall, and tried to ignore the dull ache throbbing between my thighs.

Outside, cloaked in blackness, I walked quickly, eager to get away from the apartment, not stopping until I reached the brief stretch of wooded path before the well-lit path of campus. I pushed away branches and buried myself amid the trees; I sat on the ground, puffed up with fallen leaves. I kept still, silent, and held my breath whenever someone walked by on the path. All I could see, all I could think about, was the bloodied sheet. Patrick would see it in the morning. He would see the proof. He would remember. I wanted to get it, to burn it, to hack it to shreds.

I was no longer a virgin. *No longer a virgin.* It was too soon to know exactly how I felt, but I didn't feel good. I didn't feel like a "woman." Most important, I didn't feel loved or . . . saved. I closed my eyes and recalled the one thing about sex that I *had* enjoyed: I hadn't been able to think about anything. No worries, no thoughts, no self-conscious anxiety. That had been nice. But afterwards, *instantaneously*, the thoughts were back, full force, and all of them were telling me to feel disappointed.

*

fifteen

When I awoke, after a terrible night's sleep, Faith was gone. A note lay in the middle of the floor that read: "Have a great break! Have a great life!" How had I not heard her leave? I dropped down out of my bunk, crumpled the slip of paper into a ball, and chucked it into the wastebasket. Then I picked up the phone, weary, and dialed home. All night my mind had raced and churned. I hadn't been thinking about Patrick or our evening or my loss of virginity, though; I'd been thinking of Jacob. I'd been thinking that I was beginning to understand him and what he did in a way I never had before. That for some, life might be too fraught with sadness to sign up for the whole ride. Now, in the light of morning, I missed him. I wanted to talk to someone else who'd known him.

My mother answered and began asking irrelevant questions about my midterms and whether I predicted straight A's. Instead of replying, I asked my own question, a question I had been building myself up to ask all night. I asked this: "If you had known Jacob was going to kill himself that night, what would you have done?"

Silence. When she finally replied, her voice was thick, burdened: "I would have stopped him."

"How?"

"I . . . I would have told him that . . . that . . . I loved him."

"But you had already told him that. It wouldn't have helped."

I could hear my father in the background asking, angrily, "What's wrong? What the hell is she saying?" I knew my mother must be crying. I wanted to apologize but I couldn't.

"We never thought he was going to actually kill himself," she said between sobs. "I just wish he had left if he wasn't happy. Maybe if he had moved, far away, he would still be here."

I wound the telephone cord around and around my wrist. Why had I done this? My lips trembled. This was even worse than talking about sex with my mother. And yet something had propelled me to take this step and was urging me onward. I thought about what she had just said. What would she think if I revealed that, in my sick child's mind, Jacob *had* never died and *had* simply moved far away? Would she be surprised? Would it sadden her?

"Why . . . do you think he did it?" I managed to ask.

"I don't know," she muttered, half to herself. "I really don't."

"Was it a girlfriend?"

"No."

"Did something happen to him?"

"No."

"Drugs?"

"No . . . I don't . . . *no.*"

"Then was there something wrong with his brain? Was it chemical?"

"*No,*" she gasped, almost angrily. "There was *nothing* wrong with him. *Nothing.*"

"Then . . . *why?*"

"I don't know!" she screamed, crying hard. *"I don't know!"*

A hollowness opened up in my chest and my stomach sank. She wasn't going to tell me anything. Still.

"Give me the goddamned phone," my father barked. "Why are you hurting your mother?" he accused, his shrill voice striking me like a bullet.

"I'm not," I replied uneasily. "But . . . why can't we ever talk about . . . him?"

"You have *no idea* what your mother and I talk about."

I heard a click and held the receiver, limply, in my hand before setting it back on its base. I paced the length of my room once, twice, then collapsed onto Faith's bed, wrapping my arms around me. After a few minutes I again cruised the room, finally stopping in front of the mirror. There were bags under my eyes and a tiny frown line seemed permanently etched into my forehead. I pulled the skin taut with my fingers but the trace of the line remained, and I realized that someday—someday soon—it would be deep, severe, like my mother's.

Sex had canceled out my illusions. All my years of daydreaming, all my schoolgirl naïveté, was smashed. My carefully scripted fantasies involving love and romance now seemed ludicrous. Patrick wasn't in love with me, and love wasn't going to save me. He wasn't even interested in me beyond, I was sure, sex. And whose fault was that? I knew my behavior had changed since our first meeting. I had gone from being potentially interesting to pathetic. I lit a cigarette and sat on the windowsill. Patrick's behavior, too, had changed. Which of us had changed first? I exhaled a plume of smoke and tried to tell myself that Patrick was a jerk for not caring about me or what we'd done, but recalling my behavior in his apartment, prior to our sex, I didn't blame him one bit. He had attempted conversation and I had just sat there, waiting for what would happen next, so determined had I been to lose my virginity. *If I had been him,* I thought, pinching my right cheek, then my left, *I'd have done the same. An easy lay.*

I laughed aloud at the irony of this last thought. In the space of just weeks I had given myself over to someone who now didn't even really like me. I wondered if I was the only one who'd ever ruined his sheets.

I closed my eyes and tried to recapture the sensation of penetration. It had been so . . . so violent somehow. Knifelike. Invasive. *Invading*. I should have asked him to go slower, to ease into it . . . into me . . . but words had eluded me. There was a brief moment when he was inside when the pain had lessened and I had felt connected to him, skin to skin, and from that moment—from that brief bodily link that vanished almost as soon as it was felt—I could sense that sex wasn't all pain and that this, the act of *connecting*, was the whole point of doing it. It had made the agony—the ripping and cutting and brutality—somehow worth it. But it was also what terrified me, afterwards, because I could sense that I could, I might, I *would* try to recapture that moment. The first time was supposed to be unpleasant . . . but what about the next time . . . and the time after that? *No*, I thought, feeling suddenly nauseous. I pushed down the shorts I'd slept in and studied my vagina. Too much hair. Too many folds and flaps. Too moist. I hated the sight of it. I hated it even more than before. I snapped the elastic back around my waist and looked at myself, hard. I didn't want to see any beauty at all, I wanted my reflection to be as ugly as I felt, but it wasn't and this angered me. I was vile. Base. Life was traveling in a direction I had never wanted it to go in. I had to stop it. I had to regain control. It scared me where this slippery slope might lead.

I fetched the Yellow Pages from Faith's bottom desk drawer, flipped to "Salons," and settled on a shop called the Head Place because it was within walking distance. I dialed and spoke with a man who sounded drunk, or who had just risen from bed, and made an appointment with him, with Bob, for later in the afternoon. When I hung up, I felt somewhat liberated from the weight that had been pressing on me. Yes. Without my long hair I would be ugly. Patrick wouldn't want to see me anymore. He certainly wouldn't want to touch me. And that's what I wanted, suddenly. I didn't want to be touched again. I didn't want anything inside of me that wasn't already there.

I hurried down Hillside Street, past Gampel and Jorgensen Auditorium on my way toward North Eagleville Road, where the salon I'd called lay within a strip mall that stretched less than half a block and contained the only nonuniversity activities within walkable distance. When I got there, I went inside of the Head Shop quickly. It was empty, but a little bell ding-dinged as I entered.

"Make yourself comfortable!" a voice hollered from the next room.

I took off my coat and sat on a vinyl-covered purple chair that had a long rip on its seat back and flipped through a *Vogue*, studying the perfect women with perfect bodies. I tossed the magazine back on the black lacquered coffee table, stained in several spots. The waiting room looked like it had been pieced together using discarded roadside furniture, and I hoped this meant a cheaper haircut.

"Are you Natalie?"

I looked up at the man standing in the doorway. Under different circumstances, I might have walked out without replying. He hadn't shaved, his dirty-blond hair was a mess—a bad sign in a hairstylist—and he was dressed in a white undershirt that tugged at the folds of a potbelly.

"Hi," I said, following him into the next room, where he would wash my hair. I leaned my head back against the hard white enamel sink as instructed and cringed, slightly, when his fingers slid through my long locks. He worked it into a lather, rinsed, and conditioned. When he was done, I squinted against the white light shining down into my face.

"What did you have in mind," he asked in a bored voice, "a trim?"

"Um, actually, I was thinking of something more drastic. I want it short."

"Like, to your shoulders? A bob?"

"No," I said steadily, "I want you to cut all of it off. I want it to be shorter than your hair."

He studied me for a moment before saying anything. "That won't look good on you," he finally said.

"That's what I want," I stated firmly.

"You don't have the face for it. Your face is too round. You need a heart-shaped face to pull off a cut like that."

I faced forward and looked at myself in the mirror, my soaked hair hanging like dead branches from my scalp.

"But that's what I *want*," I pleaded.

"Okay," he sighed with a shrug, "I'll cut it. But don't say I didn't warn you."

I fidgeted when he took out a pair of scissors, newly worried but determined, too. He stood behind me and gathered a large clump of hair into his fingers and cut it off at the base of my neck. Gone. Just like that. He proceeded to do the same to the rest until all of it lay in stringy clumps on the floor.

Over the next half hour, I watched as Bob cut and styled my hair into what appeared to be a man's haircut. And one thing Bob was right about was that my head was, indeed, round. It resembled a large pumpkin.

He lifted a hand mirror behind me to give me a view of my new haircut from every angle. "Is it okay?" he asked, just as bored now as when he had begun.

"Uh-huh," I replied, though I couldn't keep back the few tears that were now falling. "Thanks."

"It's what you said you wanted," he sighed, taking my Visa. "I tried to tell you."

My fingers reached instinctively for my hair, and not finding it where it usually hung, reached further until they felt the short, fine hairs sprouting from my scalp. There was a bump on top, toward the back. I bent close to the mirror and realized the hair was either cut too short there or I was now finding out I had a cowlick. I licked my palms and patted it, but it popped back up again.

"I have a cowlick," I stated simply and looked at Bob for help.

He covered his mouth with his hand and studied me, then got a rack of hair accessories from the front desk. I brightened and hoped that an accessory might have the additional benefit of making me look prettier and more feminine, too. I chose a cream-colored headband and put it on, balancing it atop the cowlick. I had to push it back further than it was meant to be placed. I backed up, a good three feet, and looked at myself in an unfocused way—in the same way that your eyes get bleary when daydreaming. *Better*, I thought, taking another step backwards, *better*. Then I focused again and bit my lip in horror.

"I tried to tell you," he repeated.

I signed the receipt. Instead of returning directly to my room, I took the long way and walked around the entire campus. Thankfully, campus was already getting that deserted-Thanksgiving-break vibe. The sidewalks were almost empty, and the buildings were dark. I was glad I had signed on to work over the break. I kept touching my hair and kicked at a rock. When I got back to McMahon, there was a stillness on my floor that was unsettling, but just when I thought I was the only one left in the dorm, Linda bolted out of the bathroom. As her eyes landed on me, they widened, comically—and if a bubble had been over her head it would have read: "Holy #$^%*&!" She clapped a hand over her mouth and ran over.

"Natalie!" she screamed. "Where's all your hair?"

I shrugged. "I cut it off."

"But . . . *why?* I mean, not that it looks bad, but it's kind of shocking, you know? Were you trying for a Mia Farrow look? *God*, I admire your guts! I could *never* cut my hair because everyone loves it long too much." She pulled at her hair, stroking it, just as two curly-gray-haired adults rounded the corner, both of their faces echoing Linda's own. Linda introduced me to her parents with great enthusiasm, then disappeared with them into the elevator. Silence blanketed the hall, again, until I heard a faint ringing that grew louder as I approached my door. I went inside and picked up the phone, reluctantly.

"Hello," my mother said brightly.

I said nothing and reached for a cigarette.

"I was just calling," she said uncomfortably, "to find out if we can come get you for Thanksgiving dinner. Bill can drive you back to Storrs afterwards, if you don't want to stay over."

"I have to work," I said.

"But not on Thanksgiving day," she said.

This was true. "I need to study," I said harshly. "I need to get a head start."

"So, does that mean you won't come?"

"Yes," I said, "it does. Sorry."

"I'm sorry, too."

I thanked her for the invite, and then I hung up.

*

sixteen

In some ways it had been nice to be on campus while it was all but abandoned, harboring only a handful of international students and fugitives like myself, and it had been *very* nice to be able to hide out, virtually unseen, with my new haircut . . . But with nothing but my reckless thoughts for company, my self-hatred had thrived. Students began trickling back into the dorm just in the nick of time. Hearing the elevator dinging arrivals and the excited yells outside my room as friends greeted one another made it easier to breathe, somehow, and calmed me, even though I only left my room for faster-than-lightning bathroom breaks.

Faith, though, still hadn't returned. I dropped my plastic grocer's bag, containing a dozen ramen noodle packets and a jar of peanut butter I had just charged to my credit card and glanced at the answering machine. No new messages. I snatched a plastic spoon and the jar of peanut butter and sat on the windowsill. I tapped my finger against the cold glass, then wiped the moisture off on my pants. It was too quiet. I slid off the sill to put the radio on. The smash hit "The Sign," by Ace of Base, sounded ridiculous, and I fiddled with the knob to find something more melancholy.

A knock at the door, along with a deep voice: "Natalie?" I stiffened. It was Patrick. I hid the peanut butter in a drawer as if it were something sordid and sat still, holding my breath, cursing myself for putting on the stereo.

"Natalie?" he tried again. "Are you in there?"

"I am," I said, hitting my forehead with my fist, "but I can't see you right now."

"Um, why not?"

"Because," I said quietly, "I just can't."

"It would be really great if you would at least open the door for a second," he continued, "because I feel pretty stupid out here."

I gulped down some water to get rid of my peanut breath and walked to the door, leaning face forward against it. I knew I might as well let him in and get it over with. "Okay," I said, twisting the knob, "but I'll warn you first: I cut my hair."

"Wow," he said, entering, "you weren't kidding. You look . . . really different."

"Yes," I nodded, taking in his good looks, his broad shoulders beneath his blue coat, "I do. And don't worry—I know I look awful. Not what you expected, right? Like ordering chicken but getting tofu, instead."

"Tofu?" he laughed, stepping closer to me. "You're definitely better than tofu. Tofu I can't eat. You, on the other hand, I could eat." He sniffed. "In fact," he said with a grin, "someone smells like peanut butter. Is that Peter Pan or Skippy?"

My cheeks burned and I adjusted my headband. Patrick placed his hands on my shoulders and drew me close. His hands glided down my back until he rested them low, on my hips. Was he *really* still attracted to me? It made me feel trapped. I didn't want to do it again. I didn't. Why else had I cut off my hair? He lifted my face up and kissed me. He told me he'd been thinking about our night together, that he'd been missing me and wanting me since. I wasn't sure it was specifically *me* he'd been missing, but I let him kiss me. At least, until he accidentally knocked off my headband.

"Oh!" I yelled, reaching up to keep my cowlick down. I scrambled onto my hands and knees to retrieve the band, which had rolled under my desk. When I replaced it on my head and stood, I noticed Patrick's hands were in his pockets, jostling his keys. *He came here to have sex with me*, I thought, nervously crossing my arms. I went and locked the door. Wasn't it only decent to have sex with him after he had made the effort to come over from his *off-campus* apartment? So what if I had walked to his place in the past, or walked home, alone, in the dead of night? *Yes, Patrick*, I thought, facing him, *you will get to fuck me. Why not?* I unbuttoned my shirt, I let it fall open and resisted an urge to cover myself, then I sat down on the edge of Faith's bare mattress, and I waited.

. . .

"How was your break?" Patrick asked.

"Fine," I replied, cinching my robe at the waist. "How was yours?"

"Fine," he aped.

After double-knotting the robe's sash, I turned around. Patrick was sitting on the floor tying his shoes: brown lace-ups. I smiled and looked around the room for something to do to make the moment less awkward. I settled on my backpack and fetched it, unloading my books and placing each on top of the other in a neat, vertical stack on my desk. Patrick then stood, towering over me, and said he'd better get going because he was supposed to meet someone (he omitted where or who or when). I nodded, laughed for no reason, and moved my headband slightly backward. His gaze fell on my new short hair, then he squeezed my arm, told me it was great to see me, told me he would call me later, told me to have a good night. I was grateful he didn't thank me.

I breathed for what felt like the first time in hours and sat, heavily, on Faith's bed. The whole thing had hurt less the second time around, as expected, and yet this time it had felt more real. More physically real. More physically enjoyable. Emotionally, I knew, it was even less real than the first time. The first time there'd been a slight hope that Patrick liked me, but this time, this second time, I knew there was no hope of that. If he had cared, at all, he would have stayed, he would have talked to me, he would have asked me about myself.

He's so perfect, I suddenly thought, extracting a cigarette and lighting it, recalling the sensation of his hands on my flesh. I loved his face—the strong jawline, the pale blue eyes, the light freckles dotting his nose. I loved his body—so lean, so silky, so unblemished. I wanted to know everything about him—his beliefs, his fears, his desires. But how would I ever know the things I wanted to know? Each time I saw him I suspected it might well be the last time. Would he really call me? Would he ever show up, unannounced, again?

It was very late and Faith still hadn't returned. I grabbed my caddy and went to brush my teeth and wash my face. Sasha was picking at a pimple, her face not an inch from the mirror. I set my toiletries down and squeezed some toothpaste onto my brush.

"Hi," she said, glancing up. "Interesting haircut. So, I saw that guy from the bar just now. Way to go. You guys an item now?"

"No," I said, adjusting the faucet.

"What!" she teased. "Do you mean to tell me that you— Natalie Bloom—are fucking someone who *isn't* your boyfriend? Wonders never cease. I'm impressed."

I shook my head. "He's not my boyfriend, and I'm *not . . .*"

"Like hell you're not," she grinned, moving to leave. "I heard the bed rattle."

When I awoke the next morning, I missed Faith more than ever. I wanted her to be there, sharing the room with me, being a body, a presence, I could count on. I thought about calling her but realized I had never gotten her home phone number. I rolled onto my side and studied a small cobweb that had been erected overnight, but no spider was in its midst. I swept it away and rubbed the sticky web off on my sheet. Maybe she really was keeping her word about dropping out. I hadn't really believed her, but she had an early class on Mondays.

Stepping on the lower bunk as I climbed down, I felt momentarily sick that I'd had sex there the day before. If Faith had done the same on my bed, I would have been horrified. But it didn't make sense, at the time, to ask Patrick to climb to the crowded top bunk. I thought of him digging into his pocket, pulling out a condom, and tearing the wrapper, expertly, with his teeth. He had turned away from me while rolling on the latex before resuming, before pressing into me. I didn't like the smell of the condom with its vague scent of synthetic chemicals. Of course . . . there had been no orgasm for me. I didn't expect one, nor did I want one. Or I didn't want the kind of attention that would possibly *give* me one. No, Patrick was my perfect lover: quick, purposeful, selfish. If he had moved his face below waist level I might have screamed, anyway. Not down there—not that place that secreted liquids and scents.

I pulled on my robe and went to shower. Standing naked in the stall, I decided I wouldn't eat breakfast. My belly was a little too soft, a little too rounded, and I vowed to do a hundred sit-ups, at least, after class.

Gwen and Noah walked out of the dorm with me, Gwen holding Noah's hand and speaking rapidly about what the two of them had done over break, interspersing her dialogue with earnest compliments on my new haircut. I smiled, said how fun it all sounded, and tried desperately to sound sincere. And when we parted, I felt I had succeeded, because neither of them had attempted to control their gleeful reportage, and neither of them had asked me a single question about my break. I was glad of this. I didn't delude myself into thinking that my friendship with Gwen could really be resurrected now that she had Noah.

I walked to class and considered my new world. Faith was gone, Gwen was as good as gone. Patrick might still be around for now, but to him I knew I was a body without a personality. I felt like I was erasing myself.

As I neared the history building, I stopped. Jack was sitting on the stone steps, wearing a red pullover and blue jeans. Two girls paused on the steps to stare and giggle at his good looks before moving past. I glanced at my watch and saw that I had no time to spare or I'd be late for class. I decided to test my invisibility—walk by without a greeting and hope that he wouldn't notice.

"Natalie?"

I reluctantly smiled, waved hello, and continued climbing the stairs.

"Just a sec," he said, standing up and joining me. "I've been waiting for you. I remembered you had a class here now, so I took a chance."

I looked at him, confused. "Yes?"

"You . . . cut your hair."

"Yes."

"It looks . . . cool. Really cool."

I sighed, heavily, and told him I was going to be late.

"Well," he continued, speaking quickly, "I was wondering if you'd want to grab lunch with me later. The last time we ran into each other you pointed out that I don't know you, and, well, you're right. But I'd like to know you."

He was speaking in complete sentences, but they made no sense. "Why?" I asked stupidly.

"Why?" he repeated. "Why . . . not?"

"I'm sorry," I replied with a nervous smile, his intentions suddenly obvious. "But . . . I'm really busy today."

"Another day, then?"

"I . . . have a boyfriend," I blurted.

His smile faltered. "Cool," he said, backing up, his arms raised out in surrender. "I thought you might, but I wasn't sure. Is it the guy you were with at the party?"

I nodded, unable to speak. His smile returned and he gave a slight bow. "Maybe I'll see you around," he said. "Peace."

I watched him round the corner, rattled. How could he have pursued me after he saw how hideous I looked? He could have had any girl he wanted. It was ridiculous that he would choose *me*. In fact, his interest made him less likable. And, besides, *I* wasn't interested in *him*. Jack needed a blond, hip sorority girl, preferably one who had her own verbal sign-off. Instead of "Peace" she would say "Ciao." I frowned. I was being unkind, but it kept me from feeling regret.

I ran down the hall to Room 181 and found a seat in the back corner instead of my usual spot. Anderson strode in a minute later, looking haggard. I opened my notebook and prepared to take notes, but the pen in my hand felt like lead. I didn't want to take notes. I didn't want to be sitting in class. What was the point? With my recent performance, how was I ever to get back to a perfect GPA? I doodled on the blank sheet of paper rather than bothering to record the date and title of the lecture.

"The last half of the semester," Anderson announced, "will focus on the post–World War II period. The Soviet Union's rise, and its subsequent fall."

He began the lecture, first talking about the Soviet Union's geography and the different kinds of agriculture employed immediately following the Second World War. I jotted down words without linking them together into a coherent narrative. My notes looked more like a grocery list: seed, corn, potatoes, poverty, winter. When class ended, I shoveled my notebook into my book bag and stood to leave, waiting impatiently behind the several students ahead of me. I barely looked at Anderson when he called out my name; his voice, my name, sounded distant, and I glanced back distractedly, without meaning to respond. But he caught my gaze and motioned for me to come up to his desk, which I dutifully did.

"Will you come with me to my office?" he asked, stuffing his lecture notes into his briefcase. "There's something I'd like to discuss with you."

"What?" I asked, surprising both myself and him. I didn't ask Anderson questions; I simply obeyed.

"I want to discuss our last meeting," he said reluctantly. "It won't take but a minute."

"Why?" I asked quietly. "I didn't misunderstand our last meeting."

Anderson eyed me. "All the same," he breathed, "I'd like to speak with you."

I shut up and followed him to his office, leaving the door open behind me. I wanted to remain standing, and so I leaned against the wall and waited. I expected more harshness from him, or disappointment, and braced for the onslaught.

"My wife died two weeks ago," he said matter-of-factly, sitting at his desk, "and I haven't been myself since, well, since she got sick. Since her stroke."

I took in his words and slackened before succumbing to sit in the chair beside his desk. "I'm so sorry," I said. "I didn't know."

"Of course you didn't," he continued abruptly. "And I'm not looking for sympathy—certainly not from one of my students."

I flinched. Tears welled and I pursed my lips, determined to stay silent.

"I apologize," he said quietly, still not looking at me. "What I wanted to talk to you about was your request before the break to write a term paper for extra credit. I've reconsidered. I would be willing to factor a paper, on your topic of choice, into your final grade. You can drop off a subject proposal by noon tomorrow."

I blinked back tears and felt a sudden, strong urge to reject his kindness. "Thank you, but no," I whispered. "I . . . I don't have time."

Anderson shot me a look of disbelief. He leaned back in his chair and stared at me, devoid of comprehension. I slipped my backpack on and prepared to leave.

"What is *wrong* with you!" he barked angrily.

His question was like a slap, and his raised voice shocked me.

"Natalie," he continued pitilessly, "I will not take no for an answer. Write a term paper. I don't give a damn if it's about your Rasputin, or about Soviet gulags. Just *write one*."

I nodded, stunned, and left.

The lobby of McMahon was packed with people, mostly girls. They were all sitting quietly on the tiled floor, listening to an older woman wearing a UConn sweatshirt as she railed against the lax security on campus, lamenting the case of a young woman who had recently been raped outside of Gampel Pavilion—which everyone knew about since it had been covered in the campus paper for two weeks straight.

"Extra vigilance is called for!" she yelled angrily. "If you see *anyone* who doesn't belong in McMahon, or even if it's someone who you *think* doesn't belong, *please* alert your RA *immediately*."

I stepped around and over the splayed bodies, eager to get into an elevator. I half-expected the woman to demand to see my ID card, which I fingered in my pocket.

Faith was stuffing clothes into a black garbage bag when I got to my room. She smiled broadly when I entered, told me honestly, but without malice—as only Faith could do—that my haircut sucked, then put her hands on her hips and announced: "I'm leaving!"

"And this is a good thing?" I asked, fidgeting with my headband.

"Yes," she nodded, lighting a cigarette. "It is."

"And why is it?" I asked, heart sinking.

"Because I'm done with this fucking school," she breathed, sitting on her bed. "I flunked two out of four exams, and I've already talked to a community college in Groton and they're willing to take me. I'll be closer to Keith and I might just get some decent grades, too. I can stay with my mom to save money."

I sank to the floor and tried not to cry. Faith, in turn, laughed.

"What's this?" she hollered gleefully. "Do you mean to tell me that you care about me? That you'll miss me?"

I looked at her and nodded. I began to sob. Faith watched, quietly, then got down on the floor beside me.

"Come on," she said, blowing smoke into my face, "you'll have your *own room*. How many people would kill for that?"

I wanted to tell her that I didn't know how I would go on all by myself. I wanted to say that I regretted never really getting to know her, and that I would try harder to get to know her now. I would help her with her classes, we would eat together, we would face the stresses of school, as allies, as friends. I dried my eyes, got my own cigarettes, and returned to the floor. "I'll help you pack," I offered. "Just tell me what to do."

Faith smiled and leaned against her bed. "It isn't like I'm proud," she said, inhaling on her cigarette before dissolving into a succession of ghastly coughs. "No one expected me to make it here—not Keith, not my mom. Not you. I'm just a dumb girl, after all. Did you know I'm usually one of *three* girls in any given class? How could I think I could actually be a mechanical engineer?"

"Because you love it."

"Loving something isn't enough."

I paused, considering this. "Yeah," I agreed, "I guess it isn't."

We finished our smokes in silence before setting to work. "Some of this stuff is yours," I said, scanning the room, "like the phone and answering machine."

"Keep it until you graduate," she said distractedly, searching through a stack of CDs.

I stared at the phone and thought that there wasn't anyone, really, who would be calling. Patrick might, possibly, call to set up a quick fuck, but he also might *not* call. Wouldn't it be better if I were unreachable? If Patrick *wasn't* planning to ever call but I no longer had a phone, I would be saved the anxiety of knowing or caring. I imagined myself returning from classes each day only to deflate upon seeing the red digital zero blazing on the answering machine, and I decided I wanted no part of it.

"No," I said, unplugging the phone from the wall and winding the cord around it. "You take it. I can always buy a cheap one at the Co-op. Or I'll ask my parents for one for Christmas. Not even a month away."

She glanced at me, raised an eyebrow, and shrugged.

"But I'll keep the mini-fridge for now," I added. "If that's okay."

After Faith departed, I lay flat on my back on the floor, staring at the ceiling. The room felt barren, deserted, and even though everyone always joked about the prison-like atmosphere of the dorm rooms, now it really did feel like a cell—missing only a lidless toilet bowl and sink. I was alone. I was sad. But within this sadness I felt alive. Palpably alive. I thought of Jacob and wondered if he, too, had found his tortured depression intoxicating in a similar way.

I removed my headband, glad to free my scalp of its sharp plastic teeth, and laid it on top of my chest.

seventeen

Week one was hard without Faith; week two was harder; week three harder still. I began to talk aloud to myself, the stereo on to drown out my voice for anyone passing in the hall. But not in a crazy way. It wasn't as if I imagined someone replying to my words, carrying on a schizoid conversation. I simply voiced the thoughts that flitted through my head. If a song playing on the radio was particularly good, I might say, "I love this song," or if I was thinking about Patrick—as I invariably was—I might say, "I wonder if he ever thinks of me."

I tied my sneakers and stretched, straightening my legs. "God," I said, looking at the now blank wall above Faith's desk, "I even miss that horrible photo of Faith and her mom." I pulled on a red hooded sweatshirt, grabbed my keys, and left to go running. But first I went to the cafeteria for a quick bite. I had been avoiding the dining hall as much as possible, and when I did go, I had tried to eat at off-hours to avoid being seen, but that day I went during the lunchtime rush. I handed over my ID card and then began walking across the room to grab some fruit and a yogurt. The table of guys who had elected themselves to survey each female, passing judgment with a derisive bark or a gleeful howl, eyed me, and as I passed them I heard the unmistakable sound of a bark. It was a single bark, but it was definitely a bark. I reached for my nonexistent hair as my face heated to a boil, and I'm pretty sure I gasped. How wrong I had been in thinking a howl was just as bad as a bark! A bark was so much worse. A bark was fatal. I adjusted my headband, then decided to leave without food.

The sky was white. When I reached the road, I walked for a while before breaking into a soft jog. The semester was grinding to a most welcome halt: two more finals, one more term paper. Almost over, but it did little to motivate. Despite my best efforts, I had managed only to write a generic paper for Anderson on women's roles in peasant society. Russian history, as a whole, had ceased to interest me. The idea of "keeping people alive"—that goal I had created for myself upon choosing my major—now seemed like a complete waste of time. People were forgotten, not only upon their deaths but in life, too.

All of the trees were leafless, their bare branches poking out over the street—but there were still the green pines, towering and plump with needles. I watched my wintry breath stretch out before me with each exhalation. A bicyclist whizzed by, too closely, and I resisted an urge to yell. I pushed myself to run hard up a hill and slowed to almost a standstill at the top, then made my way back toward campus. As I jogged, I remembered the day when Patrick had chanced to drive past. I wondered again if he had tried to call. I had hoped that the lack of a phone would diminish my obsession, but it hadn't helped. His face, his body, were always in my mind, and I replayed our brief conversations until they felt like a script, a play I had memorized by heart.

I slowed down and considered running by his apartment. It was three weeks since I had seen him, and he couldn't accuse me of desperation since I had remained unreachable, hidden in my room. A dog barked—a real dog—and it set my heart pounding. Maybe I would run *toward* his apartment, and then decide, once closer, whether to actually stop by.

A light snow began to fall, sprinkling the grass and the blacktop, vaporizing on contact. I lifted my face to feel the flakes patter my skin and took it as a sign of renewal: I *would* go to Patrick's. I would simply knock and see what happened next. If he flinched even slightly I would leave. But there was only one way to find out.

His apartment looked different, seedier, in daylight. The entire complex looked deflated. Rusted dumpsters, ripped screens, toilet paper wound around a sickly tree. I stopped some twenty feet from his door. If he were to look outside, I realized, he would think I was a stalker. With that, I casually approached and knocked. A television was on, and I stuffed my sweaty hands into the pockets of my sweatshirt as I waited.

Patrick opened up. He looked surprised but not unhappy to see me. He wore a white T-shirt and khakis and his feet were bare. I smiled and touched my headband. "Hi," I said rapidly between heavy breaths. "I was just out running and thought I would stop by. To say hi. What with the semester almost over."

He smiled and motioned for me to follow him. It was warm inside, heated to what felt like 90 degrees. I sat on a chair and folded my hands to still them as Patrick disappeared, returning a minute later with two glasses of water. I considered how thoughtful this was as I failed to suppress another smile.

"How are you?" he asked. "I tried to call you once, but it was busy."

"Oh, yeah," I replied. "I don't have a phone right now because my roommate dropped out. It was her phone."

He gave me an odd look. "That must suck," he said.

I nodded and drank half of the water down, then pulled away from the glass too quickly on the last mouthful and water dribbled onto my chin, which I rubbed away with humiliation. I looked nervously around the room, searching for something to say.

"Are you finished with exams?" I asked.

"Yeah," he said. "I just have to hand in one more paper. You?"

"Almost," I laughed for no reason. "Two to go. Can't wait."

He nodded and set his glass on the coffee table beside a thick, worn copy of James Joyce's *Ulysses*.

"Is that for a class?" I asked, pointing at it.

His eyes narrowed. "No," he replied slowly, "it's for pleasure."

"Oh," I exclaimed, impressed. I hadn't read for genuine pleasure since high school. How would I find the time? But

Patrick, clearly, found the time, and wasn't this a mark not only of his superior intelligence . . . but also of his wealth . . . his class? I was so far behind. So very, very far behind. I caught myself looking at him in awe and focused, instead, on my lap.

"So . . . why *did* you cut your hair?" he suddenly asked.

I laughed as if he'd made a joke, but he continued to look at me seriously. "I just felt like it." I shrugged, touching my headband lightly. "Do you hate it?"

"No," he replied quickly. "I just . . . I never kissed a girl with short hair before. When we . . . last time . . . I felt a little like I was kissing a guy. It was kind of freaky."

A lump, in the throat. Tears would be next.

"Sorry," he went on hurriedly. "Do you mind me being honest? I mean, it would be silly to act like I don't notice your hair . . . you know?"

I nodded and swallowed my urge to sob. "If it makes you feel any better," I said haltingly, picturing the table of guys who had barked at me earlier, "I know I look ugly. I told you that. Should I . . . should I leave?"

"No," he replied, sitting forward. "And, hey, don't worry. That's the great thing about hair: It grows. This is only temporary. My big head, however, is permanent."

I smiled as if he had just offered me deliverance. With time my hair would be long again. With time he wouldn't feel like he was kissing a guy. With time . . . with time there would be a future for us.

"Do you have any plans for winter break?" I asked.

"Not really, but my parents have a few things lined up."

"What kinds of things?"

He shrugged. "I know they got tickets to a David Hare play."

A David Hare play. Who the hell was David Hare? I pictured Patrick seated in a red velvet seat at the theater, his family beside him. They probably sat around together reading novels and discussing articles in the *New York Times*. Just the idea of going to a play with my own parents was ludicrous. The Blooms thought watching *Wheel of Fortune* was a good time—and as intellectually riveting as you could ever want.

"Why don't you come over here," he said, patting the seat beside him. "It's snowing out. We can keep each other warm."

I laughed awkwardly and debated making a joke about the tropical heat in the room but decided against it. I stood to walk over to him, but as soon as I was standing, Patrick, too, stood, and met me halfway. Taking my shoulders in his hands, he held me in place. "I still like you," he whispered, his eyes drifting to my hair, his expression giving away the slightest revulsion. Then he parted my lips with his tongue.

Before leaving, Patrick told me it made sense for us to see each other over break even though we lived ninety minutes apart. He told me we would hang out, get to know each other better. I was astonished by the proposal and broke out in a sweat at the prospect of meeting his two sisters and his parents. Didn't that mean something? Didn't it mean he was looking at me more seriously? Would his family like me? How could I *get them* to like me? And maybe . . . maybe he would invite me to come along to the David Hare play! I wrote down my home address and phone number for him on a piece of paper and took his contact information as well. I folded the slip of paper and pocketed it, deeply, in my sweatshirt so that it wouldn't fall out in transit. But just as I was leaving, a stupid grin on my face, he suggested we could each drive, we could meet halfway, and my disappointment at not seeing his home—at not seeing where he lived and meeting his pedigreed family—was fierce.

"I . . . I could drive to your town." I smiled. "It's really not a problem."

He shook his head a little too quickly. "That's okay," he replied. "It wouldn't be fair. Meeting halfway is better."

"Great," I agreed.

On my walk home I tried not to think about our sex, which had been focused on a single result, which was reached in no time flat. I had lain still underneath him and hadn't uttered a sound while placing my hands—balled into fists—around his body. I had attempted to caress his back after a minute, lightly and with what I hoped was sensuality, but as soon as I began to flutter my fingers he had finished. He had paused, laying his full weight on me, before pulling out, leaving me exposed, naked from the waist down. Then he had gulped down the last of his water and tossed me a box of tissue.

I began jogging, afraid. The words creeping into my mind ran something like this: slut . . . easy . . . pathetic. So, then, why did I feel, even *more*, the need for him to love me? To want me as a girlfriend? But instead of pondering these questions, I thought how refreshing it had been that he told the truth about my hair instead of lying. Jack had said I'd looked "cool," and now I was certain that he had lied. I looked bad, and Patrick had simply been honest. *I loved him for it.*

When I got back to my room, I locked the door and studied myself in the full-length mirror. My headband sat too far forward and my cowlick pointed skyward. I looked sad, I looked ugly. I looked slovenly in my sweats, I looked pale, I looked ghastly. Bags under the eyes. Two pimples on my forehead. Too much hair on my upper lip. Patrick would *never* be my boyfriend. How could I even entertain such thoughts? I moved close to the mirror until my face was just an inch away. Then I tipped my head back and whipped it forward, hard, cracking my forehead against the glass. I screamed in pain. I fell to the floor and pressed my palms against the welt that was already forming, and when I pulled my hands away I saw blood. I looked up and watched myself. I felt involved, yet removed, too. It was as if I was seeing someone else, watching the drama of someone else's life unfold, and I was just a voyeur. I felt bad for this girl in the mirror. The girl looked awful. The girl was in pain.

A knock sounded at my door, then Sasha's voice: "Natalie? Are you okay?"

"Yes," I shouted back. "Sorry I yelled . . . I hit my head. By accident."

"Jesus," she said, already walking away. "You sounded like you were being murdered."

The electrifying initial pain subsided and was replaced with a dull, throbbing ache. I wrapped some ice from the fridge in a towel and pressed it against my wound, wincing as the cold added an additional shooting pain. And then I decided, with a calmness that was almost disturbing, that I would skip my afternoon classes—something I had never done before, not even when I'd commuted to Eastern and had had to drive through snow and sleet.

I grabbed one of Faith's forgotten magazines and began flipping through it.

At dinnertime Gwen stopped by, and when she saw the ugly scab on my forehead she slapped a hand over her mouth and listened as I lied: I hit it on the bed frame. I was leaning over to pick up a pen, and when I stood back up—wham!

She sat down at my desk, eyeing me sympathetically. Then she apologized for her lengthy absence, due to Noah. "It's hard having a boyfriend," she explained. "It occupies all of your personal time, and then the rest of the time you're studying."

"Speaking of which," I said, "where is he now?"

"He had a group study tonight," she replied a bit guiltily. "So . . . I was thinking you and I might grab dinner together."

"Sorry," I replied, "I'm not planning on being seen for a while. I was barked at today in the cafeteria."

Gwen's eyes gaped, then narrowed, then somersaulted back into her head as she tried to come up with an appropriately aghast reply. "Don't you . . . *dare* give those moronic losers any legitimacy! I'm sure they've barked at every girl, and anyway, we should all be barking our heads off at them! And, by the way, you're beautiful!"

It wasn't fair to do to Gwen—to force her to rationalize how I could have been barked at, but I repeated myself. "I was *barked* at."

She folded her arms in a huff. "Well, you know how guys are about . . . long hair. They're cavemen! Unless they can drag us into their beds by the ponytail, they feel impotent. Your short hair . . . I don't know . . . it *threatens* them."

I shook my head and sighed.

"But you have to eat," she whined. "And we need to catch up."

I couldn't suppress a look of bewilderment. I took a cue from Patrick and decided to be honest. "It's okay, Gwen."

"What's okay?"

"I mean, you don't have to do this. You don't have to try with me. I get it. There's nothing to feel good or bad about— it's just the way it is."

She stared at me. "You've changed," she said, "and I don't care for this 'new Natalie.' "

"You never knew the 'old Natalie,' " I answered angrily. "And so what?"

Gwen stood and faced the wall. "I'm sorry you feel that way," she said calmly. "Because even though we don't know each other very *well*, I feel like we *could* be friends."

She turned around, her arms crossed stiffly across her chest, her silky hair tucked neatly behind her ears. I blanched. "Please," I managed to say, my voice trembling, "I want to be alone."

She sighed and shook her head in exasperation. "*Why?*" she

asked heatedly. "*Why* do you always want to be alone? I can't figure you out!"

"Maybe I don't *want* to be figured out!" I yelled back. "I'm not bothering anyone! *I* don't want to be bothered, *either*!"

Gwen's shoulders relaxed. "Just be careful," she said as she backed out the door, her tone ringing with finality. "Bye."

I sat, cross-legged, on the floor, and after a moment . . . guess what I did?

Yup. I cried.

Each ceiling square had approximately seventy-five tiny holes punched into it. I knew this because for a good hour, after Gwen left, I was on the floor, counting the microscopic dots.

I needed to talk to Patrick. I wanted to see him, but every time I saw myself in the mirror I was stopped by the ugly red welt on my forehead. My eyes were puffy, my face swollen with misery. I couldn't see Patrick. Not like this. But I could call him.

I grabbed some quarters and took the elevator down to the laundry room. No one was there, but a dryer was spinning, warning me that someone would soon return. I dropped a coin into the pay phone and dialed, not wanting to waste a second. When he answered and I said, "Hi, it's me," he didn't know who the "me" was. I said my name, quietly, and he spewed apologies for not recognizing my voice.

"It's okay," I said. "I've been . . . crying. My voice probably sounds raspy."

"Oh."

"Um, I just wanted to ask you something. I was wondering what you're thinking 'we' are . . . or if you're thinking that 'we're' not anything? Either way is fine with me."

Silence.

"I guess I think that 'we're' seeing each other." His voice dropped in volume and became playful: "We're lovers. Is that a problem?"

Is that a problem? "Oh, no, not at all. I just . . . I just wanted to know, that's all. I was feeling kind of like, maybe . . . you know . . . that you're not actually into me."

"Well, if that's why you were crying," he replied, unsympathetically, "you should get over it."

"No . . . I . . . it wasn't that. I . . . hit my head, really hard. That's why I was crying."

"Listen," he said, gruffly, "I've got some friends over, so I'm going to have to talk to you later. Okay?"

"Sure," I whispered. "Have a good night."

I laid the receiver in its hook and sat down in an orange plastic chair. The dryer churned in the background, humming rhythmically. Something metal intermittently clinked, and I guessed it was a button or a coin left in a pocket. Fluorescent lights glared and I looked around for the light switch, which, once found, I flicked off. I sat back down and listened to the clothes spin in the darkness. *None of it matters*, I told myself, thinking of my dead brother, deep in his grave, *so don't care*.

Two days later I was on my way to take my last exam, walking absentmindedly toward the language arts building. I had taken

Anderson's final the day before and expected a C or a C-plus. Now I was off to take my Russian final—part oral and part written—and I prayed for a less humiliating experience than I'd had on the midterm. I rehearsed my oral speech, which I'd knitted together the night before and memorized despite the grammatical errors I was sure were laced throughout. At least I would be prepared with *something*. I was so in my head that I didn't even notice Professor Anderson when I approached him, and I didn't hear him when he said my name. He reached out and placed a hand on my shoulder, shocking me.

"B-minus," he said, quickly dropping his hand to his side. "You received a B-minus for the class."

I smiled appreciatively and nodded. "I probably didn't deserve a B-minus."

He looked straight ahead, past me. "You deserved a B-minus," he said sharply, "or you wouldn't have gotten that grade."

I continued to smile, even though I felt desperately sad. "Thank you," I said. "I better get to my next class now."

"Will you be taking my seminar next semester?" he asked, a slight urgency in his voice. "I'd like you to."

I straightened and adjusted my backpack. "I haven't thought about what classes I'll take next semester. Maybe."

"I wish you would," he said, glancing at me. "I'm sorry if I wasn't . . . there for you this semester. I feel as though I've let you down. I'm afraid I wasn't much of an adviser. I don't blame you for leaving me."

"I'm sorry," I replied, lowering my eyes. "You were fine. It was me. You can't exactly advise someone who doesn't have a clue."

"Natalie, you are *very* bright," he said, uncomfortable in his sincerity. "If you'll have me as your adviser next semester, I promise to be more available. I believe you're going to go far, Ms. Bloom, and I'd like to be there to see it happen."

He gave an impression of a smile and strode off. I stared after his bulky form. I was late, as I had been for the midterm, and so again Katya would probably test me first. I touched the scab on my forehead, gently, and walked on.

*

eighteen

Two black garbage bags lay in the center of the room, one filled with clothes, the other with miscellaneous stuff: towels, bedding, shoes. Enough, hopefully, to get me through the next couple of months. I sat on my windowsill, smoking, wanting to smoke as many cigarettes in freedom as possible. My privacy was about to end.

It was a little past four but it was already dark. A cold December day. About an inch of powdery snow covered the grass below and lay delicately atop the branches of the quad's tree. I crushed out my cigarette, dumped the butts in the trash, and went to brush my teeth and wash my hands to be rid of the most overt proof of my new habit. Sasha was primping in the bathroom's full-length mirror in a backless purple-sequined halter, black stretchy skirt, and stiletto boots.

"This doesn't make my ass look big, does it?" Sasha asked, still admiring herself.

"Not at all," I answered, stunned at how grateful I felt to have been spoken to. "You look great."

"I know," she said, flashing a mischievous grin. "I have to work tonight, but afterwards I have a date. The guy is *hot*."

I grinned and began brushing. I couldn't think of a reply to "The guy is *hot*." I rinsed, spat out. "I'm leaving tonight," I blurted, my voice high and slightly hopeful, "so I guess I'll see you next semester?"

She smoothed her skirt and glanced at me. "Sure," she said distractedly.

I smiled—a smile that wasn't noted by a mirror-loving Sasha—and gathered up my items, but as I was leaving she asked me to hold on. I turned around so quickly I dropped my toothpaste and had to scramble to pick it up.

"You shouldn't care so much about what people think of you," she said, placing her hands on her slender hips. "You seem, like, fucked-up lately."

"Really?" I asked with genuine interest. "Do I really?"

"Absolutely," she said without sympathy. "One hundred percent. You were cooler when you just studied. Now you walk around like a scared dog. People can smell your fear."

I squeezed the tube of toothpaste until the cap looked like it might rocket off. I didn't have a response to "The guy is *hot*," and I didn't have one to "People can smell your fear," either, so I just adjusted my headband, nodded, and returned to my room.

My brother Bill didn't wait for me to open the door before pushing it open himself. He was overweight by some forty pounds, with a long, scraggly beard, and he looked hulkish in his black Harley sweatshirt and ripped jeans. He laughed when he saw my short hair, but otherwise we skipped pleasantries and began gathering stuff to stow in his van, parked in the dorm's loading zone. Ten minutes later, I pleaded for an extra minute to search for any left-behind objects and raced upstairs. The overhead light was on, and the cement-block walls looked frigid and bald. The stripped mattresses looked pitiful, the wood-veneer desks cheap and neglected. It wasn't much to look at, but it was mine. I took a deep breath and held it for a moment before exhaling.

"What took you so long?" Bill asked with irritation when I climbed into the van.

I pulled my seat belt across my chest. The van rattled and wheezed, and I hoped it would get us home. The heating system was on the fritz and I zipped my coat. Empty bags of Doritos and Fritos, empty KFC buckets, and general disarray littered the floor, and I kicked at the debris before planting my feet down. We passed the information booth where I worked three times a week, and I felt relief gathering with each second that I moved farther away. At home I wouldn't feel I had to prove anything to anyone, and I was looking forward to watching crappy shows on TV, not reading about the history of anywhere. My relief faded, though, when Bill started talking.

"You feel any smarter?" he asked, diving right into his trademark humor. "'Cause you don't *look* any smarter."

I forced myself to laugh and shrugged.

"You know what I find funny?" he went on. "I find it funny

that all these kids go to school, yet they don't have any *common sense*."

I wanted to ask him how he would know whether college students had common sense, since he had never spent time on a campus. But instead I nodded and said, "I know," and vowed to be in complete agreement with anything he had to say for the entire ride.

"But what *pisses me off*," he said, turning onto the highway, "is that all you *graduates* get all the good-paying jobs. I make a lousy eight bucks an hour doing shit work, while these college scum get twenty bucks an hour. Now, is that fair?"

"No," I answered, staring out the window at a house blazing with Christmas lights.

"You're damn right. What do *you* know that I don't know?"

"Nothing," I answered.

"You're not being wise with me, are you?"

"What do you mean?" I asked innocently.

"Just don't sass me," he warned. "I mean, I drove all the way up here to get you, so I don't want *any* fucking sass."

I sank lower in my seat and stared ahead. I wanted to tell him that I highly doubted that I would find a job that paid twenty dollars an hour and would probably continue working at the cable factory for an unspecified amount of time. Probably years. There were many college graduates who stayed at the factory for years. Who sank into the job until that was just what they did—until they lost the drive to search for other employment. "I really appreciate the ride," I offered, trying to sound sass-free.

He kept his eyes on the road. He wasn't going to make this easy.

"I did terribly on my exams," I offered. "I got my first D this semester."

"No shit?" he asked, grinning victoriously. "How the hell did *that* happen?"

Before I could reply, he laughed, told me to forget it, and looked happy the rest of the drive home.

I spent a few minutes greeting an ancient but loyal Biffo in the driveway. His black wiry hair had grown tougher and was matted in thick clumps around his floppy ears, and I promised him a good brushing. Then I stood back and surveyed the house, trying to view it as Patrick might. Even in the dark, you could tell that the white house was filthy. Who knew when it was last painted? Before I was born, I suspected. A beat-up bicycle, a rotting Big Wheel, and miscellaneous dirty, sun-bleached toys were strewn through the front yard, belonging, apparently, to the new tenants living on the second floor.

My mother was standing at the sink, peeling potatoes in a blue dress with a gold sash tied around her thick waist. Her shoulder-length bob had recently been dyed dark brown, and ever since she'd done it, I felt like I was with a stranger. I missed the salty gray I had known all my life. I imagined what Patrick's mother looked like, and I pictured a conservatively dressed WASP with ash blond hair and manicured nails. My mother glanced at me, then dropped a potato and clapped a hand over her mouth in astonishment. "I *love* it!" she hollered, taking in my own new appearance. "You look so . . . so *modern.*"

"That's one way to put it," Bill laughed.

She came close and inspected my head from every angle while murmuring approval upon approval, then let out a sigh as if she were viewing me on my wedding day and just couldn't get over what a vision I was. I hate to admit it, but it made me smile in the same way as when she'd oohed and aahed over a bad drawing I'd done as a child. She nodded one more validation, then busied herself with clearing off the table for dinner, which was a major task. It was littered with old mail, a motorcycle helmet, a plant that had probably died months before, and various tools: a screwdriver, a wrench, a box of nails. I studied my mother as I helped gather the mail into a single pile. She was sixty-seven years old. My father, seventy-four. The number of times they'd been mistaken for my grandparents was too many to count. My father had always seemed plain ancient; he had false teeth by the time I was eight. My mother, though, had never looked her age, kept young, according to her, by her children and her job—waitressing at a local dive called Yummies.

I ducked into my old bedroom, which adjoined the kitchen. To me it was still Jacob's. After he died, my parents decided it was time I had my own room, and within a month his things had been put in the cellar and my things transferred in. I let Biffo in and closed the door, then collapsed on the bed and stared up at the water-stained ceiling. The blue throw rug was stained yellow smack in the center . . . but by what? I couldn't remember but felt it had something to do with a spilled bottle of nail-polish remover. I recalled the one time I'd had a slumber party, when I turned eleven, a year after Jacob's death. My parents had dragged in two mattresses—both covered with urine stains—for me and my friends to sleep on, causing me to become mute for the rest of the night. Even the pillows passed out were stained yellow in spots. Were those stains a result of piss, or drool?

Did it matter?

I grimaced and imagined what Patrick's room might look like: wainscoted walls, a wooden bed, a braided blue rug straight from the pages of a Pottery Barn catalogue . . . not to mention the twenty-inch-screen television next to the sleek black laptop. I dug in my bag and snatched the slip of paper with his phone number. Biffo lay at my feet and started whining as he scratched frantically at the fleas or ear mites that were causing him distress. I sat up and petted the coarse hair on his head, and he looked at me with sad, cataract-filled eyes. He had acquired an old-age stench, and no one wanted to be near him. My father screamed at Biffo to get away, my brothers raised a threatening hand until he cowered and sought another place to rest his body. I bent down, hugged his smelly body close, and whispered, "I'm so sorry."

Biffo farted. The room swelled with a sickening aroma, compounding the stink that already existed. I leapt up and ran into the kitchen to escape the noxious fumes, and Biffo followed, so I shooed him outside. He looked in at me, head cocked, and then curled into a ball on the porch, resigned.

It was freezing out. Just 18 degrees Fahrenheit.

I opened the door and the dog trotted in happily. Gratefully. Wagging his tail.

I could hear the screen door squeak open again and again as my five brothers began arriving for my homecoming dinner. People always idealize what big families are like. "That must have been so much fun!" they say, or "Holidays must have been a *blast*." And the truth is, yes, sometimes it was fun. But you can't squeeze that many different personalities into one little house and not expect trouble. And I worked hard as the sole female sibling. My brothers didn't know how to relate to me, and as I got older they knew even less. I was always going to be their baby sister, and I was always going to be teased: It was the only way they knew to communicate. In the past that had been okay, but I wasn't sure I could take it this visit.

Adam and Phil still lived at home. Adam was sort of a recluse; Phil drank too much, smoked too much, and watched too much TV. Bill was a stout Harley-loving, beer-drinking man who had moments of surprising sweetness that were too often superseded by manic rages. Danny, the only one who had married, worked as a car salesman, while his wife, Vera, had a white-collar job at a baby-food factory. What this white-collared job *was*, what she *did*, hardly mattered. She worked in an office, wore heels and pretty suits, and was thus regarded with a mixture of awe and suspicion. Mark was the eldest and the angriest, but he took out his aggression through organized boxing. Phil, unfortunately, took his anger out on innocents—

he had a special knack for harassing parents with toddlers, babies.

"Where's our bratty kid sister?" I heard Mark shout.

"Shhh," my mother scolded. "She's reading."

Bill guffawed. "So what? Is she too good to spend a little time with her family?"

"Yeah," Mark concurred, laughing along, "maybe we should teach her some *common sense,* since she has none of *that.* No college can teach it, either, *that's* for sure."

After rereading the same sentence ten times and still not absorbing it, I put the book down. It was a copy of *Ulysses,* the novel Patrick had been reading the last time I'd seen him. But just looking at the massive hardback copy I'd checked out of the library made me yawn. I braced myself as I pulled the door open. All of my brothers were standing around the table, stuffing their hands into a bag of generic-brand potato chips. As they took in my new short haircut, they pretended to gag and retch.

"*Whoa,*" Mark yelled jovially, punching my arm too hard in greeting. "You're looking even more ugly than usual."

"Har, har," I replied, giving a light punch in return.

"Yeah," brother Bill joined in, also delivering a punch— though lighter than Mark's. "Not to mention pasty. Maybe you should try one of those tanning beds."

"I know. I can't remember the last time the sun graced my skin."

"*Woooooo,*" Phil whistled, clapping his hands in mock reverie, "What are you now, a poet, too?" He pitched his voice an octave higher and repeated my sentence in a Southern drawl:

"Ah simply cahn't *remembah* the lahst time the sun graced mah skin."

My mood sank as my smile stretched wider. I couldn't help but think of how Patrick would view this scene. They were hicks, jerks, idiots. *Would you say,* I wanted to challenge Phil, *that line was more Dickinson or Plath?* Instead I laughed along with everyone else.

"So, Natalie," Danny asked. "Does the short hair mean that you're, like, gay?"

My father came into the kitchen and picked up a plate, signaling it was time to eat. He was an imposing man, heavyset and tall, with the same brush cut he had had since he was in the Navy, but every time I saw him now he looked older and more fragile—nothing like the enraged man I had grown used to in childhood.

"Dad," Adam said, "what do *you* think of Natalie's haircut? I know I just lost my appetite."

"Shut up," my father warned without a trace of amusement in his tone. He scooped some mashed potatoes onto his plate and ladled on gravy, served himself a broiled chicken drumstick and a sizable portion of canned corn. He scanned his children, still grouped around the table, and didn't seem to notice that my thick mane of hair had gone missing: "If I see anyone with more than *one* chicken leg on his plate," he cautioned, "there's going to be hell to pay. Understood?"

Everyone nodded. I wondered if they minded being spoken to like children. I was just eleven years old when my father retired, a year after Jacob's death. We had grown close in our own way, with me as sidekick, following him wherever he went, whether to the grocery store or the dump. I smiled at him now and got into line behind Vera, and as I served myself, my brothers commented on each and every thing I did as if they were sports commentators watching a game: "Look at how much chicken she took—what a carnivore!" "Yeah, but did you notice how she barely took any string beans? I'm gonna tell Mom!" "All I know is that she's looking F-A-T. Are they serving her lard at school? Yum yum!" The entourage then moved into the dining room, where two tables had been pushed together to make room for everyone. I sat beside my father to shield myself on at least one side from my brothers and touched my belly surreptitiously. I *had* gotten fatter. My fat roll felt thicker. I sat more upright to stretch it out.

"Dear," my father called to my mother, "get in here. We have to say the prayer."

She was busy cleaning up and making sure everyone had water, napkins, silverware, but per his request she took her seat opposite him, aglow in smiles but without food. "You say it, dear," she urged.

He looked down at his plate and muttered his standard refrain, spoken as quickly as humanly possible. My mother then left to retrieve her plate and the salt and pepper, and when she returned, my father noted that there was no chicken leg on her dish.

"It's fine, dear," she said, smiling. "I really don't want any."

"Horseshit!" he yelled, eyeing all of the plates surrounding the table. "Which one of these bastards took more than one?"

"It was me, Dad," Adam volunteered sheepishly. "I didn't know we could only have one."

"What do you *mean*, you didn't *know* . . . I SAID ONE CHICKEN LEG PER PERSON!"

"I must have been in the bathroom," Adam lied.

"So your mother who MADE THIS GODDAMNED MEAL doesn't even get to eat a GODDAMNED CHICKEN LEG?!"

I listened to the back-and-forth outburst and kept counting to ten, over and over, hoping that by the third time they might finish and move on. Already I had pushed my leg to the rim of my plate, intending to save it for my mother. I asked Bill to pass the butter and slapped a pat onto a piece of white bread. I chewed on the airy dough, barely tasting it. My other brothers continued to shovel food in, using fingers instead of knives to help secure food onto forks, splattering their faces and shirts with potato and chicken grease in total disregard. Biffo raced from one end of the table to the other in his pursuit of scraps and offerings. I imagined Patrick viewing the scene and turned crimson, realizing that not even I had bothered with a napkin. I grabbed a paper one from the middle of the table and placed it on my lap. When my father finally returned to his plate, Bill attempted to change the topic.

"All I know," he said, elbowing me hard in the side, "is that Natalie sure doesn't look too good. Right?"

My brothers laughed and nodded. I said "Ha ha," excused myself, gave my mother my chicken leg, and tossed my scraps into the garbage. I rinsed my plate and loaded it into the dishwasher. Then I went into the bathroom and scrutinized my face, inches away from the cloudy mirror. I did look pasty. I touched my cheek and thought it had the texture of white bread, then I closed my eyes and tried to recall Jacob at a Bloom family dinner, but I couldn't. I wondered, in fact, if anyone in my family would be able to.

*

nineteen

It was early, but when I emerged from my room, hollow-eyed and crabby from yet another bad night's sleep, Phil was already up, sitting at the kitchen table, reading the local paper while drinking straight from a jug of orange juice.

"I just don't get it," he said brightly, leaning back in his chair. "Didn't anyone ever tell you that guys *hate* short hair?"

Back in my room I looked in the mirror. Two small pimples had developed right at the hairline, but with cover-up they'd be negligible. I sank to the floor and did 150 stomach crunches. Then I sat on my bed and stared at Patrick's number, my heart thumping. Maybe I would call him. I could ask him how it was to be home. I could ask him how he, himself, was doing. I could suggest that we meet. Sometime. Anytime that was good for him.

My armpits grew moist; my breathing felt shallow. I retrieved the cordless from the kitchen and resealed myself in my room. I pressed "Talk," but as soon as the dial tone rang out I pressed "End." I knew I should wait for Patrick to call me, especially since I had called him last—and it had gone so badly. At the end of that last call he said he would call me, and he hadn't. But how could he? I didn't have a *phone*. Maybe he had forgotten this and *had* tried to call, only to be frustrated by an endless busy signal. Or maybe he had misplaced the piece of paper on which I'd written my home number? I considered this and picked up the phone again. If I called and he was indifferent, I would simply throw away his number and I would forget about him. I would.

"Hello?"

A man's voice. A familiar voice.

"Patrick?" I asked breathlessly.

"No, this is his father. Just a minute."

The receiver clicked onto a surface as his father yelled for him. I feared I was calling at a bad time—it was too early!—and he would be irritated to hear my voice. My breathing felt erratic. My armpits were now drenched. I ran my fingers through my hair and knocked off my headband, which fell to the floor and rolled under my bureau. My head felt naked.

The first part of the conversation went well. Patrick recognized my voice without me having to identify myself, and he answered the two questions I had prepared—"How are you?" and "Is it good to be home?" I proceeded to tell him how I was and how I felt to be home: I lied and said I was "fine" and that it "was great." Then I pinched my cheek over and over in the same spot until it throbbed.

"You think you might want to get together sometime?" I blurted.

"Yeah," he replied. "That might be good. How about tomorrow night?"

Might be good. He asked, again, if I'd be willing to meet halfway, and we decided to meet at a mall in Waterford, in front of J.C. Penney's, at eight p.m. Next I had to get my father to agree to lend me his pickup, and I prayed he wouldn't check the odometer beforehand. My only other obstacle? Cash to refill the gas tank that would surely empty on the long trip.

I hung up, dropped to my knees, and felt my way through cobwebs as I groped for my headband. My mother knocked on my door and peeked in just as I put it back on my head. "Rise and shine," she sang. "We leave for church in ten minutes."

I stared at her, knowing full well I had no choice in the matter. I searched for something to wear, but all I had brought home was jeans and sweaters. My mother was of the generation that believed a proper outfit was required for mass. Apparently, God preferred his adherents in pressed slacks and crease-free blouses. I put on black jeans and a blue sweater and went to meet my parents in the kitchen. My mother wore dark-green pleated pants and a white, lace-trimmed blouse. She looked me over and shook her head.

"You are *not* wearing jeans," she ordered.

"But, Mom," I pleaded, "I only brought jeans *home*. I have no choice."

"You can wear a pair of my pants, then."

I looked at her as if she had lost her mind. Had she noticed the great bulge of her stomach area, in contrast to my flattened abdomen?

"Black jeans are better than blue jeans," I replied, trying to sound as authoritative on the subject as possible. "Let's go."

She sighed but gave in when she looked at the clock over the refrigerator. My father ambled into the kitchen bundled in a bright-red jacket, and we all braced against the cold and climbed into the Buick. It was foggy out, and as we quickly approached the church, I thought how ominous it looked with the top of its red-brick steeple disappearing into white mist.

Sitting between my parents in the pew, I studied the gilded columns lining the aisles, the white-marbled altar, and the angels painted amid clouds tinged pink, luminescent, on the ceiling. Sundays had always been the worst. It was the one day of the week when it was difficult to fully deny Jacob's suicide. Especially just after his death. I would stand beside my mother during mass as tears spilled down her face, and instead of trying to comfort her, I had only been concerned that kids from school would witness my mother crying—my mother *publicly crying*—and would then know that I was lying. My brother had not simply moved to Florida, my brother was dead, dead by his own hand. I would watch her grief-stricken face and inch away from her in the pew, trying to distance myself from whatever it was that was making this woman—this person I suddenly didn't know—cry. *I'm not with her*, I would hope to convey as people turned to see who was sobbing, occasionally even smiling at strangers to express my own bemusement at her behavior.

I knelt and knit my hands together, and was relieved when the choir began its last song, signaling the congregation to leave. But walking out again, flanked by my parents, I felt suddenly small and wished I could stay with them—just the three of us—and wished even more that they could protect me. I wanted to feel protected. The blank expanse of adulthood was everywhere before me.

After supper that evening, I found Bill watching TV with my father in the den. He was reclining in the baby-blue La-Z-Boy, its footrest shredded from too many feet over the course of too many years.

"Hey," I said, eyeing the TV, "could I clean your van for ten bucks tomorrow?"

"I'll give you seven, but it has to be cleaned inside and out."

"What's three more dollars?" I whined, now looking at him. "Please? You paid me ten the last time I did it."

He didn't reply and continued watching the show—a *Dateline NBC* segment about a mother and daughter who were murdered in their motel room. The murderer was never caught.

"Get out of here if you're going to talk!" my father yelled suddenly, belatedly.

I looked at him in His Chair, the chair no one else was allowed to sit in. Not even if he wasn't at home. It, too, was worn, its seams pulling apart and exposing yellowed foam. His head was tilted back so that he could see because, like Biffo, he had cataracts.

"Eight bucks," Bill said severely. "Now quit bugging us."

*

twenty

The next morning I started first thing on cleaning the van, which Bill had left for me in the driveway. I wanted to get that out of the way early so I could spend the rest of the day preparing for my date. Four hours and several warm-up breaks later, I finished and Bill returned to inspect the van, whereupon he told me, without fanfare, that I had done a shitty job and that he would give me a buck instead of the eight dollars he'd agreed to.

"What do you mean?" I asked through gritted teeth.

He opened the driver's-side door and pointed to a grease smudge a foot in length.

"Oh," I breathed, hopeful, "I can clean that in just a sec. Okay?"

He slammed the door and shook his head, folding his arms over his burly chest. I ignored his gestures and dunked my hand into the murky pail, wringing out the sponge and gingerly stepping around him to open the driver's-side door. Bill stepped back and leaned against it, his face a steely blockade. He dug into his way-too-tight jeans and pulled out a wad of crumpled cash, then selected a wrinkled, ripped dollar bill and dropped it on the ground. "I drove you home the other day," he said humorlessly, climbing into the van, "using *my* gas. So this is fair. This is how the *real world* works."

A moment later he had backed down the driveway and disappeared around the corner. I watched the gleaming white van drive away. The sponge, which had started out a bright neon yellow but was now dingy and gray, dripped through my clenched fingers. I gasped. The world felt so still, and I felt like I had to stir it, shake it, make it move. I pocketed the dollar and went inside to throw on some sneakers, then ran out the front door, letting my feet carry me away without really thinking about where I was going. But soon it became clear. I turned down a dead-end street—Nelson Drive, the street where Jacob had shot and killed himself—and stopped. I sat on the curb between two flowerless azalea bushes. Decrepit suburban homes lined the street, differentiated only by color (white, pale yellow, celadon), and I wondered if Jacob had chosen the spot for a reason, or simply because it was close by and he couldn't wait to finish himself off.

A bird flew near me, and I watched it hop a few steps atop the yellowed grass before fluttering onto the bush to my right. We were alike, Jacob and I. My other brothers took their anger out on the world and on each other; Jacob and I only took our anger out on ourselves.

I filled my lungs with icy air and pushed myself off the

ground. I circled over the spot where Jacob's car was last parked, and then I moved my body forward until I was slowly jogging again.

That night, after combing through my closet fifty thousand times, I opted to wear my ivory cabled sweater since a sweater, even a bulky one, falls against the chest in a way to emphasize the breasts. Even if it might hang off of them and droop over the stomach and hips like a tent. This, I hoped, would bring less attention to my face and short hair. I studied my curves and acknowledged that the sweater did little to compliment my skin, but it was more prudent to focus on tangible assets. Tits.

My father was in His Chair, dozing off to the local six o'clock news. "Hey, Dad," I said, taking a seat in the pale-blue recliner next to him. "Can I borrow the truck?"

"How far away do you have to go?" he asked gruffly.

"Not far," I lied. "Just about twenty-five minutes."

"That's too far," he said, definitively.

"It isn't," I objected. "I'll put gas in it."

He turned away to play solitaire on the table beside his chair, and I waited as he flipped cards. If he wasn't intending to lend the truck I'd have already heard so.

"Refill whatever gas you use," he ordered, "and no later than midnight."

"Thank you!" I yelled happily. I settled into the recliner and stole a few glances at him, now so old and wrinkled. Once, and only once, when he and I were returning home from an outing, my father had told me he loved me. Granted, it had been in a joking voice and prompted by something the radio DJ had said. I remember replying, also in an insincere voice, "I love you *more*." We'd gone back and forth then, each saying the word "more" louder and longer than the other, like an improvised game, until we were parked in the driveway. Then we got out of the car, slammed our respective doors, and went into the house: I to my room, he to the living room. The game was never repeated.

I crossed my arms and sat forward. Did my father remember that day? Probably. And if he did remember, I thought, getting up to leave, would it make him feel the same mixture of cheer and revulsion that the memory evoked in me, all those years later?

My mother was washing dishes when I slipped past her on my way out. "Don't *you* look nice," she said with an eager smile.

"No," I replied severely, "I don't."

"I know I keep telling you this, dear, but I love your new haircut."

I shook my head, frowning, and looked for the keys to the truck.

"Which friend are you going to see?"

"Does it matter?" I shot back. "She's just a friend from UConn. Okay?"

"Just be careful," she said quietly, focusing back on the pile of pots and pans in the soapy water and looking as if she might cry.

I murmured an apology and let the door slam behind me. It was dark out, and cold. I tilted my head back and was relieved to see that the sky was clear and bright with stars, promising neither rain nor snow. The truck's gas gauge read three-quarters full. Would the dollar Bill had paid me, coupled with two dollars in spare change I'd found in a drawer and another two I had managed to borrow from my father, fill the tank back up to the same level?

When I got on the highway, I kept my speed between seventy and seventy-five miles per hour. Traffic was light but fast; for every car I passed it seemed as if four passed me, whizzing past in red-lit blurs. It was surreal to be going to meet Patrick. The last time we'd seen each other we'd had sex with almost no dialogue beforehand, and I wondered what it would be like to be with him, out in public, where dialogue, I imagined, would have to occur. It made me feel hopeful, but anxious, too, and I prayed our conversation would happen naturally, without too much effort. This could be my chance to show him what I was really like, to allow a true relationship to develop.

I found a parking spot near the J.C. Penney entrance and looked in the mirror. I adjusted my headband and applied more pink lipstick, forgoing an earlier conclusion that the color didn't suit me. Patrick was already there, his hands buried in his blue coat pockets. My heartbeat quickened as I got out of the pickup and approached him.

"Hi!" I said cheerfully. "I hope you haven't been waiting long?"

He smiled and folded me in his arms. "Not long at all."

I hugged him back, feeling strange and awkward. A slight scent of cologne filled my nostrils, and I breathed in, surprised that he had bothered with it.

"I figured we could grab a quick bite at the food court," he said, pulling away. "You haven't eaten yet, have you?"

I told him I hadn't and glowed: So far it appeared this was a real date. We would have dinner, and maybe a movie, afterwards, at the multiplex down the street.

We walked to the plaza filled with fast-food eateries: McDonald's, Burger King, KFC, and Taco Bell, their logos reminding me of the garbage I had cleaned out of Bill's van. Patrick led us into the line at McDonald's. When he reached the clerk, he ordered and paid, then stood aside to let me place my own order. I blushed, realizing that I had expected Patrick to pay for me, but as it quickly became clear this was not going to happen, I put on a brave face and ordered a hamburger for eighty-nine cents and a cup of water. Tap.

Four dollars left for gas.

We took our individual trays and found a table next to the purple-neon Taco Bell sign. I watched him wolf down a double cheeseburger and large fries and nibbled slowly on my own burger to make it last. I decided not to interrupt his meal with an attempt at what was sure to be poor conversation. Better to let him finish. Better to let him talk first.

He tossed his empty wrapper and carton in a nearby trash bin, and I jumped up to do likewise. Then he took my hand (he took my hand!) and began walking me through the mall, past the clothing boutiques, kiosks, and pretzel stands, until we reached our point of origination at J.C. Penney's. "What do you feel like doing?" he asked, smiling, fingering the hole in the armpit of my corduroy coat.

"I don't care what we do," I replied, hoping he wouldn't suggest a movie since I didn't have the cash for a ticket and didn't want to reveal this to him. "Whatever is fine."

"Maybe we'll go for a drive?" he asked, draping his arm over my shoulders.

"Great," I agreed, nodding my head up and down. "Your car or, um, mine?"

He grinned and led me outside to his Saab. I slid into the black squeaky leather and pulled my seat belt on. My palms were sweaty and I rubbed them roughly against my pants. My pickup was close by, and I eyed it, suddenly wishing I were in it.

As we drove, the car filled with the dreamy voice of Morrissey crooning about shoplifters and girlfriends in comas. Soon we were in boondocks territory. There were no street-lights, only the rare car's headlights flashing past on barren back roads. Patrick hadn't said a word since getting in the car, and I felt myself spinning in the wall of silence, wondering, desperately, what I could say to break it, the music notwithstanding. It seemed that we should have a lot to say, from discussing our families to talking about current events or the unclear "future." But each time I thought I had come up with a sentence, it remained unspoken, closed in my mouth. He pulled off the road and drove up a dirt drive that didn't seem to lead anywhere until I spotted a "Park Closed at Sunset" sign about a hundred yards ahead—at which point a chain had been drawn and locked to prevent cars from proceeding further. I glanced at him, my smile still broad, and said the obvious: "It's closed."

"That's okay," he said, parking and lowering the stereo's volume. "I thought we could hang out here. A friend of mine who lives nearby told me it's safe."

Safe for what? "Okay," I replied, nodding. "Great."

He undid his seat belt and pressed the release button on my own, then leaned in, but before he could kiss me I blurted, "I'm reading *Ulysses*."

He paused and eyeballed me. "Do you like it?"

I nodded.

"I don't believe you."

He began to kiss me then, while fondling my breasts through my sweater. I kept my eyes open and tried to feel like this was all good and that it was just what I wanted to do, even though I burned with embarrassment. I wanted to know *why* he didn't believe that I was enjoying that monstrous book. Had he insulted me . . . or was I just annoyed that he had guessed correctly? And if it *was* his favorite book and he knew that in fact I *didn't* like it, did that mean, to him, we were incompatible? *How important was* Ulysses *to our future?* He drove his tongue into my mouth, then pulled my sweater over my head, unbuttoned my jeans, and sat back, expectantly, as I wriggled out of them. He, in turn, unbuckled his belt and unzipped his fly, maneuvering a very stiff penis up and out of his boxers.

"Could you lick it?" he asked thickly, tilting his head back against the seat.

Ulysses and its imperatives evaporated. I froze. I had done it already once, but I had been drunk at the time. Now I was stone-cold sober, and I didn't want to lick it. I didn't think I'd be any good at it, and that—more than anything else—terrified me. I wondered who else had licked it and if Patrick would be comparing licks and grading us, in which case my GPA was sure to drop even further. But I had to do it . . . because how was I supposed to get out of it? I hesitantly circled my tongue over its head, then up and down the shaft, flinching as it jerked upward in tiny spasms.

"Put it in your mouth," he ordered, slightly impatient, "okay?"

I did as I was told. It wasn't hard to do. It was just a matter of moving my head and mouth, but not too much, which Patrick controlled with steady pressure to the sides of my face. I kept my eyes squeezed shut tight. I tried to think of how I felt the first night when I'd met him in the library. I tried to think that this was love, and this is what I was thinking when it all came to a very quick end as a warm, sticky fluid shot into my mouth. It tasted acrid and made me want to gag, but, not knowing what else to do, I swallowed.

And this time, Patrick did thank me.

I drove home at a steady 85 miles per hour, though I didn't need to speed; I wasn't so late, and it was stupid of me to risk getting a ticket that I didn't have the money to pay. But I couldn't seem to cede any pressure on the accelerator. It felt good to press down on the pedal, propelling myself, fast, through the darkness, the taste of his semen still lingering on my tongue. A green sign promised gas and food in two miles, and I pulled into the Mobil station conveniently located just off the highway and pumped my four dollars' worth in, shivering under white floodlights—and barely cursed when the gas gauge didn't tilt up to the three-quarters level I had promised it would. It went up halfway, and that would have to be good enough.

The one thought that played, and replayed, in my head?

I love him.

*

twenty-one

I was almost twenty-one years old and I was dating. We met twice more that first week, me winning a few dollars from my father each time with the promise that I would pay him back. An efficient routine was established: burgers at McDonald's, a drive to our "closed at sunset" park, then a drop-off at my truck back at the mall. When Sunday arrived, I lay still in bed, staring at the stained ceiling. My parents were angry because I hadn't gone to mass, nor had I helped with lunch. I had to redeem myself. How else would I get them to keep lending me the truck?

Patrick was everywhere I looked, he was everything I wanted. I rolled onto my stomach and buried my face in my pillow. I was in love. Patrick, however, was not. The knowledge of his disaffection hung around my neck like an ever-tightening noose, with no signs of loosening, and I grimaced as I recalled a brief conversation from the previous evening. He had simply asked me what I'd thought of Camus' *The Stranger* in a way that demanded my knowledge of the book. I had frozen beside him and stuttered out a few syllables that revealed my utter ignorance: I hadn't read it yet; was it new? The shift in his attitude afterwards was instantaneous. I had feebly attempted to save myself by delivering a rave review of *Ulysses*, but my words had felt hollow; I was the dummy of a ventriloquist, and not a very talented one at that. How could I explain the absence of books—and curiosity—throughout my twenty years of life, my knowledge of Russia notwithstanding? Here he was, *trying* to give me a chance to win his heart and respect, but I was failing. I knew. I was just an easy lay in his eyes. A poor unread girl with a deficit of learning and zero appreciation for the arts. My high GPA meant nothing. In my world, Edvard Munch was pronounced like "Crunch." John Donne's last name sounded like "Don." Patrick, meanwhile, continued to cement the perfect vision I had of him. Every time I saw him it seemed he grew *more* attractive, *more* interesting, *more* learned. So what if I fell short? The emotional and intellectual imbalance was worth it. *It was worth it!* Things could change. Our rapport could improve. I could read the novels he mentioned. I could listen to the music he deemed "essential." In this way Patrick's feelings could grow until they more closely matched my own. It was possible.

I was using what little leverage I had. At first I told him I wouldn't be able to meet him once my winter-break job started, but when we were parting the night before, I had grown desperate at the thought of not seeing him and said as I got out of his car that, come to think of it, I could see no reason why I couldn't meet him after work a couple of times during the week since I was on the eight-to-four shift. It would be difficult to engineer, but it was necessary. It was necessary if he was to learn to love me. I had smiled with relief when he nodded and shrugged, and had tried in vain to read meaning into his nod and shrug on the long drive home.

I sighed now and climbed out of bed to stare at my reflection in the mirror. My hair was a lost cause, but even my features were flawed to me suddenly, and I wondered how I might make them *less* flawed. I grabbed some tweezers and plucked at my brows until I'd plucked one hair too many on the left side, making it look like a crescent moon. So, I did what I had to do: I plucked the right side until it matched the left. I rimmed my lips with a pink lip-liner, then filled them in with a red lipstick. I tried smiling, I pretended to smoke a cigarette, I imagined being cool and witty and interesting. But I looked ridiculous, and, worse, I had nothing to say to Patrick, not even in the privacy of my own room. I ran to the bathroom and washed my face. My newly plucked eyebrows made me look surprised. But, then, I was surprised. By everything.

A blast of static buzzed and I fumbled in the darkened room looking for the alarm's snooze button. It was 7:10 a.m., my first day back to work, and a whimper escaped my lips as I threw off the covers, shivering. I showered, dressed in my worst pair of jeans and a gray sweatshirt, grabbed my mandatory safety goggles, and fetched my prepacked lunch as I headed out the door.

It was freezing in the pickup cab; I rubbed my hands together and let the engine warm before shifting into first, then second gear, and took back roads, driving far too fast, cutting corners and skimming into the oncoming lane in my effort to not be late. I found a spot at the back of the parking lot and sprinted to the factory—a four-story brick complex that, I thought, had probably been quite attractive at one time but now showed the degeneration of decades of wear and tear. Just like most of the people who worked inside of the place.

I hurried to my work station, or "cell," the official description of the work environment. Each "cell" had a "cell leader," and my leader was named Joanna—a hostile, unattractive woman in her late thirties with permed blond hair and thin, colorless lips. I took the only open stool, slipped on my safety goggles, nodded a hello to my fellow pluggers—noting that I had worked with all of them in the past, save for two young women who looked like they should still be in high school—and immediately grabbed a black cord, pulling it taut before separating the wires by color. This particular cord had seven wires to color-coordinate, and I knew I would be dreaming of the sequence that night, seeing it before my eyes in the same way that the sun leaves glowing spots if you look at it too long: green, white, black, red, orange, blue, brown. Green, white, black, red, orange, blue, brown.

"Don't clip them too far down," Joanna warned as I used a pair of scissors to even out the wires before inserting them into a plug. "We can't mess up on *any* of these. There was an order fuck-up, and we barely have enough cords to fulfill *our* order."

I nodded and nudged my goggles, wrinkling my nose to stop them from slipping, a source of irritation throughout the day. I touched my headband to make sure that it, too, was in place. It was.

Most of the people who worked on the third floor were pluggers, and the majority of pluggers were women. Men worked on the first two levels, either making the cords themselves or in the shipping department, loading the finished products into boxes for distribution. Bill worked in shipping and, thankfully, our paths rarely crossed, especially since he was on the graveyard shift. Women were confined to plugging because of their smaller hands, which, it was believed, made working with tiny wires easier. But there were a few male pluggers, and George was one of them. George was a bit of a goof, but of all my cellmates, he was the nicest. He coughed and swallowed what sounded like a large amount of phlegm, eliciting disgusted groans from the two young women I didn't know. He blushed and ran his fingers through greasy-looking black hair before speaking. "What have you been learning lately, Natalie?"

I clamped my plug to the cord and shrugged. I smiled at him across the table, hoping he would read in it an attempt at friendliness but also a need for silence.

"Come on," he pushed, "what is it again that you're majoring in?"

"Russian history," I whispered.

"What?" he hollered, letting out a deep laugh. "Did you say *Russian history*? What the fuck for? You wanna be a Commie or something?"

I laughed, the same laugh I used with my brothers to concede that, yes, I was an idiot.

"Seriously," George said. "Why Russian history?"

I thought of how Patrick and I had had this same conversation once upon a time. How the conversation had been coherent and fun. What had happened to me—to *us*—since then? Why did Patrick no longer kid around or flirt? Things had seemed normal at one time. Possibilities had been in the air. It wasn't just in my imagination.

"I don't know," I finally answered, clamping a cord before realizing the blue wire was where the brown wire was supposed to be. I held the cord up, extending it toward Joanna, who guessed my mistake and grabbed it.

"If you can't plug and talk at the same time," she warned, "then keep quiet. You're not paid to have a good time here."

Joanna tossed me back the cord to redo and I nodded at her, relieved to blindly plug for the next eight hours straight, with nothing else to think about but my love.

Patrick answered on the third ring and I said hello and laughed afterwards as if something funny had been said, as if the "hello" we had each uttered contained a hidden joke. He replied to my laugh with silence.

"I, um, just got home from work a few minutes ago," I said, pinching one of my cheeks hard. "God, I *hate* being a plugger."

I waited for him to ask why I hated it, or simply to acknowledge my statement with an "mmmm," but he said nothing. Maybe he had nodded.

"You just fit these little wires into the plastic plug tips— you know, the kind you snap into telephones?—and then clamp the wires to the thing. Pretty fascinating, huh?"

"Yeah."

I laughed, thinking his "yeah" was sarcastic and meant to make me laugh—only he didn't laugh along and the silence suddenly seemed stony and severe.

"Did, um, you have a nice day?"

"Yeah. No complaints."

"What . . . what did you do?"

"Nothing. I watched TV and smoked some pot. I did a little writing."

"Oh, cool."

I started to perspire. I had thought I might tell him about Joanna and the other pluggers in my cell and that it might evolve into a full-fledged conversation. I had fantasized about it all day: We could talk about personality types and discuss work environments in a sociological and class-based context, and in this way we would deepen our understanding of each other. The conversation would be charged, intellectual, satisfying. Patrick would learn new things about me, and I would learn new things about him. We would realize we had the same perceptions of reality and the same views about people and their varied psychologies.

"What, um, were you writing about?" I managed to ask.

"I don't talk about what I'm working on."

"Oh," I said. "Of course. Is that because it's, like, an intrusion?"

"Exactly."

"Oh. Well, I, um, I should let you go," I stammered, laughing again for no reason but wanting to appear easygoing. "Maybe we can get together tomorrow night?"

"Sure," he replied distractedly. "Same time and place?"

"Great," I said happily. "See you then!"

Just before arriving at J.C. Penney's—while primping in the rearview mirror—I nearly collided with a bright-yellow semi. The giant truck appeared out of nowhere, and while I swerved in its blind-spot region it had jerked to the left, coming within an inch of demolishing my little pickup, and, consequently, myself. I screamed and beeped and almost drove into the oncoming lane. The truck sounded a long, angry honk, then repeated the honk when the first had finished. I pulled into the mall's parking lot, found a spot near the entrance, and was glad to see that Patrick wasn't waiting for me yet. I buried my face in my hands and tried to collect myself by slight degrees from the scare of what I was certain had been a near-death experience. I wondered if I was feeling relief that I wasn't dead, or simply relief that I had barely avoided a possibly very *painful* death— with sharp glass and steel gouging into eyes and flesh and organs. Did my fear mean that I didn't have suicidal tendencies, or did it merely mean that I needed to carefully choose my method of death—a calmer death that wouldn't involve excessive blood loss? Did I feel happy at that moment to be alive? I looked in the mirror and noted the fear in my eyes. I might not have been happy, but I was certainly relieved to be breathing.

A knock at my window startled me, eliciting a small scream from my throat. I smiled and laughed mechanically when I saw Patrick.

"Hi," I said, opening my door, a frozen smile still etched on my face. "I almost got into an accident. With a semi. I'm pretty freaked out about it, actually."

He put an arm around my shoulders and ushered me toward the mall's entrance.

"It really scared me," I pressed, stopping abruptly in the J.C. Penney lobby. "I could have been . . . I could have been killed."

Patrick stopped and looked at me, and his mouth spread into a kind smile. "You look okay to me," he said. "Just don't think about it. Nothing happened."

I followed him to the food court and paid for my hamburger. We ate quickly, mostly without speaking. He briefly told me about a funny show he had seen on HBO, and I laughed as if I were currently enjoying the episode; and just to drive home the fact, I kept mindlessly repeating "That's funny." He told me he sometimes considered writing for television, but he worried about "selling out." I nodded knowingly, imagined him hanging out with TV stars and found myself blushing for no reason at all. Then we moved on to the "closed at sunset" park.

I lay across the backseat with my sweater and bra pushed up around my neck and my head hanging out the opened door to give Patrick a more comfortable position. It was he, after all, who was excessively tall. I tried to hold my head up to keep the blood from rushing to it, but the head can be a heavy thing when gravity is weighing on it, and after a while I just let the blood collect, resigning myself to the fact that Patrick would most likely finish soon. When I saw the bright headlights of a car approaching, it was difficult to absorb that it was a real car and not a figment of my imagination. I was so dizzy. But when I saw the telltale flashing blue and red lights whir from the vehicle's roof, I hit Patrick's shoulders and pleaded with him to stop.

The policeman parked and walked slowly up to the Saab while we wrestled to pull our pants on. I, however, panicked, gave up, and was just able to lay my pants across my lap in a desperate attempt to hide my naked vagina when the man's flashlight beam lit up the car's interior. I touched my hair and was dismayed when I failed to feel the hard plastic of my headband. Patrick moved into the driver's seat and handed over his license and registration, which the cop grabbed roughly from him.

"Your license, too," he ordered, shining his flashlight beam directly into my eyes.

I asked Patrick to get my pocketbook, which he found beneath my white underwear—the kind you buy three to a pack. I fumbled with the zipper and handed over my entire wallet, needing both of my hands to keep my pants safely lodged on top of my naked body.

"*Just* your license," he snapped, refusing to take it.

My pants shifted as I let go of them to open my wallet; my hands shook as I extended my license. A shiny gold wedding band glinted on his ring finger as he took it from me, and this little detail made me feel even worse. He studied my photo for a long minute before handing it back. I guessed he was making sure that there was no statutory rape taking place. I wanted to beg his forgiveness; alternatively, I wanted him to tell me I was a no-good whore. I would adamantly agree. Instead, he berated Patrick that if he ever dared to "park and fuck" on public lands again he would arrest him for lewd conduct and loitering. Patrick nodded and kept repeating "Yes, sir" in as soft and polite a voice as I had ever heard. When the cop finished, he put his flashlight on me once more.

"Don't get yourself into trouble, miss," he warned sternly. "Keep your pants *on*."

I grimaced painfully in the beam of light. Hot, milky tears slid down my face. When he finally moved away and got back into the police cruiser, I gratefully pulled my pants on and found my headband, then got out and slid into the passenger seat. Patrick drove back to the mall. Neither of us spoke or commented on my weeping. When he parked beside my truck, he rested a hand on my shoulder, and I instinctively touched it, needing its warmth and comfort. Needing him.

"Don't worry about that asshole," he said softly but with anger. "I know another place we can go to next time. Fuck that pig."

I touched my headband before unclasping my seat belt, then I forced a smile, leaned in, and gave him a perfunctory peck on the lips. He didn't smile back, not even a forced smile like mine. I hurried to my truck. The air inside the cab was stale and cold, but I was relieved to be in there. I watched him drive off, not waiting for me to follow. Then I looked at myself, hesitantly, in the rearview mirror and picked myself apart, mercilessly. I thought *I look pale*, and *I look ugly*, and that sort of thing. When I got home, I went inside and lay on my bed, not bothering to even kick off my shoes. I glanced at the brass crucifix hanging on my wall that had once briefly lain on Jacob's casket, a trinket my mother had bestowed upon my room despite my utter fear and loathing of it, and now, for the first time . . . I liked it. It was Jacob's parting gift to me, a reminder that when all else fails, there *is* a way out. And Jacob was showing me the way.

A big-brotherly thing to do.

twenty-two

Christmas had passed much as any other day of the year. My family gave me gifts like socks, and I, in turn, bought each of my brothers a set of blank audiotape cassettes, on sale for $1.99 at Radio Shack. Why spend my hard-earned money on *them*? I had Patrick to buy for, and I had chosen a brown leather journal that was far too expensive, and yet not expensive *enough*. I had wrapped it carefully in red foil paper and tied a silver bow around it, and when we saw each other just after Christmas I had thrust it at him. He tore the paper off as I said, in a whisper, "It's for you to write in," and he had thanked me but then informed me that he only wrote on his computer. "Oh," I'd said. I was only slightly surprised that he hadn't gotten a gift for me, and it felt presumptuous of me to even think that he *might* have given me something. So, when he apologized for coming to see me empty-handed, I felt, oddly, like I was a bad person, like I had caused him to feel guilty, and I ended up apologizing back. I decided not to inform him that my birthday fell on the twenty-eighth of December—just a day or so away—because, well, just imagine his guilt then! But the thing is . . . I don't think he felt guilty at all.

Work, in the meantime, added new social anxieties to my life.

People thought I was a college snob, and I confess I did little to convince them otherwise. There were a few other college kids working at nearby tables, but they kept us separate for some reason—maybe they thought we'd goof off with one another?—and while they usually became a chummy clique after a few days, I stayed away from them, too. I just wanted to plug my plugs and receive some money for it. I wanted to be invisible.

At my table were two high school dropouts: Becky and Tara. Becky Brinkley had dark, wavy hair that was brittle from excessive blow-drying. She wasn't pretty, but she wasn't unattractive, either. Her sidekick, Tara Sparks, was a dumber, uglier version of Becky with a horrible case of acne. Together, they thrived on gossip and pried into everyone's lives.

"Do you have a boyfriend?" Becky asked me one morning, a smile stretching across her wide face.

I smiled weakly and lost track of my color-coordinated wires. I wished Joanna would order them to shut up, but she seemed to view Becky and Tara as needed entertainment. I shrugged.

"Is that a yes or a no?" Tara chimed in.

It would seem to be an easy question.

"I'm dating someone," I said, the words sounding strange and foreign on my tongue.

"That's so, like, *adult*-sounding," Becky laughed. "Like something your mom would say. What do you do on your 'dates'? Go ballroom dancing?"

The table erupted in a wave of laughter, and I laughed along, pushed up my goggles, and gingerly slid a seven-wire sequence into its plastic plug.

"What's his name?" Becky pressed on.

I went to say his name but found I couldn't. I felt as if I had made him up and if I said his name aloud it would sound fake.

"It's not serious," I dodged.

"Do you like *him* more, or does he like *you* more?"

"I . . . I don't know," I stuttered.

"Is he dicking you around?"

I didn't know what "dicking me around" would consist of, but I was interested in hearing her definition. "What do you mean?"

"Is he playing you? Is he a *dick*? Because I'm getting the feeling he is."

Joanna threw a finished plug on a pile of cords, then heaved herself off of her stool, announcing that she would soon return. Becky watched Joanna until she disappeared down the corridor, and when she was certain the coast was clear, she leaned over the table toward me: "So, what—is he good in bed? Is that why you stay with him?"

"*Excuse me*," George interjected. "I really don't want to hear any *girl talk* right now."

"Why not?" Tara laughed. "We could probably teach you some good pointers."

The conversation shifted, thankfully, to George and his sexual education and what makes a girl "hot," and I resumed working . . . but my hands shook so badly it rendered my task all but impossible.

I was about to choose my ivory sweater again when I spotted a black shirt that had been mine when I was in, say, the fifth or sixth grade. I tried it on and felt my breathing constricted by its tight fit. It was clearly too small, and yet it was just right: My breasts looked great. Large and round. So what if I developed welts under my arms from where the material cut into my flesh?

That night, as I neared the mall, I looked at myself in the rearview mirror and erased the deep furrow between my eyes by smiling, exposing my fairly aligned top white teeth. Patrick could never see me looking so serious. He could only see me as happy. Happy, happy, happy.

I parked and raced to stand by the entrance. He wasn't there yet, and he wasn't there ten minutes later, either. I glanced, repeatedly, at my watch. Elevator music could be heard drifting from loudspeakers inside the mall, and after another minute I allowed myself to escape the cold by waiting in the lobby. Some thirty minutes later, he finally arrived. He was high. His bloodshot eyes were a dead giveaway. I resisted an urge to ask what had delayed him because I did not want to be a nag. He asked me if I was hungry and I shrugged. He shrugged back with what was clear irritation and waved for me to follow him to his car. Had a new ritual begun, one where dinner was no longer a requisite part of the date? Now it would just be a Saab ride to sex.

"My friend told me about a quiet place," he said, stuffing his hands into his coat pockets. "I doubt anyone will bother us."

"Great," I said, grinning broadly. "Where?"

"You'll see," he answered mysteriously, giving me a little wink that I accepted with gratitude, as it suggested friendliness, flirtation.

We drove along a barren back road skirted by tall pine trees. I told him, haltingly, that I had finished reading Willa Cather's *Death Comes for the Archbishop* the night before. I had enjoyed it. He had been right, it was wonderful. Cather's voice *was* pure and unaffected. I hoped he would recommend other novels.

He slowed down and turned left into a cemetery.

"What did *you* think of the book?" he asked dryly.

I studied the slabs of granite bearing epitaphs as a chill ran up and down my spine. I swallowed as the car came to a halt.

"I thought . . . I thought," I stuttered, "it was interesting."

I didn't want to have sex in a cemetery. It would be sacrilegious. Cemeteries meant death, and death meant Jacob. I didn't want to think about Jacob. But it was too late: I pictured the slab of granite that marked his plot. Hadn't I always felt like he could see me above his grave? Hadn't I always feared visiting him there, feared that I, too, would be sucked into the earth and left to rot? I closed my eyes and waited for Patrick to suggest my next move as my thoughts turned even more macabre.

Jacob, I thought, must be a skeleton, although it was possible that some flesh might still be sticking to his bones because of the embalming and the concrete crypt encasing his coffin.

" 'Interesting'? Is that it?"

I was surprised that he was still talking about the book. How could I express my view when I was terrified of saying something he would deem stupid? Moreover, how could I formulate an academic opinion when I was horrified by what I was about to do amongst the dead? But he wanted me to say something more. I forced myself to think about the novel. There were two French missionaries. They went to New Mexico. They succeeded in getting the Mexicans to embrace Christianity. It had been interesting. I looked at Patrick and slowly nodded. He shook his head and didn't try to mask his disapproval. Then he studied me, and his next sentence seemed like a test of sorts: "It's interesting . . . that Cather was a woman. So few have added anything to the development of art or science or culture. I think that's why I admire her so much. Her talent is such an anomaly."

My heartbeat quickened. I wanted to call him a misogynist, but I wasn't entirely sure how to pronounce the word. "That's not true," I said meekly.

"Well, then, prove me wrong," he challenged, his tone entertained. "Name ten women, right now, who rank up with Hemingway . . . or Einstein."

"There's . . . there's," I choked, "a lot of women who've . . ."

I looked out the window and my eyes came to rest on a gray slab bearing the words "Helen Josephine Provost: Beloved Wife and Mother," and as I scanned the epitaph my brain stopped trying to think. I turned back to Patrick and saw that he was eyeing me in a way that was not dissimilar to my brothers. He was trying to get a rise out of me.

"I can't think of any right now," I said quietly, ashamed.

He laughed, somewhat angrily. "That's just *great*. Way to go. So, do you want to get in the backseat," he asked resignedly, "or should we find a place on the ground? It's cold, but at least we can stretch out."

I smiled. "Whichever," I said. "You choose."

He sighed, clearly annoyed that my indecisiveness seemed to have no boundaries, then got out and circled around several graves before finding a spot. He waved to me to follow.

"You don't think anyone will come?" I asked shyly, resisting, ever so slightly, for the first time. "It seems a little weird to, you know, do it in a cemetery."

Patrick didn't comment and sat down on the dried, spiked grass. I hesitated for another moment: "I'm scared of cemeteries."

He took my hand and pulled me to the wintry ground. He cradled my head in his palms and brushed my lips with his own. I wanted to kiss back, but my lips were pursed and refused to relax, so after another awkward attempt he moved on. I pushed my pants down, he did the same, and the sex commenced. I stared at the sky, stared at the moon, and tried desperately not to read the names on the gravestones around me. A rock jutted painfully into my back and I focused on the rhythmic pain rather than on the death surrounding me. My tight black shirt chafed against my armpits, and I thought how silly it had been for me to wear it since Patrick wouldn't even see it. There would be no occasion for me to remove my coat. I looked at him: His eyes were closed, his lips gently parted. I loved his brow line, the structure of his face; I longed to study his face for hours.

When it was over, I smiled and said, "It's cold."

He nodded in agreement and buckled his belt. "I'm free tomorrow night," he reported without looking at me. "Want to meet again?"

I stood and brushed off my pants. "Yeah," I replied. "Great."

We climbed back into the Saab and Patrick slid a Smashing Pumpkins CD into the stereo.

"Oh, I *love* the Smashing Pumpkins," I said, picking up the CD cover and reading the listed tracks, happy to have something to do on the drive back to the mall . . . but the truth was, I had only heard one Smashing Pumpkins song—the one that played constantly on the radio, the one that began "Today is the greatest day I've ever known." I didn't know any of the lyrics after that.

*

twenty-three

It was a cruel twist of fate. A cord slipped through my fingers and fell to the floor. I hopped off my stool and bent down to retrieve it, and on the way back up my forehead clunked against the metal band that rimmed the Formica table. Tears sprang to my eyes; I grunted to keep from yelping in pain. The blow didn't break the skin, so no blood gushed forth, but an unsightly purple-and-yellow bruise quickly appeared and spread outward as the day wore on, like a paper towel soaking up a spill, making the bruise I had self-inflicted a month ago seem minuscule by comparison. Joanna asked me if I wanted to go home, but I declined and said I was fine, it was just a bruise—and I needed the money. I reported that I hadn't slept the night before, which was certainly why I had misjudged the distance between my skull and the table. Joanna then seized on this revelation and warned me not to file for workers' comp. I sighed, rubbed my forehead, and winced. I would have to cancel with Patrick. I had no hair to hide behind, and no amount of makeup would conceal the damage. I knew this without seeing the bruise. I could feel it, and feeling it was worse . . . although I kind of liked the pounding throb of pain beating against my skull and hoped it might make the day go by faster. But no. Pain never makes things go faster. Pain makes things slow down.

Becky asked me if I wanted some of her Tylenol and dug into her bag, pulling out the pill bottle along with a compact. She flipped the compact open, reached across the table, and held it out until I finally took it. First I saw the fluorescent lights reflected in it, but then I saw my face, saw my bruise, saw my ugliness. I popped two Tylenol, turned my back to the table, and continued plugging. "Shit," I whispered.

"Yup," Becky said sympathetically. "That bruise is *butt-ugly.*"

"It's not *that* bad," George said without conviction.

My head spun. It felt like it should have felt when I'd actually banged myself. A delayed reaction. I put my cord down and held my head gently, elbows resting on the table. How could things get any worse?

"Either go home or get back to work," Joanna said dispassionately.

It was my birthday. I searched for my time card and punched out. It was noon.

My breathing felt light, like it might trail into nothingness in a few short minutes. Patrick answered on the second ring.

"Hi," I said, forcing my tongue to form words. "I can't make it tonight. Sorry."

"Why not?" he asked.

Let the facts speak for themselves. "Because I hit my head on a table at work."

"You have a headache?"

"Well, yes, it's very sore."

"I bet it's nothing a few beers won't cure. I'll bring a six-pack along."

I laughed—laughed a little too loud, a little too long. "I can't. I have a terrible bruise right in the middle of my fore-head."

"Well . . . you know . . . we *could* just meet at the cemetery? That way no one will see you at the mall. And, come to think of it, they won't have to see *me*, either. I scare people. Trust me."

I laughed again. I had expected him to say "Okay," but right now it felt like he really wanted to see me. Maybe he was starting to care? It was just a bruise. Ugly, yes, but superficial.

"I'm just going to warn you, then," I said, borrowing the term from Becky and regretting it the moment I parted my lips: "I am *butt-ugly*."

He surprised me: He laughed.

I laughed.

We laughed together.

I dabbed foundation on my bruise and blended, but the sickly mark was undeterred and seemed to take on an even uglier tinge beneath the flesh-colored makeup. I backed away from the mirror, hoping it would be less noticeable at a distance, but if anything it was more so. It was like a bull's-eye, the center of the half-dollar-sized bruise a deep purple and the rim a putrid yellow. But I had said I would go.

I pulled a sweatshirt on, left the safety of my room, and entered the kitchen, where my father and brothers Phil and Adam were sitting down to dinner. My mother was at work. Phil and Adam whistled, predictably, when they saw me. I spooned out a dinner of mashed potatoes and broiled chicken as they tore me down, one insult at a time, seemingly in honor of my birthday. I couldn't fake-laugh as I normally did and stiffened under the weight of their infantile assaults.

"Shut up," my father demanded, waving a finger at them before turning his attention back to me. "What time will you get back?" he asked, a slight whine edging his voice to indicate his displeasure with me for borrowing his vehicle *yet again*.

"A little late," I replied. "I'm sorry, Dad, but this time it's really important."

"I bet," Phil rejoined. "I bet it's for something *real* important."

I arrived first at the graveyard and parked on the graveled turnout. I left the truck running to stay warm, then decided it was better to be cold than waste precious gas that I would only have to replace. I buttoned my corduroy coat up, put my hands in my pockets, and tried not to think about my stark fear as I helplessly studied the tombs and graves lit eerily by the moon. If Patrick wanted to make this a regular routine—meeting here rather than at J.C. Penney's—I wouldn't agree to it. No. That would be too much to ask. I shivered and jumped when I heard what sounded like footsteps. My breath quickened and I told myself, again and again, that it was my mind playing tricks on me. I double- and triple-checked that the doors were locked; I glanced repeatedly into the cab behind me to comfort myself that it was empty. But my nerves stayed alert, terrified, and I couldn't resist the idea of a serial killer arriving, or a rapist, or a gang of bored young men. I noticed empty beer bottles beside a grave. Was this where locals came to get wasted? What would they do if they discovered me? The trees were bare, the slabs of stone black and icy in the night. I tried to beat back the creeping dread I always felt before seeing Patrick—a dread I tried to tell myself was nothing more than nerves, resulting from excitement and love . . . if not love *from* him, then at least *for* him. But there was another, more powerful dread right then, and it had nothing to do with him and everything to do with death itself.

He was late. Glancing at my watch for the fiftieth time, I calculated that he was exactly thirty-seven minutes overdue. How could he be late? If it were the mall I could understand, but he was late to a *graveyard*. How . . . awful. My feet, warmed by a thin pair of socks and black lace-ups, went numb, and I wriggled my toes in an effort to create heat. *Maybe he won't show up,* I thought, suddenly horrified. *Maybe he never intended to come at all.* I considered starting the truck up, if only to heat the cab for a minute, but resisted. *It's colder in Russia*, I thought, thinking of my studies for the first time in ages, *and I bet it was much colder when Rasputin was tossed into the river to die.*

The glare of headlights flashed across the gravestones and I twisted the key in the ignition, heart pumping, ready to peel out if it was anyone other than Patrick. When I determined a moment later that it was, indeed, a black Saab approaching, I relaxed a touch and removed the key. My hands shook as I tried in vain to make a few last-minute touch-ups: I maneuvered my headband atop my cowlick and put on a coat of cotton-candy-pink lipstick. I unbuttoned my coat to expose my cleavage and disregarded my erect nipples poking my shirt in the cold. My bruise was ugly, but not so noticeable in the dark. I climbed out and ran to sink into the shadows of his car.

It was warm and reeked of pot inside. Patrick smiled at me with unfriendly eyes and pointed to my feet: A Budweiser six-pack was wedged under the seat. "For you," he said benevolently. "I've brought my own beer for myself."

I smiled with an eagerness that was humiliating but which I couldn't suppress. I snapped a beer off of its plastic manacle, flipped back the tab, and took several gulps as we listened to the same Smashing Pumpkins CD as the night before, the volume low. I began to drink faster, finishing my first beer and opening another as Patrick put back a tall bottle of Colt 45. I became aware of how loud my swallows sounded; each time I gulped I glanced at him to see if he had noticed and been disgusted by my thunderous slurps. I had to say something . . . I had to distract him. He was wearing an orange T-shirt under his jacket, and, with the help of my beer, I asked if he'd worn orange in tribute to pumpkins.

"What the fuck are you talking about?" he asked.

"Pumpkins," I said quietly, forcing my lips into a smile as I pointed at the stereo display. "You know . . . Smashing *Pumpkins?*"

He didn't respond, and he definitely didn't laugh. I considered saying I was "butt-ugly" in hopes of pleasing him, but a joke told more than once never elicited genuine laughter, only contempt.

Instead, I giggled.

"What?" Patrick demanded.

I offered a pitiful shrug of my shoulders as he glared at me with what appeared to be complete dislike. It was his first direct look since we'd met and his eyes settled on my bruise, reminding me of my appearance, but also of the dull throb beating against my skull, and for a second I thought I was having an aneurism.

"I have a headache," I said suddenly, finishing off my third beer. "Maybe I have a concussion or something."

"It'll pass." He shrugged. "But we definitely made the right call to meet here instead of at the mall. No offense."

He turned the volume up and music blared from the car's speakers. I pressed my hands against my ears. The pounding in my head grew worse, and a wave of nausea radiated through my stomach and gave me that swimming, dizzy feeling that precedes a release: I leaned my head back, I drew in a deep breath, I swung my door open, and I vomited, my puke splattering all along the side of his car.

"Jesus Christ!" he shouted angrily. He got out and walked over to see how dirtied his car had been made. I got out, too, but stayed a few feet away, like a dog that had just misbehaved. I drank from my beer to rid the taste in my mouth and sank down onto my haunches. I tried to think of how I could amend what I had done, but nothing came to me. I wanted to flee, to cry, to do or say something, but all I could do was stare at the ground with a feeling of flatness, of frozen inertness.

"Fuck it," he said after a minute with a shrug.

We got back into the car and I began apologizing, profusely. "It came out of nowhere," I pleaded. "I'm just not feeling well."

"Clearly," he said tersely. Then, more kindly: "Sorry. It's just that I washed my car yesterday. But, hey, don't worry about it. I'm glad you opened the door."

He lifted the armrest between us and took out a plastic bag filled with pot and quickly rolled a joint. He inhaled deeply and handed it to me. It hurt, but I held the smoke in for as long as possible before letting it seep out. I hoped the high would alleviate my humiliation, but if anything I soon felt worse: The smell of my vomit suddenly engulfed the car. I glanced at him; I thought I saw his nostrils flare and presumed that he, too, was bowled over by the smell. My migraine began to throb with increased pain. A cluster of nearby trees, lit by the moon, looked like an immense, sinister monster, their branches reaching out toward the car, toward me. I shrank into my seat and rubbed my eyes, refocusing until all I saw was the forest, the blackness filling the gaps between and behind the tree trunks.

He gestured to the backseat. I smiled, amazed that he wanted to have sex, given my vomit and the unmistakable hatred I had seen in his eyes. I shrugged off my coat and climbed between the two front seats; I kicked off my shoes and pulled off my pants, noticing, as I did, the journal I had given him wedged under the front seat. Then I lay back and waited for him to open the door at my feet, waited for him to climb into me—an event that took place quickly and ended soon thereafter. I tilted my head back slightly and looked out the window above me as he drew in, drew out. I should have felt worse than I did. Tears should have been streaming down my face. That's what would have happened if my life were a movie. But I didn't feel like crying. I didn't feel, actually, much of anything. I felt drunk, I felt high, but other than these drug-induced conditions, my emotional state remained frozen.

Afterward, I dressed quickly, maneuvered myself into the passenger seat, placed my hand on the door handle, and began pulling it toward me, began opening the door to leave, then hesitated. There was something to say now. There was something to talk about. I looked at him and relaxed into the seat, my apathy helping me along.

"What?" he asked, glancing at his watch.

"Do you remember," I asked spontaneously, "when we met? At the library?"

"Yes," he replied, checking his watch again. "Why?"

"Why did you talk to me?"

Silence.

"I don't know. I thought you were cute. I don't know what you're—"

"It's just that," I interrupted quietly, "maybe we shouldn't . . . do this anymore."

"What do you mean?"

"I mean, it's just . . . sex. You know?"

He looked at me, looked out the windshield, looked back at me again. "There's just one more semester," he said with resignation. "We might as well keep meeting until we finish. I'll be going to New York after graduation, anyway."

"Oh," I replied, as if he had just explained exactly why we should continue meeting and screwing. "But," I continued, my apathy melting with the trembling of my bottom lip, "you don't even like me."

He didn't answer, but he shifted in his seat uneasily.

"We'll just keep meeting until graduation." He shrugged.

Anger. Anger flickered somewhere deep inside. "Don't . . . shrug," I said impulsively, my voice dropped low.

"What?" he said.

I drew in a long breath. "Why . . . why were you late tonight?" I asked stiffly, the anger rising, rising, rising.

"Was I?" he shrugged again. "Sorry. I had a few things to do before I left."

"I'm in a graveyard," I said steadily, anger contained, erupting slowly, slowly, slowly, "And you were *forty-five* minutes late."

"Jesus," he snapped. "You're going to give me shit?"

Fingernails, digging into palms. "I'm afraid of cemeteries," I said, my voice intensifying, expanding. "I *told* you that. And do you want to know *why* I'm afraid of cemeteries?" I asked, shaking, shaking, shaking. "My brother is IN one. *That's* why. My brother fucking KILLED HIMSELF, you fucking, fucking, FUCKING *DICK*!"

I got out of his car—his shiny black Saab—and slammed the door. I backed away: one step, two steps. I watched him prepare to leave as I reached, reached, reached to the ground and lifted a football-sized rock over my head, hurling it, a moment later, at the shiny car, aiming for the windshield. The rock cracked the glass and thin lines spread across the windshield in several directions as my makeshift weapon rolled onto the hood and then to the ground. And then I, myself, was on the ground, beating it with my fists as a deep, mournful scream shook my body and pierced the stillness, the silence, the blackness of the night.

Patrick knelt beside me a moment later. "Stop screaming!" he yelled, trying to restrain my flailing arms. "What the *fuck* did you do that to my car for?"

"All you do is *FUCK ME*!" I yelled, my voice even louder, booming and shrill. "And I *LET* you! I fucking *LET YOU*!"

"Okay. You're crazy," he laughed as he backed away. "This has been a total waste of my fucking time. You should pay for my goddamned windshield, but I'm not going to make you because that would mean *seeing you again*."

He got back into his car and drove away, heading off to his home—his large suburban home in the good part of Connecticut, the place where families don't bother to cut coupons or think twice about filling up their vehicles with premium-grade gas—where his mother was like June Cleaver, his father like Ward, only smarter. I continued to scream and pound the earth until my rage subsided and slowly, slowly, slowly, my sanity returned. When I had spent myself, I rolled onto my back and stared up at the night sky, chest heaving, for one, two, three minutes. Then I crawled to my feet, climbed into my truck and sat on the cracked tan leather. I found my keys and squeezed them tightly until the metal chafed and made me wince. The fear I'd felt earlier at being in a cemetery was gone, and I viewed the graves and epitaphs ahead of me blankly, as if I were instead looking at nondescript rocks rather than tombstones. My anger, too, was gone, but the emotions replacing it were conflicted, confusing, unclear. There was relief, but rising up and above that was a deeper, thicker distress than even I was used to.

What had I done?

My hands and feet were numb and my breath plumed out before me in a frosty cloud. I started the engine and began driving along the blackened road. It was one o'clock in the morning and it seemed like I was the only one on the worn, potholed street. When I got to the highway, I moved into the right lane to travel north toward my town, but at the last second I swerved into the left and went south. I just wanted to see where Patrick lived. And maybe I wanted to see him, too. Maybe I wanted to talk to him. Maybe I wanted to take back my words, my behavior . . . everything. I pressed on the gas pedal and flew past exits until the one I wanted blazed green and white. It was crazy because I didn't know where he lived, but I knew his address, which I had gotten one night from information in one of my obsessive, longing deliriums, and memorized as if it were a captivating poem. I pulled into a 7-Eleven and asked the cashier, a string bean of a guy with Coke-bottle glasses, how I could find Harmony Road—imagine, a road called Harmony!—and the clerk actually knew and gave me easy-to-follow directions. I found the street, a dead end, within minutes, and as I drove along it, pins and needles pricked at my skin. I was excited and scared. Scared and excited. Each house I passed seemed more impressive than the one before. One had Roman columns; another, more modern, seemed to be built entirely of glass. I found Patrick's house at the end of the cul-de-sac, a two-story traditional with a big yard and big trees, number 550. My heart raced as I took in his black Saab glinting in the driveway, looking forbidding as it reminded me of all that had gone wrong, its cracked windshield giving it a menacing stance. I switched off my headlights, parked, and stared at the house, biting at my nails. The first story was brick-faced, the second story pale yellow. There were no lights on inside—even their Christmas tree, still up, was turned off—but a lamppost glowed bright near the front doorstep, and tinier lights lined a brick walkway leading up to the entrance. A white-latticed gazebo stood beside the house, surrounded by some sort of garden, and next to the gazebo there was a small pond that reflected the moon in its smooth surface. But the house, as beautiful as it was, was just a house. A house where Patrick happened to live. And I knew, with increasing certitude, that there was *no way* I was going to ring its doorbell. There was *no way* I was going to scream Patrick's name or beg to see him. The scene was as it was supposed to be: just there. The only thing *wrong* with the scene was that *I* was there, invading the calm with my internal calamity that infected no one but me. A dog suddenly started to bark, a large-sounding dog, and I spent a brief moment wondering if Patrick had ever mentioned a dog, but I knew if he had I would have remembered, because I would have cherished the name of the dog like a lover's secret, and as the barking grew more frantic, I started my truck up and zoomed away, eager to leave the place where Patrick lived. But as I drove along the dark street I dreamt up one last fantasy. As tears blurred my vision, I imagined plowing my little truck into a telephone pole in an explosive head-on collision, and all that would then follow: Patrick, flying out of his house, would see my vehicle in flames, would run to it, would try to get to me, but, finding me lifeless, would wail in disbelief and grief, would feel the worst sorrow possible. He would cry, he would realize . . .

I couldn't think of what he would realize.

And that was when I almost blew it all.

There was a real tree—*a real fucking tree*—straight ahead of me. It was a giant deciduous pine with a very thick trunk, and it threatened to make mincemeat of me in about two seconds flat. I flicked my wrist and tires screeched as I swerved, barely missing it, but miss it I did, coming to an abrupt standstill in the middle of the road. Tension buckled at my joints, making them steely and unbendable, as I understood something in a stark new way.

If you sought death, it found you.

My body began to shake. The air seemed to be leaving the cab. My mouth opened and I sucked, I gasped for oxygen, but there wasn't enough. I was suffocating. I found my voice and forced out words: "Help me."

No one came.

Somehow, I reapplied my foot to the accelerator and, after an hour and a half of steady driving (with a quick pit stop for gas), I finally pulled into my own driveway. My house, decrepit though it may have been, had never looked so good to me. I tip-toed inside and into my room, or into Jacob's room, and imme-diately removed the crucifix from the wall—the one that had lain on his casket—and buried it in the back of my closet be-neath a bag of clothes I had meant to donate years ago.

I fell onto my bed.

I left the light on.

I went to sleep.

twenty-four

How do you move on when you're in quicksand?

I stared at myself in the bathroom mirror. Dark, puffy circles sagged under my eyes, but internally I felt far worse. I felt stripped, hollow, barren, racked with nausea.

I was going through withdrawal.

I hopped in the shower and hurriedly washed, amazed that my body wasn't black and blue. How could everything ache so badly? I closed my eyes, wishing I didn't have to go to work, and yet happy that it provided me with something to fill the time with. The day stretched endlessly before me. Twenty-four hours of misery.

"What time did you get home last night?" my mother asked when I exited the bathroom. She was wearing a floral housecoat and faded pink slippers, and she looked older than usual, almost elderly.

"I don't know," I replied, pitching an apple into my lunch bag.

She fixed her eyes on me. "Have you been crying?"

She may as well have asked me if I had just masturbated, so invasive did I find the question. My heart closed up, like a fist, and when I said the word "no," it came out sounding vicious, like a growl. She took a step back.

"I don't want you staying out that late again," she said. "I don't care if it was your birthday. I was worried."

Her words made me want to laugh. If she only *knew* what my nights out had consisted of.

"You shouldn't worry," I said and slipped out the door.

The harsh fluorescent light pained my eyes and I wished I had sunglasses on instead of goggles. I rubbed at them and tried to focus on the plugs, but the colors mixed together, and I kept messing up by putting the white wire where the green one was supposed to be.

"What's wrong?" Becky asked after my third mess-up in a row.

Her question, innocent though it was, triggered tears to start sliding down my face, silently, one after the other. "Nothing," I replied, wiping at them frantically with my shirtsleeve.

"Doesn't look like nothing," George added.

I tried to smile but the tears came faster.

"It's a guy, isn't it?" Becky asked.

"Of course it is," Joanna said.

"Guys are *assholes*," Tara added.

"Hey!" George protested.

"Don't worry, George," Becky shushed. "You're not a *real* guy. To us."

Everyone at the table was looking at me, expectantly. I felt like I owed them an explanation. I felt like I had to say something.

"This guy . . . " I began.

"I knew it!" Becky interrupted.

". . . dumped me last night," I continued, my voice cracking. "Or maybe I dumped him, too. I'm not really sure. But I'm afraid it was a big mistake."

"Doubtful," Becky replied, throwing a finished plug in the middle of the table.

"Why do you say that?" I asked.

"This was the guy you've been 'dating,' right?" she demanded.

I nodded.

"Were you happy? 'Cause I don't see how you could be truly happy with someone who was dicking you around."

"How do you know . . ." I asked, letting the sentence drop off before completing it.

"Come on," she sighed knowingly. "It was *so* obvious."

My tears started to dry up. Fast.

"So," she asked again. "*Were* you happy?"

I thought about it. I shook my head.

"I rest my case."

I conceded the point, but I still felt sick. Infatuations don't just end. They die slowly, with great effort. Not picking up the phone to call Patrick that day and in the days that followed was a vicious struggle. My feelings kept me up at night with deranged, hysterical insomnia. I managed not to call him; I just wasn't able to stop thinking about him. And why not? I was good at thinking about him. So, I thought about him at work. I thought about him while watching TV. I thought about him in the car, while talking to my parents about the weather, and while sitting on the toilet. I imagined what I would say to him and how I would apologize. I imagined him calling *me* and putting an end to my agony. I imagined starting over. Again.

As the days passed and the phone remained painfully silent, I became more proactive. Whenever I felt myself going to that dark place, I played a game of solitaire, and it helped. It really did. It forced my mind to focus. King, queen, jack, ten . . . there was an order that had to be followed. Even my job as a plugger forced me to think basic, concrete thoughts: green, white, black, red, orange, blue, brown. This, too, helped. It pushed Patrick to the periphery. He was still there, but blurry.

And then life began to intrude, as it must. Faith called me out of the blue one day. We spoke for an hour, or, as usual, *she* talked, filling me in on the latest details of her life. Keith had proposed on Christmas morning, she had said yes, and would I please be her maid of honor? I resisted an impulse to offer my condolences and readily agreed, and met her one Saturday to help her find the perfect wedding dress—a simple white sheath that made her glow—and within two weeks she had tied the knot after finding a justice of the peace in the Yellow Pages. Then, another day, I randomly decided to call Gwen. I got her home number from information and phoned her, divulging what had transpired with Patrick. Unloading the sordid details made them lighter somehow, easier to carry. She, herself, had broken up with Noah, and it was both surprising and a relief to find out that she, too, battled her own insecurities around love (she was prone to jealousy and could hold a grudge for an eternity).

Days began to roll by, each *slightly* less torturous than the one before. TV helped. Books did, too. I stopped playing solitaire all the time, and this, I thought, was a positive step toward recovery. But recovery from *what*? A broken heart?

Absolutely not. It had never been about hearts or love or sex. It had never been about the *guy*. Period.

"Natalie," my mother called, "come watch *Jeopardy* with us. It's the *college* edition!"

Ever since my rock-bottom night with Patrick, and in spite of turning twenty-one, I had become my parents' child again, joining them each evening for a rock-block TV marathon that began with game shows, moved on to prime-time sitcoms and nighttime soaps, and finished with the nightly news and late shows (I preferred Letterman, Dad liked Leno). Neither of them had inquired about this new routine or questioned the thick, devastating silence that surrounded me. I knew that after my mother had innocently asked me if I had been crying, the morning after my apocalypse, she had at least suspected something sad had transpired with a "boy," but she carefully side-stepped my sadness while still warning my brothers to let me be (which I appreciated).

I closed the book I was reading, rolled off my bed, and opened my bedroom door.

"Oh, good." She smiled. "Quick, it'll start in just a minute."

I followed her into the den and took my assigned seat at the foot of the couch. As the contestants were introduced, I glanced up at the mantel, noticing Jacob's high school graduation photo, the only photo of him that still remained on display. Then, without really thinking about what I was doing, I got up and stood in front of it and studied his face, impressed by how handsome he had looked for the shot. He wore a 1960s-style brown suit with white stitching along the seams, a white oxford shirt and a red tie. He was smiling, and it looked like a real smile, happy and warm.

"What are you doing?" my mother asked uncomfortably from the couch.

"Looking at Jacob," I replied, unnerved by his name passing my lips.

"Oh," she replied, letting the sound fade into silence. A moment later: "Look—one of the categories is American History. I bet you'll get all of those."

My father told me to quit blocking the TV, and I retook my seat at the foot of the couch. I tried watching Alex Trebek for a moment or two, but none of his words registered. A weighty silence filled the room, and when a commercial break began I got up to leave.

"He would have turned thirty-one in November," my mother blurted out. I looked at her, saw her eyes grow moist, saw her bite her lip to keep from letting a sob out.

"I'm sorry, Mom," I said.

She waved her hand at me as if she were shooing away a fly and then brushed away the few tears that had dripped out of her eyes. "Look," she said, pointing at the television eagerly, "it's back on. I hope the girl in the middle wins."

My father cleared his throat. "Me, too," he agreed.

There were things much sadder than me.

I sat back down, I watched the show, and that was that. This may seem anticlimactic, but . . . had I pressed my mother to talk about Jacob and she *had* opened up, right then and there, and told me everything she remembered about him—would that have made him any more real to me? No. I could collect the bits and pieces of his life and store my fractured memories in my brain, but I would never see him for who he was or who he could have become . . . And that was okay. Jacob had made a choice. He had sought death and it had claimed and absorbed him. It wasn't up to me to remember him, because he wasn't mine to remember. I may not have been entirely aware of this as I sat staring into the blue glow of the television set, but it was beginning to sink in.

*

twenty-five

"There's the information booth," my mother said as we turned into campus, pointing out each site like a tour guide. "And there's the duck pond. Look at all the ducks!"

"Never mind them—look at all the damn kids!" my father chuckled. "What I wouldn't *give* to feel young like that again."

I smiled and undid my seat belt. It was the start of spring semester—my last semester at UConn—and I felt like I'd come full circle: still damaged goods, but ready to reacquaint myself with anal-retentive compulsions. I had even gotten my books ahead of time and begun reading them, determined to raise my GPA back up to its former lofty heights. But as I stared out at all of the students hanging out, greeting one another, my old panic slipped back. It was strange to return to a place where Patrick was. I felt my mind drifting toward him. What if we bumped into each other? What if he came to see me? What if . . . I kept asking myself, *What if?* I shook my head, ordering myself to shut up. We *weren't* going to see each other, and that was great. I reminded myself that he was an asshole. I reminded myself that if we had had anything left to say to one another, it would have been said. I just didn't want any surprises. But I got one, anyway.

While my parents parked, I took the elevator up to the seventh floor and went to my room, but when I entered I blanched: A girl was sitting at Faith's desk. She had long, pin-straight brown hair and looked far less surprised than me.

"Hi," she said, standing up. "Are you . . . Natalie?"

I nodded.

"I'm Jennifer," she said. "I guess we're . . . roommates."

"I thought I was going to have my own room," I stated bluntly.

"Yeah, well," she replied with a dimpled smile, "tough luck."

I smiled back. Dimpled people always seem friendlier, somehow. She was dressed casually in jeans and a black sweater, but there was something edgy about her. A tiny diamond stud glittered in one nostril, and she had lined her eyelids with a black liquid that gave her an Egyptian, Cleopatra-like look. She walked to the window and picked up Faith's old purple ashtray. "Please tell me you don't smoke," she said.

"No," I stuttered. "I mean, I did, but I never *really* did. I mean, I sometimes do. Did."

"Are you telling me you never inhaled?" she laughed.

I reddened but grinned. "Something like that."

"Anything else you don't do that I should know about?"

"I don't . . . snore," I offered.

"Excellent," she said. "Then I won't pick my nose in front of you."

We laughed, and I knew that something different had begun. My parents came up a few minutes later and Jennifer was overly polite and friendly, and after they left we talked some more. Like me, she was a history major, although her focus was on Latin America, but we came from totally different backgrounds. She was from Guilford—that lush green suburb filled with golden retrievers and sprawling backyards—but I found myself not caring too much because it seemed like *she* didn't care. She had money and I didn't. She was an only child and I wasn't. She was an extrovert and I was an introvert. Ironically, at twenty-one she was a virgin and, of course, I no longer was. But it was okay, and I was more or less uninhibited as we talked—whether it was a discussion about the best way to eat a sundae or about our places in the infinite universe. I told her about Patrick and Jacob, I warned her about Sasha, I even ended up talking about Jack. Our conversation flitted from one subject to another, without any apparent order or rationale, but always effortlessly, without apprehension.

I, Natalie Bloom, had made a friend.

"Why would you switch roommates for your last semester?" I asked.

"I spent the fall in Guatemala," she replied, "studying *español* and all things Mayan. While I was away, my old roommate got a boyfriend and moved off campus."

"Wow," I breathed, genuinely impressed. "What was *that* like?"

"You mean, was I pissed that she ditched me?"

"*No,*" I said. "*Guatemala.*"

A rhapsodic look came over her face. "It was heaven," she sighed.

For the next hour she told me about her travels—from the villages she had stayed in to the intense beauty of the country. Her Spanish had vastly improved and, after graduation, she intended to return to hone her language skills even more.

"You're so brave to do something like that," I said.

"No," she replied, "just really, really lucky."

Sasha's new roommate stood next to me in the bathroom, brushing her teeth. She had the misfortune to have severe acne, giant bifocals, *and* silver braces. On top of all this, she was overweight and had hair the color of mud. I wondered if she was a freshman, which would be odd since Sasha was a senior, like me, but her metal-mouth made her look prepubescent. I wondered if Sasha was being kind, and since I was sure she was not, I felt bad for her. This, then, made me do something I had never before done.

"Hi," I said, introducing myself. "I'm Natalie. My room's next to yours."

She smiled through a mouthful of toothpaste, the green scum of which dribbled over her chin. "I'm Lee," she gurgled after spitting out. "Nice to meet you."

I tossed my paper towel into the garbage can and went to leave, but as Lee went back to scrubbing her teeth, a shell-shocked look on her face, I paused. Maybe Lee didn't need a friend, maybe she was handling her transition with Sasha just fine . . . but I knew that if I was in her position, I'd be a wreck.

"Sasha's okay," I said. "Don't let her scare you."

Lee wiped her mouth with a paper towel and then burst into tears—messy tears that quickly led to loud, honking nose-blows. I was surprised and not sure what to do, so I just stood there and asked her if I could do something, anything.

"I just," she stuttered, "I just . . . I just . . . I just . . ."

"Take a deep breath," I suggested.

"I just *don't like her*," she wailed. "She's so . . . *mean*. I'm going to Housing tomorrow to switch out. I think I might sleep in the lounge tonight."

Just as I was about to tell her that that was probably a good idea, Sasha came in, dressed in a black minidress and stiletto boots.

"What's wrong, Lynn?" she asked in faux horror, winking at me. "Did someone take away your candy? You should see her chocolate stash, Natalie. *That* should be illegal to keep in a dorm room."

Lee swallowed her tears and looked stricken. My heart began to beat wildly with fear and anger as I built myself up to say something.

"Her name's Lee," I said, stunned that the words in my head had found their way out.

"Whatever," Sasha replied, ogling herself in the full-length mirror, forgetting us completely.

"Stuff it, Sasha," I said.

Sasha and Lee both looked at me, jaws dropped. *Stuff it?* I thought incredulously. *Is that the best you can do?* My hands began to tremble, my guts entered my throat as everything in me told me to run. But I forced myself to stand still. I waited for Sasha to shove me, I waited for her to cripple me with a dagger-like observation, but instead she just looked me up and down and then resumed admiring herself in the mirror.

"Whatever." She shrugged. "Hey—what do you guys think of this dress?"

Lee looked at me as if Sasha had just spoken in code, which, in a way, she had.

"It's great," I lied.

"I love it," Lee blurted.

"I know," Sasha agreed, yanking at the neckline to show off more cleavage. "I *know*."

I slipped out, unnoticed, now, by both Sasha *and* Lee, who had tentatively stepped closer to Sasha and was saying something about how the dress made Sasha look like a model, causing a beaming smile to glow on Sasha's face. When I returned to my room Jennifer was already asleep, and it was odd to see a mass of loose brown hair where Faith's stiff blond hair had always been. I dressed for bed and, as was my ritual, stood before the full-length mirror. I applied some Clearasil and plucked a few errant hairs from my brows—a necessity ever since that first plucking. Then I removed my cream-colored headband, put it back on my head, removed it, put it on, removed it. My cowlick had all but disappeared, and my hair, while still short, was lengthening, even if it was in that awkward, in-between stage. But I looked older without the headband. I looked better.

I snapped the plastic band in half, then tossed it, where it clattered at the bottom of my garbage can. Jennifer groaned. I whispered, "Sorry," and then climbed into bed, happier than I'd been in ages.

Life, for the most part, went back to normal: The pre-Patrick normal where studying took up all of my time and evenings were spent at the library—fourth floor, same carrel—although a few key changes had taken place. I now had someone to eat with in the cafeteria, and occasionally Jennifer even joined me at the library. But the biggest change, by far, happened on Friday nights, but *only* on Friday nights, since I allowed myself just one night of depraved activity per week.

"We're going to a party in Terry Hall," Jennifer announced the very first Friday of the semester, over lunch, beginning it all. "I heard about it in my sociology class."

"I don't . . . think so," I said, still determined to be the person I used to be, more or less single-mindedly focused on my GPA. "I should probably study."

"So study before we leave!"

I nodded, despite my inner voice telling me to be firm on the matter. We returned to our room and, after reading quietly for a few hours, Jennifer finally slammed her own text closed and said, "*Vámonos.*"

So we went. Two full floors of the dormitory were in darkness except for the purplish glow of black lights, which illuminated not just your teeth but also your undergarments if you happened to wear the wrong clothes. Luckily, my own remained hidden beneath my heavy black sweater. It was almost impossible to move down the halls, though, so packed were they with people, their hormones almost visibly on display. Pulsating dance music deafened. We were handed two red plastic cups of beer and sloshed them down, and then we returned for more, and then more, and more. Within an hour, two guys had cozied up to us, but all I remember is that they both had dark hair and seemed somewhat muscular in their white T-shirts. Fast-forward to the next hour, when Jennifer began making out with her guy, and then I, too, began sucking face with my suitor. Finally, people began dispersing, and so did we, providing fake names and phone numbers to our inebriated partners.

And so began our Friday-night hookups. Instead of shying away from them, I began to look forward to them and eagerly went. With Jennifer by my side, I tackled all those college experiences I had been missing, collecting them haphazardly—never quite certain if I was truly enjoying them or simply doing them, like mandatory homework. There were the occasional late-night hot-chocolate moments, but so much of the college experience, after all, revolves around booze and its not-so-pretty baggage. The rituals surrounding our Friday nights were sadly predictable: We'd get drunk, make out with strange guys who all, in my memory, looked exactly alike, and who gave kisses as wet as Biffo—tongues lolling, licking, lapping—and who never inspired the libido to move past neutral. Then Jennifer and I would walk home in the wee hours, get sick, and suffer through horrendous hangovers together. I'd generally feel guilt and remorse the next day; Jennifer wouldn't, claiming it was the last time in our lives we would behave so recklessly. And then, of course, Gwen and Jennifer had hit it off, so sometimes we were a threesome; and sometimes Gwen would bring along a friend or two, which made me feel like I was part of some impenetrable, beautiful clique. I'd pass lonely-looking girls and want to say, "Hey—it's not what it looks like," but, in reality, I knew that it *was* what it looked like. I had made friends. I could refer to people who knew me and actually seemed to *like* me, too. So, then, why did I feel the dread I imagine adulterers must feel as they live their lives clandestinely, fearing that each illicit kiss might be espied by the wrong person?

I'm not sure.

On some level, though, I missed being a dreamer. I missed the pursuit of my perfect Romeo. I was having a good time with Jennifer and Gwen, but drunken make-out sessions weren't exactly fulfilling, and I had a hard time treating them as cavalierly as my new friends seemed to. Yes, there was something "fun" about hooking up with random people that you would never see again, but it was "fun" in the same way that squeezing blackheads is fun. It was perverse fun. Ultimately, it was a waste of time. Yet I kept doing it. Every Friday night. Was it to prove my own attractiveness? Was it the safety of anonymity, where no feelings could be trampled upon? Or was it a desperate attempt to *feel* something again, after Patrick had so casually discarded me, like a used condom?

If so, my hookups failed in all of the above. I was still empty, still searching.

Still embarrassed.

Thankfully, not everyone knew of the Friday-night me. To Professor Anderson, for instance, I appeared to be my old self in his class: utterly prepared and able. Even Linda remained somewhat in the dark, but that was mostly because her own life had changed. No longer did she stop by unannounced or prattle on to anyone who happened to be standing near her. In fact, about two weeks after the semester had started, it struck me one day that I hadn't *seen* her since my return. Concerned, I walked down the hall to her room and knocked, realizing, ashamedly, it was the first time I had ever visited her. When she opened the door and saw me, she smiled with something like gratitude and dragged me inside. Her room had the same Monet print that I had displayed across one wall, and the rest of the decor was flowery, pastel. Linda, though, was not her usual made-up self. She wore puffy sweats, her face looked bereft without its glittery powder, and I smelled no vanilla in the room at all. She looked like she'd been crying.

"How was your break?" she asked, not pausing for me to reply. "And how do you like your new roommate? She seems nice. Kind of pretty, right? I heard she lived in Costa Rica or something. Does she have a boyfriend? I was kind of hoping you and I might room together this semester. How's Faith? I can't believe she dropped out and got married. Did you hear about how Sasha was arrested the other night? For a DUI? She didn't have to go to jail or anything, but she had to pay a HUGE fine."

Then, again not pausing, she filled me in on all of the details of her own life. Her parents had bought her a car for Christmas—a Honda Accord, teal with a gray interior. She and

Ian were still meeting secretly, and she hoped he would finally break it off with Samantha soon. He had promised her, and she believed him, but if he failed to do it she was okay with it because she had her eye on a new guy, someone named Billy who had just moved into the dorm and was hot, hot, hot. Oh, and she had been chosen out of hundreds, or possibly thousands, or maybe even tens of thousands of candidates for an internship at the Smithsonian in Washington, D.C.

"Isn't that exciting?" she finished, almost breathless.

"It is," I agreed.

She grew pensive and pulled at her hair. "I'm not sure if I should go, though," she said.

"Why not?"

"Well, I would really miss my family and friends. Besides, I have this fantasy that Ian and I will travel together after graduation. Maybe to Europe. We could get a Eurail Pass and backpack. Wouldn't that be cool?"

"But . . . I thought you just said he was still with Samantha? And that you have your eye on someone new?"

She shrugged as if these were irrelevant details. I was in no position to hand out advice, yet I did.

"Fantasies aren't real," I said.

She laughed, bitterly. "Ian sure *felt* real when he was with me last night."

I frowned. I considered telling her about my adventures with Patrick, but something held me back. For one thing, I didn't think she would hear a word I said, but for another, I simply didn't want to. Even though I had told Jennifer and Gwen some of what had happened, in general I wanted to bury the experience, stow it away, never look at it again. I shivered, willing the thought of him away.

"Do you want to go to the game on Saturday night?" I asked. "Jennifer was able to get a few tickets."

"Can't." She smiled. "Sam has to go home for the weekend, so Ian and I are going to go see a movie in Willimantic."

I paused. Linda had no idea how unhealthy her love life had become. Not only was a guy clearly using her, but there was a third party involved. Linda was a mistress *and* she was deceiving Samantha, someone she had once claimed was a friend. Anyone else would have despised Linda for this, but, after Patrick, I had lost all claims to moral superiority. If I were Linda, which wasn't too hard to imagine, I probably would have convinced myself that Ian was in love with me, that even though Samantha would be hurt, true love couldn't be denied. I didn't want to hear the lies that Linda was telling herself. I was eager to leave.

"Have fun," I said.

She nodded and told me to have fun, too.

I walked to class. Or, specifically, I went to Anderson's seminar, a special course dissecting the revolution that resulted in glasnost and perestroika—a fitting topic since I was now determined to approach my own life with more openness and less rigidity. When I had showed up on the first day, I had wondered if Anderson would greet me, but in his typical fashion he didn't comment on my appearance or show any reaction other than slightly raised brows. I was glad that he hadn't taken me aside and welcomed me back. It was what I expected of him.

When I reached the history building, I had a few minutes to spare and went to sit on my old favorite perch at the water fountain. It was a beautiful day. The sun was out, the sky was pure blue. It was cool but not freezing. Pleasant. I looked down at the pool of water and tried not to think about anything at all.

"Ms. Bloom."

I looked up, and there was Professor Anderson, dressed in a steel-gray suit and a red tie. I smiled and he sat down on the fountain's edge with me. He looked tired and, well, lonely, and I resisted an urge to ask him how he was.

"Have you thought about what you're going to do after graduation?" he asked.

I shook my head. I told him I thought I might work at the factory for the summer in order to save up some money.

"How would you like to work for me?"

"Excuse me?"

"I need an assistant. A researcher, if you will. I'm writing a book covering pre-Soviet Russia and I can think of no one better qualified to assist me."

I smiled, flattered. But then I realized something, and it hit me, hard.

"I'm sorry," I said with urgency. "But . . . no."

He looked surprised. Genuinely surprised.

"It's just that," I hurried, "I don't think I want to . . . stay here."

"You'd rather work in a factory?"

"No," I stuttered, "no . . . I guess . . . I guess I'm not sure

305

what I want to do. Would it be all right if I took some time to think it over?"

"Of course," he said, standing up and checking his watch. "We'd better get to class now."

I walked with him into the building, relieved—but from what I wasn't sure.

Another Saturday arrived, and I spent another day nursing a wicked hangover and ruing the previous night's activities. That morning I had told Jennifer that this was *it*—I was done having my face mauled by drooling boys who couldn't grow facial hair.

"What exactly is the big deal?" she'd asked, truly perplexed. "It's just *kissing*. It's harmless!"

"It isn't," I'd replied, Patrick lurking in my mind. "It's . . . *demeaning*. I feel disgusting today. I don't know how you *can't* feel disgusting."

It was our first argument. She told me I was being judgmental, and we volleyed back and forth, stating our cases while pleading with the other to see it from our own point of view. In the end I assured her that I in no way thought *she* was disgusting and even convinced her that any disgust I felt was for myself, alone. I blamed it on my Catholic upbringing—the perfect catchall excuse for feelings of guilt related to anything sexual. By late afternoon we were both feeling better and were excited and ready for a new night of fun.

I put on some mascara and stared at myself in the mirror as I prepared to go to the basketball game at Gampel Pavilion, the very arena I had walked past on countless evening treks to and from the library, listening to the roar of the crowd inside. The Huskies were playing Duke—and it was strange even to *know* this. It was even stranger to pull on a UConn sweatshirt, to wear my school colors—blue and white.

"Will you hurry up already?" Jennifer whined in a matching sweatshirt.

I smeared my lips with gloss and brushed my hair, pinning my bangs back with a blue bandanna, which made me look a little cooler than I actually was.

"Come *on*," she pressed. "They're waiting for us. The game is going to *start*."

We hurried down the hall to Gwen's room, where she and her friend Christina, a full-bodied Latina with silky hair and gold jewelry that glowed against her brown skin, were doing shots and appeared to be in no rush to leave. Jennifer threw up her hands and joined them on the floor, waving me to follow.

"We'll just do *one* shot," Jennifer insisted, "and then we *leave.*"

Peppermint schnapps. It tasted like a vodka candy cane— too sweet and too powerful to fully enjoy. We proceeded to do three each and then struggled to stand again and go out the door, flushed and giggling. McMahon was virtually next door to Gampel, so we skipped, arm in arm, to the arena, joining the throng of students who were also making their way inside. Bodies pressed close, but I felt insulated from the crowd by my friends, and I eagerly pushed forward along with everyone else.

Our seats were way up in the bleachers, but we didn't care. We climbed up to the second-to-last row and filed in, Jennifer and Gwen dancing along to the music blaring throughout the place, urging everyone to get excited for the game. I clapped along, but there was no way I was going to dance. Within minutes the two teams poured onto the court and the crowd went wild. It was contagious. I started yelling, too, even though I had no idea what was going on. I had wondered if I would find the game boring since I had never watched one before, but it was anything but. I found myself hollering with glee whenever the Huskies scored; I found myself booing every time Duke scored. It built to a crescendo when the two teams were tied, and overflowed to bursting when UConn won with a basket just seconds before the final horn sounded.

It was more than just fun. It was important.

And then I ran into him. Not Patrick. Jack.

He was right in front of me as we pushed our way back outside, and all it would have taken from me was a slight tap on the shoulder to get his attention. Jennifer spotted him and nudged me, not realizing I knew him, and I smiled at her, agreeing with my eyes that, yes, he was very good-looking. When he disappeared with his friends, I admitted to her that it was Jack, the guy I'd told her about.

"You're kidding me, right?"

I laughed and looked away.

"Let me get this straight," she said. "That totally hot guy asked you out. You said no. And now you're single and you didn't even say *hello*?"

I nodded.

"*Why?*" she shouted. "What the hell do you have to lose?"

"He probably has a girlfriend by now." I shrugged.

"True," Jennifer agreed. "But what if he doesn't?"

I frowned, thinking that it didn't matter if he did or did not have a girlfriend. Noncommittal hookups were one thing, but Jack was something else entirely. "After Patrick," I explained, vaguely, "I'm done with men."

"Yeah, right," Gwen laughed, joining in.

Christina, Gwen's friend, suddenly ran ahead of us. "Come on!" she yelled. "Let's go to Carriage House! I heard there's going to be a huge party there tonight."

I flushed and glanced at my watch. Carriage House was the off-campus apartment complex where Patrick lived. Just as I was about to offer an excuse as to why I couldn't go, Jennifer squeezed my arm. "You won't see him," she whispered in my ear. "And if you do, you'll ignore him. And anyway, *we're* with you. We'll protect you. I swear it."

I resisted a bit more, but halfheartedly, and before I knew it we were there. Hundreds of students filled the dead-end street, drinking, making out, smoking cigarettes and joints. Gwen found a keg line and we followed, blindly. Then we drank, just as blindly. Then we scoured the scene for attractive guys, but none were found. I kept glancing toward Patrick's unit, which was in total darkness. I searched for his black Saab, but it was gone.

Then I got very, very drunk.

The next thing, or the next thing I *remember*, I was kissing some dirtbag, a beefy guy with acne and a prematurely receding hairline. Never had I let any of my hookups have roaming hands, but with him, I allowed him to grope and cop more than a few feels. He gave me a hickey so large I was certain it was the size of his fat head. So flagrant and obscene did we become, in fact, that Jennifer, Gwen, *and* her friend, Christina, finally pried me away from the dirtbag with real force, telling the guy to shove it as he protested.

"What are you doing?" Jennifer asked, clearly appalled.

"What?" I asked angrily, falling backward and hitting my butt, hard, on the pavement. "*What?*"

"Let's go," she said, and as we walked back to McMahon, I sobbed, I cried, I despised. Oh, and I vomited into a trash can outside our dorm . . . and it was at that point that we bid adieu to Gwen and Christina, who looked relieved to be free of me.

"I'm sorry," Jennifer whispered once we were back in our room. "We never should have gone there. I feel so stupid."

I climbed up to my bunk and buried my face in my pillow.

"Do you forgive me?" she asked. "Please?"

I grunted a noise that was supposed to mean "yes," but I couldn't bring myself to look at her.

"I get it now," she said, turning the lights off. "I get it."

And although it was a Saturday night, that was how my Friday-night hookups came to an abrupt end.

The big question remained: If I didn't want noncommittal hookups and I was done with men, then what *did* I want?

I didn't know, but I wanted something. It didn't have to be a fantasy, but it also didn't have to be disgustingly real. It could be something else.

It could be . . . friendship?

Yes, friendship, I lied to myself as I sat staring at the student directory on my lap about a week later. There was his name and number: Jack Auburn, Brock Hall, 466-3230.

"I'm Going to the Lounge to Study," Jennifer announced purposefully and slipped out, and after another moment's hesitation I dialed.

"This is Jack," a voice said.

"Do you always answer the phone that way?" I asked, the words flying out of my mouth uncensored.

"What way?"

"By . . . saying your name instead of hello?"

"Yes," he replied factually. "It saves time. People always confuse me with my roommate. Who is this?"

"Oh. This is . . . my name is . . . Natalie Bloom. We were in a—"

"I know who you are," he cut in. "How are you?"

"Good," I said. "How's your . . . frat?"

He laughed. "I guess you haven't joined a sorority, huh?"

I smiled. "I haven't dyed my hair blond, no."

"I think it's time you experienced a different *kind* of frat, Natalie. Are you busy Friday night?"

My pulse sped up. "I am," I said. "But do you run?"

"Run?"

"Yeah, like on roads and trails and paths. Like for health."

"Not . . . typically. But I *can* run. Are you asking me to go running with you?"

I gulped. "Yes."

"When?"

"Maybe right . . . now?"

"*Now?* It's seven-thirty at night!"

"Oh. So . . . you can only run in the daylight?"

He laughed. "You live in McMahon, right?"

"Yes."

"I'll meet you in the lobby in twenty minutes. Peace."

I hung up, shocked, then told myself not to stress, because I was only pursuing a *platonic* friendship with him, and, as if to emphasize *how* platonic this friendship would be, I pulled on my large red hooded sweatshirt and baggy black sweatpants and re-sisted the urge to even *glance* into the mirror on my way out (well, maybe I glanced, but I didn't focus). I ran downstairs and sat at an empty table, waiting, and stood when I saw him climb-ing the steps outside.

"I'm sorry," I apologized when he opened the door, letting in a draft. "It's probably too cold out to run. It was a stupid idea."

He frowned, slightly. "It wasn't stupid. But we don't *have* to run. I just wanted to see you. How've you been?"

He sat down at the table and, after a moment's hesitation, I joined him. I smiled, weakly. "I've been okay. Good. What about you?"

And then he just dove in and started talking. He told me about a guy on his floor who had picked a fight with him over something silly—he was upset that Jack hadn't asked him to play poker one night and had felt excluded—but the fact was, Jack had thought the guy had gone to see his girlfriend and wasn't even around at the time of the card game in question. I, then, ended up telling him about how I had felt jealous when Gwen had gotten a boyfriend—but mostly about how I could be overly sensitive and—who knew?—maybe Jack's friend was sensitive in the same way.

"Why are you so sensitive?" he asked.

This question then moved us on to one of those heavy but exciting conversations where you hypothesize about "why you are the way you are," trading stories back and forth. Yes, it was self-indulgent on both our parts as we released biographical details and reported past wounds and present worries, but it was self-indulgent—decadent—in the best possible way. For the two hours or so that we shared the scraps of our selves, I learned more about him than I'd ever learned about Patrick. Even in the midst of our conversation I became aware of certain things: I wasn't perspiring heavily (my armpits stayed dry), nor was I overly tongue-tied or worried about saying the wrong thing. Was it that it *was* platonic? But no. Before he went back to his dorm he leaned in and kissed me. My heart fluttered, but in a different way than it had with Patrick. With Patrick there was always the sense that my heart might just give out and go into full-on cardiac arrest, but with Jack it just fluttered, like a whisper, hinting at something wilder, but something that would never cause me to, um, die. After he'd pulled away from the kiss, biting my bottom lip first, I looked at him, wondering what to say, and then I just said what was on my mind: "You're a good kisser."

"You, too," he said.

"Don't lie," I retorted.

Then he'd grabbed me, hard, and kissed me again, and we'd stood there, making out, for at least a half an hour, oblivious to passersby and the cold, impersonal lighting above us. It was nothing like my random hookups. It was nice. Better than nice. When he finally told me he had to leave, though, he said something that reminded me of Patrick, and it was like a blast of frigid air.

"I like you," he'd said.

I recoiled, and Jack saw it.

"What?" he asked, alarmed. "Did I say something wrong?"

My instincts told me to reply, "No, of course not," but I ignored them. "Why," I forced myself to ask, "do you . . . 'like' me?"

Instead of saying "I think you're cute," as Patrick had, or some other predictable line that really says nothing at all, he told me I was interesting. That may sound just as glib and pointless, but after Patrick had made me feel about as interesting as a steel-girded doorknob, I was relieved, and what's more, I *believed him*. He couldn't have cared less if I had read *Ulysses* or the Hundred Greatest Books Ever Written. He didn't care if I had acceptable bands like Nirvana in my music collection or embarrassing ones like Wham! And it wasn't because Jack was a dimwit. He was extremely well-read—his mother was a professor of literature, and he was doing a double major in law and statistics. He *was* smart. He just didn't make me feel dumb, or uncertain. Ever.

Jack became my boyfriend. My first boyfriend. He was sweet and generous and romantic . . . but here's my dirty little secret: It was harder to be with him, in some ways, than it had been to be with Patrick. Being with someone who *genuinely likes you* poses certain challenges for someone uncomfortable with intimacy. I kept expecting him to see me for what I was and to come to his senses. I kept expecting my own insecurities to rise up and ruin everything. I was quick to self-deprecate and to urge him to do things without me, but he persisted and, slowly, I grew comfortable with him.

Comfortable was foreign, but good.

After searching around for twenty minutes, I finally found the building I was looking for. It was so far on the outskirts of campus it might have been considered off-campus. I walked into an office in total disarray: Brochures and flyers and booklets were scattered all over the place, and posters of faraway places, many torn and not even centered, hung from the walls with yellow thumbtacks.

"Hello?" I called out into the empty room. "Is anyone here?"

An older woman popped her head out from around the corner. She wore tortoiseshell glasses, a tomato-red cardigan, and Birkenstocks. There was something comforting about her, like a kindergarten teacher.

"Yes?" she asked.

"I was just wondering," I stuttered. "I was just wanting . . . to get some information about studying abroad. In Russia."

"*Russia.*" She beamed. "How wonderful! It's always France or England. I can't remember the last time someone wanted to go to *Russia.*"

I smiled, feeling like I had answered a question correctly, and followed her into a smaller room in back. Her desk was as cluttered as the entryway.

"*Russia*," she repeated breathlessly, flipping through a file cabinet. "There are some *wonderful* programs there. Were you thinking Moscow? St. Petersburg?"

Hearing the names of those two cities spoken aloud, hearing her ask me about them in a way that made it seem perfectly feasible for me to actually *choose* one of those places to go and *live in*, made my hands start to tremble.

"I don't know," I managed to reply.

"What year are you?"

I told her I was about to graduate and asked her if it was too late to study abroad; she assured me it wasn't, so long as I could pay. I frowned. She, in turn, smiled.

"There are scholarships." She shrugged. "And you can apply for financial aid."

She gathered a pile of brochures and books for me to look through and sent me on my way. "Hurry," she said as she ushered me out. "The deadlines for this summer and next fall are just around the corner."

I walked back to the dorm, gripping the materials she had given me like contraband. I knew I had set something in motion and that it would keep moving forward if I allowed it to.

If I allowed it to.

I altered my course and went to see Jack. I knocked, he opened the door, and he looked . . . he looked . . . *delighted* to see me. We embraced, kissed, and fell onto his bed until he pulled away suddenly and whispered, earnestly, "I think I'm in love with you."

I answered, in a jokey voice, "I think I'm in love with you *more*."

He grinned and pushed me back onto the bed, moving his face downward.

"No," I pleaded, pulling at him to return to face level.

"Please?" he asked.

I sat up and crossed my legs. The semester was nearly over, and we'd come close to having sex—clothing had been shed, three bases had been covered—but each time he tried to slide home I'd stopped him at the last moment. I was afraid. It wasn't that I feared he would be like Patrick, or that I was in danger of spiraling out of control again; it was more that I was uncomfortable with his sincerity. Whenever we began to get intimate, he'd start saying sweet nothings into my ear, things like "You're so beautiful," or "I love being with you," and the truth is, I wanted him to zip it. I was worried that agreeing to intercourse might send him into Shakespearean soliloquies that I in no way could match, even if I'd wanted to, and I'd end up murmuring stupid safe things like, "You're nice," and "I like your hair," as I turned various shades of crimson, finally rolling out from underneath him with a slew of pathetic apologies. But beyond this, I wasn't quite sure what to make of my own physical pleasure. When he touched me, *down there*, I felt things I had never felt with Patrick, and certainly not with any of my hookups. My own arousal still seemed unsavory to me—gross, even—like the way a bruised, rotten banana makes you feel when you accidentally sink your fingers into its mushy flesh, and the idea of oral . . . no, no, *no*.

"I think you'll like it." He smiled.

I shook my head.

"I promise to stop if you don't."

I shook my head again, more vehemently.

"Close your eyes," he ordered.

I opened them, wide.

"Then you leave me no choice," he said, rummaging through a desk drawer until he located a set of handcuffs.

"Forget it," I said, standing to leave.

He bear-hugged me and moved me back to the bed. He clasped the cuffs around my wrists, and I let him. I squeezed my eyes shut, hard, and lay my head back on the pillow. Tears started to fall as my pants slipped over my hips, followed by my underwear.

"Stop," I said.

He didn't stop.

"*Please?*" I begged.

He kept going, and after a minute I relented, but I couldn't believe it, I couldn't believe I was allowing . . . I couldn't believe how . . . incredible it felt.

"Holy shit," I said.

Warmth spread throughout my body, filling it with happiness. Ardent, insane happiness. I gasped and bit my hand to keep from screaming.

So *this* is what it's all about, I thought.

"Did I lie?" he asked, coming up a moment later for a kiss and unlocking the handcuffs. I could smell myself on him, and though it wasn't as disgusting as I would have thought, I pulled his pillow over my face, embarrassed. I wasn't sure what to say or how to behave after experiencing something so new. The pleasure he had given me was so mind-bending that I was afraid if I moved or acknowledged it I might implode. For a few seconds I had had *zero* control, and it had been ecstasy. I was in shock. He kept trying to take the pillow away, but I held it, firm.

"Are you okay?" he asked, concerned.

I relaxed and let the pillow fall off my face, and nodded, eyes still shut. Then I realized what I was supposed to do. I sat upright.

"I'm sorry," I hurried, reaching for his zipper. "You must be waiting for me to . . ."

"No," he said quickly, pushing my hand away. "I'm fine."

"But . . . then . . . don't you want to, I don't know, brush your teeth? Drink some water? Or Listerine?"

He laughed. "In a minute."

I nodded and smiled. Then I told him I wanted to go to Russia.

.   .   .

It was *never* about the guy.

It was *never* about the sex.

It was *never* about love.

Really.

The sprawling lawns of campus were a dark, lush green as I walked slowly across the Student Union's open field toward my dorm. It was warm, and students ran about in shorts and sandals, tossing Frisbees and soaking in the late-May sun. I had just taken Anderson's final exam, and I had wanted to linger after class, but I was meeting Jennifer for lunch in the cafeteria and didn't want to be late. My backpack slipped off my shoulders and I pulled it back on as I passed two girls in bikinis, sunbathing, their skin slick and shiny with oil. I stared at them, openly, just as the guys passing by them did. Why not? They clearly wanted to be ogled, or else they would have chosen a less public spot. Still, seeing them was a reminder of sorts, and I checked my tank top to make sure I wasn't showing too much cleavage, and, of course, I wasn't. Not by a long shot. Some things had changed, some hadn't. I continued to be self-conscious, but there *were* moves in the right direction. A guy walked by me and smiled, and where once I would have averted my eyes, I actually smiled back. Then a girl walked past and said, "Hi," and I found myself saying "Hi" in return. Two girls grinned. A solo girl nodded. *Another* guy flashed his pearly whites and offered a cool-sounding "Hey." When had everyone become so damn friendly? Had they *always* been this friendly? Or was the sun warming people's moods along with the temperature? But then I overheard three girls lamenting their imminent graduation and their sadness that their time at UConn was ending, and, just like that, my own remorse settled in my throat. My days of traipsing across campus were over—that beautiful campus of green grass, ivied buildings, and cow-dotted fields that I had so longed to be a part of—and it seemed sad that they should be ending, then, when I finally *was* a part of it and had even built some friendships. I mean, I actually spent time with people *outside* the library, *my* library, my first true love. I eyed Homer Babbidge Library already with a nostalgic eye, zeroing in on the window where I had spent so many nights studying, but also dreaming, and I couldn't quite fathom that I would never sit there again.

But sadness, these days, no longer clung to me with a parasitic need. How could it? I was far too excited.

There was so much to do before I left for Russia in less than a week. For a full year! Anderson had helped me decide on a postgraduate program at St. Petersburg University, but it still seemed unreal. How *could* it be real? But all the paperwork was done, all the visas applied for, all the bureaucratic red tape lifted. It frightened me that my impending adventure would put me even further into crippling debt, but Anderson assured me that completing the program would open up otherwise closed doors afterwards, even more than if I'd chosen to labor over his book. And I had to admit: I couldn't wait to leave, to find a brand-new life in such a historically rich place. My only persistent regret about going was Jack, but he was off to an internship at a Stamford law firm for the summer, and then to law school in the fall. And, besides, I didn't want to live my life around him, or around anyone. If we were meant to be, later, we would be, and if we weren't, that was okay, too.

We weren't, as it turned out—my year in Russia turned into two years—but it really was okay. Other loves—both for him and for me—presented themselves. Good choices, bad choices, okay choices. Even, finally, the right choice, where I could finally speak comfortably of love.

This took a very long time.

A group of guys sat on a stone wall at the edge of the field, and as I approached, I scanned them absentmindedly. One of them, despite slouching, looked very tall, and before my brain made the connection my heart had already identified the person and stopped. Patrick. He was sitting in the middle and making the others laugh. I stopped in my tracks and did a U-turn, not wanting to be spotted, but it was too late. He called out my name and, when I didn't turn around, he ran to catch up.

"Hey," he said, tapping my shoulder. "Can I talk to you?"

I stopped as my hands began to shake. I had already done one of the things I had promised myself I would never do if we ran into each other, which was pause to talk. I looked at him and tried not to admit that I still found him attractive. He was wearing a gray T-shirt under a black windbreaker, and he had recently had a haircut that made him look younger, more innocent.

"Wow," he said, stuffing his hands into his pockets. "It's been a while, huh?"

I shrugged, nodded, and looked over my shoulder, itching to move on.

"I was going to call," he continued, "but . . . after what happened the last time . . . well, I just thought it would be better if, you know."

There were so many things to say in response. Too many. I ran my fingers through my hair, which was now almost to my shoulders. I crossed my arms and forced myself to look at him. "I do know," I agreed.

He seemed uncomfortable and glanced back at his friends. "I've thought a lot about what you said that night," he said, "and I'm sorry about . . . the cemetery . . . and your brother. To be honest it freaked me out being in a graveyard, too."

The reference to our secret meeting place and Jacob made my pulse quicken; my forehead furrowed into a deep frown.

"Just for the record," he continued, touching my shoulder gently before retrieving his hand, "I never *wanted* to be a 'dick,' as you put it. I guess I *was*, but I didn't *want* to be. You, like, shriveled up and acted like I was a god or something. I have way too much self-hatred to be anyone's god. And then," he teased lightheartedly, "don't forget—you tried to kill me with that rock."

I reddened and knitted my brows together even more. "I shouldn't have done that," I said. "I'm sorry I hurt your car."

"Don't worry about it." He shrugged. "It didn't cost that much to replace. Anyway . . . I was pissed at first, but, then, I don't know, I felt bad. I shouldn't have left you there like that. That was wrong of me."

I swallowed the urge to cry and shrugged. His kindness, his willingness to talk, was surprising. But I was unwilling to expose myself to him ever again. His gaze traveled over my body appreciatively. Longingly.

"You look good," he said evenly.

His confidence was so familiar and yet so . . . troubling. I focused on the ground, breathing in, breathing out. "I have to go," I finally said. "Bye."

With an about-face, I headed back in the direction of his friends and my dorm, and as I approached the clique of men, still perched on the stone wall, I tried not to be bothered by the way they were eyeing me with strained, muffled hilarity. Were they rating me? Was I a six? A seven? Maybe . . . possibly . . . an *eight*?

"Natalie," Patrick said, trailing a step or two behind. "Wait. Listen."

I stopped.

"I just want you to know that, in the beginning, I really *was* into you."

It wasn't like I was going to argue with him, and, besides, I almost believed him. It annoyed me that he'd said that, though, because he might just as well have gone on to say, "but then I got to know you better and realized I, um, *wasn't* into you." Why say anything at all? Did he think a statement like that would wipe the slate clean and absolve him of any questionable behavior? Or was he suggesting I had been a different person at our first meeting (arguable), and, so, really, all successive events were *my* fault because *I* was the one who had not been who I had initially seemed to be? Of course. *I never wanted to be a dick. I really was into you.* Poor Patrick. I nodded and turned away, again, desperate to flee from the source of my prior addiction.

"Look," he went on, following closely at my heels, "I'm having a few people over on Friday night after graduation. You should stop by."

A slow, involuntary smile crept onto my face. Why respond to his invitation? Why divulge anything about myself to him? For what? But I did, anyway.

"I can't," I said with relief, facing him, "I'm leaving for Russia."

"Really?"

I nodded and blushed, furiously, proud of my final courage. What can I say? Part of me—the sick part—was flattered and, while not exactly interested, curious as to why he was asking me to his party. Was it merely friendly? Or was he hoping I might return to being the girl who initially interested him at the library? No. Most likely, he was hoping for a quick, noncommittal lay before moving on to the truly worthy women of Manhattan. But it was okay. I was walking away. I was *walking away*. In another moment Patrick and his friends would lose sight of me and Patrick's temporary interest would evaporate. And then my own cheeks would pale and I would meet my roommate and tell her about the encounter, and then this, too, would pass, until the memory of my last meeting with Patrick blurred and became . . . a footnote. A postscript. And then I would travel across an ocean, and a continent, and then . . . what?

What?

Before entering the cafeteria, I sat down on the cement steps. I was glad I had seen him one last time, and I don't think it was for closure. I think it was simply because I was already forgetting, even then, what he had looked like.

Jacob.

Patrick.

Jacob.

Patrick.

I do remember you.

Just not very well.

I pulled open the door to the cafeteria and searched for

Jennifer's face amid the sea of students, and when I spotted her I waved hello. And as I neared the table of guys who enjoyed barking and howling like dogs in heat, for once I looked straight at them. They were a sad-looking bunch. Not a *one* was noticeably attractive or even interesting looking. Somehow this shocked me, and I'm not sure whether my thoughts were evident on my face or if I just wasn't listening closely, but I didn't hear any howls *or* barks as I passed by. I heard nothing. And I hear nothing, now.

acknowledgments

Thank you to Paul, for kick-starting me to write in the first place, and for everything else.

Thanks, also, to John Rechy, for being such an inspiring teacher, and to Julie Gray, who gave up walks along the Seine to read several *way* too thick drafts.

Good old-fashioned encouragement—a vital necessity—came from Marion Brown (or "Mom"), Rosemary Brown-Wright, Kim Charneski, Alessa Angle, Wes Bausmith, Van Khanna, Jessica Garrison, Erin Moylan, and Hillary Fogelson. Carol Wiggins, Ann-Marie Brown, and Amy Jackson helped me recall things I had all but forgotten about the UConn campus. And Luis and Drusilla Ortiz helped me with my darlings, J. & M.

I am indebted to my fantastic agent, Mary Evans. I am grateful above all to Sarah McGrath, my wildly gifted editor, as well as to Geoff Kloske, Sarah Stein, and everyone else at Riverhead.

Lastly, a very special, warm note of gratitude for Kerry Kohansky—the most assiduous reader and staunchest of allies a writer could have.